IN THE DARK

Published by Phaze Books
Also by G.A. Hauser

Man to Man
Miller's Tale
Pirates
Teacher's Pet
Vampire Nights
Two In Two Out
Double Trouble
Top Men
In The Dark

IN THE DARK

G.A. HAUSER

EXCEPTIONAL EROTIC FICTION

This is a work of fiction. Names, characters, places and incidents either are the product of the author's imagination or are used fictitiously, and any resemblance to any actual persons, living or dead, events, or locales is entirely coincidental.

A Phaze Books Production
Phaze Books
an imprint of Mundania Press LLC
6470A Glenway Avenue, #109
Cincinnati, Ohio 45211-5222

To order additional copies of this book, contact:
books@mundania.com
www.mundania.com

Cover Art © 2010 by Stacee Sierra
Edited by Stephanie Balistreri

Trade Paperback ISBN: 978-1-60659-593-0

First Edition February 2011

Production by Mundania Press LLC
Printed in the United States of America

10   9   8   7   6   5   4   3   2   1

FOREWORD

Under certain conditions, human beings can react in unusual ways. Nature has provided us with instinct and reflexes to help protect us in the event of danger or fear. For instance, the response of the flight or fight impulse is part of our primal brain and can help us make the correct decision in a pinch.

But what about the urge for affection, touch, or even lust?

In which conditions do perfect strangers reach out to one another for comfort, closeness, or simply to get their rocks off? What causes rational people to react slightly irrationally and perhaps do things they wouldn't normally do? Like cheat on loved ones, have a sexual encounter with someone they do not know, or fall head over heels in love at first sight?

There are mysteries to the human psyche that people may conjecture about, hazard a wild guess, or divulge their own failings in similar situations.

But...does anyone really trust themselves when opportunity knocks?

And what if these chances come in the form of hot hunks that make offers one cannot refuse?

Who knows what we should expect when 'life happens'? Especially when those contacts are In The Dark.

—GA Hauser

CONTENTS

IN THE DARK OF NIGHT

ELEVATOR MEN

Brad was exhausted. Finally the end of the week had arrived. His briefcase in hand, he stood at the elevator on the tenth floor and exhaled deeply, wishing he was already home and had a beer in his fist, relaxing. He loosened his necktie and opened the top button of his starched shirt collar.

A handsome man in a navy blue short-sleeved shirt and the same color blue trousers approached and stood near him waiting for the elevator. Over his left shirt pocket read the name 'Kent'. He was carrying a small toolbox and appeared as tired as Brad felt.

The building was almost void of occupants as most took an early out to get a jump on the weekend. It was the same every Friday. Brad tended to be the last to leave his office and by the time he was going home, the structure had cleared out. It was as if Fridays were half-days in some businesses. He wasn't as lucky. He worked a full day.

Though Brad was lost in thought, he found he had been staring at the man's profile too long. Brad jumped slightly when Kent looked at him. A blush rushed to Brad's cheeks at being caught admiring the guy. As quickly as he could, Brad evaded those lush blue eyes.

The elevator doors opened, sliding back soundlessly. Trying to be a gentleman, Brad waited for Kent to enter. It seemed Kent was being polite as well. They laughed at the awkwardness of their indecision and ended up entering side by side, brushing shoulders.

"Christ, I must be tired," Brad chuckled, "I feel brain dead."

"Ditto." Kent pushed the button for the lobby.

The doors slid shut.

"Uh..." Brad wanted to speak to this man. He enjoyed his adorable smile. "Working on the computers?"

"Cables."

"Ah." Brad nodded and tried to occupy his thoughts with something other than the appeal of this stunning man.

The elevator jolted sharply and the interior went dim.

"Uh oh." Brad looked up at the numbers that were no longer illuminated over the door.

"Crap." Kent rubbed his face tiredly.

"What do you think?" Brad asked. "Power outage?"

"I assume so. What else can it be?" Kent pushed a few buttons, including the emergency one. They waited. Nothing happened.

After a long pause where neither of them spoke and Kent continued to push at the buttons on the panel in vain, Brad cleared his throat nervously. "You, um, have to get home to the family?" Brad had no idea why he was asking him that.

"No. I don't have a family. I'm single. Shit. I'm just fucking exhausted. It's been a long week and I was looking forward to putting my feet up and having a damn beer." Kent set down the toolbox he was holding and ran his fingers through his dark thick hair.

"I hear ya. I'm beat as well." Brad licked his lips as he eyed Kent hungrily wondering what kissing him would be like.

"What do you do?"

Waking up from his fantasy, Brad answered, "Accounting. I'm Brad." Brad reached out his hand.

"Kent." Kent shook it warmly.

"I know." Brad pointed to the nametag on Kent's chest.

"Oh. Duh. And you think you're brain dead?" Kent laughed.

Brad set his briefcase down and they stood in silence a moment. "You don't think this will go on for a long time do you?"

"Christ, I hope not." Kent took his cell phone out and flipped it open.

"Anything?"

"No signal."

"I'm not surprised. This is an older building and the walls are thick. Especially in this contraption."

Kent stuffed his phone back into his pocket.

Another silent few minutes passed.

"At least there's a dim emergency light," Brad whispered. "Be frickin' insane if it was pitch-dark."

"Why? Are you claustrophobic?"

Seeing Kent's slightly amused smile, Brad chuckled. "No. I don't think so. But trapped in a pitch-black elevator with the cable guy?" The incredibly hot cable guy? Lucky me!

"Shut up." Kent laughed at him.

Dimples appeared on Kent's face, causing Brad's attraction to rise. He wondered if the feeling could be mutual. Doubting the guy was gay, and knowing he fantasized encounters with straight men all the time, Brad tried to calm his lust and exhaled a deep breath.

He leaned against the back wall, crossing his arms over his chest. "You think it's just this building?"

"No way to know."

"I didn't feel an earthquake. Did you?"

"No." Kent grinned. "Man, don't get panicky on me."

"It's just that California's known for them. You know."

"You need a teddy bear?"

Brad grinned at Kent's wicked smile. Okay, I'll play. "You got one in your box of tools?" Brad wondered if this was Kent's version of flirting, and hoped to hell it was.

Immediately the expression on Kent's face changed from a silly grin to dead serious. Chills rushed over Brad's skin.

"You...ah..." Kent cleared his throat nervously. "You interested in 'tools'?"

Holy fuck! No! It can't be! Brad felt his knees go weak. "Did you just ask me what I think you asked me?"

Even in the dimness Brad could see Kent's blush. "No. Never mind."

"Christ, is it hot in here?" Brad loosened his necktie so it hung down his chest and popped another button open on his shirt. Suddenly he was a raging inferno.

Slowly, sensually, Kent met his eyes. "Very fucking hot,"

he hissed, giving Brad's body a glance from head to toe.

Gulping down a dry throat, Brad connected to Kent's gaze and they stared at each other intensely. Am I hearing this guy right? Very fucking hot? And he was staring at my dick? No. I'm hallucinating.

Brad's heart pounded in his chest at the look of lust he was receiving. "You...think it'll be a while?"

"Could be. Could be hours."

"Damn." Brad's dick went rock hard.

As if he were trying to be casual, Kent stepped closer. But in the tiny elevator box, they weren't exactly miles apart to begin with.

Brad caught the scent of his cologne and sweat. He closed his eyes and inhaled deeply. "Fuck you smell good." Did I just say that?

Like that was what he needed to hear, Kent pressed his body against Brad's, nailing him to the elevator wall aggressively. "You think I smell good? Grrr... So do you."

"Holy shit," Brad whimpered as Kent reached between his legs and took snorts of his neck.

"Nice dick. Jesus." Kent stroked Brad's cock as it pressed against Brad's thigh and down his pant leg. "Yum. Love your cologne. Mm!"

"Holy-fucking-shit..." Brad repeated, closing his eyes as Kent licked his chin tentatively. Brad perked up and blinked at him.

"Do you kiss?" Kent crooned sensually.

"Hell yeah." He wondered when the lights would turn on. Would they get down and dirty, and caught?

"This is so hot." Kent stroked Brad's cock harder. "I was hoping you were into it, you know. With us being stuck like this."

"I'm into it." Brad panted. Staring at how incredibly good looking Kent was, Brad made a tiny nervous move towards his lips.

At the gesture, an explosion of passion erupted from Kent. Grunting in surprise, Brad was slammed back against the wall again and a hand shoved down his trousers as a tongue made its way inside his mouth. Wow! It was very clear Kent liked to dominate and Brad was becoming his eager slave.

Brad let out an agonizing moan in delight and dug his fingers into Kent's hair, deepening their kiss.

With the assistance of Kent's hand, Brad's cock was set upright and stroked hotly. He was about to combust.

Kent parted from his mouth, breathing hard as he pushed Brad's suit jacket down his shoulders excitedly. Brad was almost hyperventilating he was so primed.

His jacket, his tie, his starched light blue shirt, ended up in a pile on the floor by the toolbox and briefcase. As Kent lapped at Brad's nipples like a wild man, he struggled to open Kent's shirt buttons. Helping him, Kent licked and stripped his shirt off simultaneously. Once they were both topless, he drew Kent's mouth back to his, dying for more deep tongue kisses.

Brad's trousers were opened and shoved downwards as an aggressive tongue was fucking his mouth. He sucked hard on it, yearning to taste Kent's cock. Breaking the kiss to gasp for air, Brad watched in the dimmest of light as Kent stripped him of his bottom half of clothing. Brad's dick popped out of his briefs, standing stiff and hard. No hiding the attraction now, was there?

Kent moaned and was about to get to his knees when Brad began opening Kent's pants. Time to see what's behind these dark blue trousers, buddy.

As if getting the idea quickly, Kent kicked aside his work boots and yanked off his clothing. Soon they were both just in their socks, staring at each other's bodies in light that was no more than a candle flame.

"Holy fuck." Brad ran his hands down Kent's silky sides. "And you think I have a nice cock?"

"Wanna suck it?"

"Yes!" Brad admired Kent's perfectly cut hairless chest and abdomen, salivating at the sight of his torso and long curving engorged dick.

Kent went for Brad's mouth again as they both fondled each other's cock eagerly. Slowly Kent urged him to the floor of the elevator.

"Christ, I wish I had lube. I'd love to take that up my ass," Brad hissed as Kent kissed him behind his ear, making him tingle.

"A bottom?" Kent purred with enthusiasm.

"Uh huh...love it." Oh, yes, baby, bring it on!

Growing more forceful, Kent shoved Brad to lie on his back, spreading Brad's legs wide. As Kent licked from Brad's balls to his ass, Brad groaned loudly before he shut his mouth and wondered if they could be heard outside these four walls.

The minute his rim was wet with saliva, Kent finger fucked him. Brad was going insane, writhing on top of a pile of their clothing. "Ahh! Oh, yes! Kent! Holy fuck!" Brad bucked against Kent's fingers and prayed, "Christ, I hope the lights don't come on now."

"Me too." Kent chuckled. "I want to be quick and I want to be slow. You know?"

"Yes." Brad moaned and raised his hips to get Kent's finger in deeper. "Fuck, that feels good."

As if he had just thought of it, Kent spun around and straddled Brad's face. The minute that big engorged dick was bobbing in front of him, Brad gripped it at the base and drew the entire length into his mouth. At the same time, his prick was plunged into Kent's hot mouth. Arching his back and groaning, Brad fucked that wet orifice and felt his balls tighten up deliciously. The daring deed brought him up quickly. Well, Christ, I was already fantasizing this. And here it is!

Brad had visions of the lights turning on, the door opening, and a crowd of people standing at the next floor gaping at them in awe. So what? Fuck it if they can't take a joke.

Brad felt a pulsating throb from Kent's cock push past his lips. He increased his suction and speed. Kent's full-mouth moans made Brad's skin prickle with passion. Kent was obviously geared up for the blast as well.

Tasting a sweet drop of pre-cum on his tongue, Brad grasped Kent's balls and pressed his index finger into Kent's ass. Instantly Kent came, thrusting his hips deeper into Brad's mouth. It was all Brad needed. He clamped his eyes shut and shot out his load into Kent's mouth. Squirming, Brad sucked until he couldn't taste Kent's cum any longer.

Slowing down, continuing to mouth Kent's long organ, Brad ran his hands lovingly over Kent's tight ass, sighing at how good his skin felt as well as his intoxicating scent.

Feeling his cock slip out of Kent's mouth, Brad heard him panting to catch his breath. The light flickered. They both froze.

"What does that mean?" Brad asked in terror. "Is the power coming on?"

"No. I don't think so. That emergency light actually just got dimmer. I think the generator is most likely overloaded."

"Good. I can't move. Fuck, Kent. That was amazing."

"No shit." Kent licked his dick.

Nudging Kent to spin around, Brad urged him to meet face to face. When Kent was on his hands and knees over him, Brad cupped the back of his head and brought him to his lips. The taste of his own cum coated Kent's tongue.

Kent dropped down heavily on top of Brad, sealing their sweaty, naked bodies together. "I can't believe how good you feel." Kent moaned.

"Me neither." Brad held Kent's rough jaw. "Not to mention, you're fucking gorgeous."

Kent laughed shyly. "I could say the same about you."

"You...ah, dating anyone?"

"Not at the moment."

"No? Really? You're single and available?" Brad wriggled his hips under Kent's.

"Why? Interested in the cable guy?"

Even in the sparse light he could see Kent's eyes twinkle impishly. "I am."

"I don't want the lights to come on. I want to suck you again."

Brad chuckled and squeezed Kent with his knees. "No way of knowing, is there? I mean, ten hours or one minute."

"Nope. No way of knowing." Kent kissed Brad's chin.

"What will we do if the door suddenly opens and we're caught like this?"

"Do you give a fuck?" Kent asked. "Are you out?"

"I'm out, yes. But...what if a bunch of secretaries or office clerks caught us?"

Kent pushed his hard cock against Brad's ass. "Sounds wicked."

"Are you into exhibitionism?" Brad licked Kent's face.

"A little. Could be hot."

He paused to stare at Kent a moment. "I love the color of your eyes. It's a good thing I got a peek at them earlier because I can't tell their color in this weird light."

"They're blue."

"I know. Perfect." Brad dug his hand into Kent's hair. "How old are you?"

"Thirty. You?"

"Twenty-five."

Brad heard a noise. "What's that?"

"No clue."

"Christ, our luck this thing will plunge to the basement."

"It won't. Do you normally panic at times like these?"

"No. Not normally. Only when I'm stark naked with a nude man lying on top of me on the floor of an elevator in a blackout."

Kent began laughing. "I like you."

"I like you too." Brad drew him back to his mouth. Closing his eyes as they kissed, Brad could feel the tiny box they were in vibrate, or maybe it was his body vibrating with renewed excitement. "You got any lube in that tool box, Mr. Cable-guy?"

"Wish I fucking did." Kent placed the head of his cock against Brad's ass.

"I have a rubber in my wallet." Brad closed his eyes, imagining shoving his hips up and slipping that big dick inside.

"Is it lubricated?"

"Yes, but..."

"Get it."

At the teasing tone, Brad smiled wickedly. "If I can find my pants."

"Find them."

Brad leaned up on his elbows and felt around the pile of clothing. Meanwhile Kent sat up and popped open his toolbox, rummaging around.

Locating his wallet, Brad opened it up and squinted in the dimness to find the small package tucked behind his credit cards.

"Bingo."

"You have something?" Brad stuffed his wallet back into his pants pocket, holding onto the rubber.

"It's a gel hand cleaner. Really slick stuff."

"Geezus, do I want that up my butt?" Brad reached for the bottle to get a look at it.

"It's harmless. Just some of that antibacterial shit."

Seeing exactly what it was, Brad shrugged. "You think it'll eat latex?"

"You do worry too much."

The minute Kent's fingers began sliding the slippery gel inside his back passage, Brad stopped worrying. Jerking breaths and whimpering moans were the only communication he was able to produce at the moment.

The condom was taken from his fingertips. Brad was ready for number two. Lights stay off, lights stay off.

"Oh yeah," Kent hissed as he pushed in.

"OhmyGod." Brad arched his back and purred.

"Smooth as glass...perfect."

As Kent drove in deeper, Brad's cock throbbed in tandem. "Yes, that's it. God, I love a good fucking."

"You're going to get a good fucking, pretty boy."

Brad smiled. "Good."

A hand on each leg, Kent gripped Brad's knees and pushed them backwards against Brad's chest, exposing his ass for a better screwing. As Brad watched, Kent's gaze was glued to the connection between his legs.

"Yeah. Yeah..." Kent pumped more assertively.

A chill of pleasure washed up Brad's spine. He moved his hand to his own cock and began stroking it. It seemed the sight of him touching himself sent Kent to a new level. Kent thrust his hips madly, grunting like a wild hound.

The internal massage was perfect. Brad quickened his hand motion and sprayed cum all over his own chest, gasping from the intensity.

"Yeah! Oh, yeah!" Kent plunged in deeply and Brad could feel Kent's cock shudder inside him as he came.

As they recovered they both moaned in pleasure.

"Geez! I love fucking you!" Kent panted.

"Good, because I love you fucking me." Brad laughed.

"Oh, Christ, this is too funny. Caught in a goddamn elevator and screwing our brains out? Do you see the humor in this madness?"

Giving his cock one last good thrust inside, Kent pulled out. "I do. Are you shitting me?" He started laughing. After he pulled off the condom he asked, "What the hell am I supposed to do with this thing?"

"Stick it in your tool box."

"No!"

"Yes! You can't leave it in the elevator."

"Put it in your briefcase."

"Now you're being silly," Brad replied.

"Shit, this sucks." He gingerly laid the spent condom in with his tools. "My luck I'll forget it and one of my co-workers will spot it."

Brad chuckled. "Just say you're hot with the chicks."

"Yeah right. That they'd believe." Kent shook his head.

"No? Your co-workers know you're gay?"

"They suspect it. I haven't come out and said I am. It's none of their business, is it?"

"No. I suppose not."

A pause followed and they heard noises from deep below them down the elevator shaft. An engine, a hum of something cranking on? More generators?

"Should we get dressed?" Kent asked. "You think the lights will come on soon?"

Brad wrapped his arms around him and held onto him, inhaling his skin. "One more minute."

Releasing a deep sigh, Kent closed his eyes and rested on top of Brad. "This is so nice."

"I know. I wish we were in my bed." He rubbed Kent's back and neck.

"We'll fall asleep. You watch. Then the door will open and I'll be mooning everyone."

Brad smiled. "And what a moon it is."

Chuckling at the comment, Kent nestled his face into Brad's neck and exhaled deeply. "Will you see me? You know, after this?"

"Yes. Are you kidding me?" Brad caressed Kent's skin

lovingly.

"Good. Very good." Kent's body relaxed, weighing heavily against his.

Brad delighted in Kent's weight. So what if the lights came on and they were discovered. There was nothing wrong with being with a man as beautiful as Kent, was there?

∽≈

It was still pitch black when Kent opened his eyes. Jolting slightly, he realized he and Brad had fallen asleep. Trying to see his watch in the dim light, Kent hissed, "Christ," in dismay.

"What?" Brad moaned groggily.

"It's been an hour and a half."

"Really? Maybe we should get dressed. The lights should be coming on soon."

"We were asleep. It felt so nice to sleep on top of you." Kent caressed Brad's face gently. "I can get used to this." He couldn't believe how much he liked Brad. It was as if he'd been bitten by the infatuation bug.

To Kent's delight, Brad leaned up to kiss him.

At the touch of their lips, he felt another spark of arousal. "I don't want to get dressed."

Brad ran his hands down Kent's back to his ass, squeezing it. "Can you come to my place? After this?"

"Yes, I would like that. Very much."

"Good!" Brad hugged him.

Slightly nervous they would actually be discovered naked in the elevator, Kent suggested, "We should get dressed. Just in case."

"Yes." Brad nodded.

Kent slid off of him and sat up, staring at Brad as he searched the floor for his clothing. "You're really nice looking. How come you're single?"

"I just broke up with my partner." Brad held up something. "My briefs or yours?"

"Does it matter?" Kent laughed.

"No. Not really." Brad laughed with him.

"If we get it wrong, we'll swap at your place later."

"True."

Making his way to his feet, Kent found his own clothing and began sliding his briefs and trousers up his legs. When he had his shirt on and was buttoning it, he glanced up at the tiny emergency light again. "Shit."

"What?"

"Is that a fucking camera?"

Brad spun around in panic. "Oh God. Please tell me you're joking."

"I'm not. Do you see a lens? Or am I imagining it?" Kent got to his toes for a closer look. "You think it went out with the power?"

"Holy fucking shit. I hope so."

"It did." Kent tried to convince himself. "Yeah. It must have." On camera? Could what he and Brad had just done be witnessed by someone? No. I'm being stupid.

They both stared at it.

"No way anyone was spying on us." Brad shook his head.

"No. We're just being paranoid." Kent tucked in his shirt.

"Who cares?" Brad slipped on his shoes. "If they were? So what? Maybe they got off on it."

"I know I would." Kent smiled, very glad Brad was there to make him feel good about it.

Once they were dressed, Kent watched as Brad folded his tie and shoved it into his jacket pocket. When Brad had stopped moving, Kent trapped him against the elevator wall again. "Amazing how we met."

"Something to tell the grandkids?" Brad teased.

"Yes. Exactly." Kent wrapped his arms around him, holding him. "I've been waiting for a man like you."

"That's very flattering."

"I mean it." Kent rocked him in his arms.

"I hope I don't disappoint you."

"You won't." He kissed Brad's neck. "My perfect bottom."

"Grrr..." Brad nibbled his earlobe.

"You'll get us started again."

"Yeah? So what? What if we're stuck in here for hours? Or overnight?"

"Damn, I'd just hate that!" Kent teased.

"Tongue. I need your tongue."

Kent made for his lips, kissing Brad passionately. It may just be a crazy night trapped in an elevator, but it felt so good! And Brad seemed to be as into him as he was into Brad. He was sick of being single, of one-night stands. He wanted a man in his life. And Brad was one hell of a beauty.

Crossing his fingers behind Brad's back as he embraced him, Kent said a tiny wish to himself that this was not just a trick of the darkness, and he had found his prince.

Surveillance

"Shit." Ted looked around their office.

"Power's out." Bill flicked the light switch up and down.

"The emergency generator should kick on."

"It has." Bill opened the door to the hall. A dim light was glowing.

Ted picked up the phone and dialed. "Yeah, this is Ted Green from the security department. Are the lights out by you as well?"

Bill chewed his lip as his partner rubbed his shaven head while he spoke on the phone, the sparse light reflecting on his mocha skin.

"Yeah. All right. No. Hey, nothin' we can do. Okay." Ted hung up.

"Well?"

"The whole city is out."

"No shit?" Bill crossed his arms over his chest.

"No shit. Go get the transistor radio over there."

Finding it on a dusty shelf near some tools, Bill handed Ted the tiny radio. "Are there batteries in it?"

"There should be." Ted turned it on and tuned through the static to hear a voice.

"...high sustained winds have knocked out power to over one hundred thousand people in the Los Angeles area... emergency crews are being summoned across county lines..."

"Sounds bad."

Ted nodded. "It does."

A whirring noise made its way to their office. A dim light lit and the security monitors blinked on.

"I think that was another generator kicking in, right?" Bill asked.

"Yes. There are three of them in the basement. I think they're on timers so they start up one at a time."

"Right." Bill nodded, rubbing his chin. He leaned over the desk to see the picture screens on the five monitors. "Fuck."

"What?" Ted peered over Bill's shoulder.

"Someone's stuck in the elevator." Bill looked back at Ted for his reaction.

"Oh shit." Ted squinted at the dim image of two men, one pushing buttons on a panel in vain.

Bill sighed sadly. "Poor guys. Nothing we can do at the moment."

"I'd call the fire department but my guess is they have their hands full. They look all right in there." Ted shifted closer to the screen.

Bill smiled sweetly at his partner. "Being an ex-cop you're too nice to the first responders, Ted."

Ted laughed. "Yeah, I know. I should pester them like the rest of the general public."

"What should we do?"

"Let's just keep an eye on things. At least the security monitors are working. It's after five on a Friday and almost everyone's gone home anyway."

"You're the boss." Bill pulled up a chair and surveyed the five monitors.

"I wonder how many trees are down. It's going to be hell driving home later." Ted rubbed his eyes and yawned.

"We should stay on until our relief comes, Ted. We can't leave the building unsecure in a power outage, can we?"

Ted looked wearily at Bill. "You do realize that may not be until morning."

A warm tingling sensation washed over Bill at the thought of hanging around with Ted for longer than their usual shift. "I don't mind. I like working with you."

"You need a damn life." Ted chuckled.

"I know. Sorry. I'm pathetic. All I have is this job." Bill admired Ted's wide biceps as he stretched his arms over his head in a catlike gesture. *And you.*

"Why don't you go out?" Ted asked, folding his hands on his lap. "You're young, not too damn ugly."

At the covert compliment, Bill smiled. "I'm shy. I can't do the club scene."

"You're shy?" Ted's eyes lit up in surprise. "You? Bill Patton? The one who gets drunk at the Christmas parties and sings karaoke?"

"Shut up." Bill shoved him playfully. It was like moving concrete Ted was so muscular.

After giving Bill a smile, Ted looked back at the monitors. "What the fuck?"

"What?" Bill leaned over his shoulder.

"Am I seeing things?"

"What?" Bill asked anxiously. "What do you see?"

Ted pointed to one monitor. "I could swear there were two men in that elevator."

"And?" Bill struggled to make out the dim shapes on the screen.

Ted gripped Bill's uniform shirt and drew him over to see. "Are they kissing?"

"What?" Bill's heart stopped.

In silence they watched. "That can't be two men."

Bill could see clearly it was. His body went haywire. "Holy shit."

"What are they doing?" Ted leaned closer, adjusting the shadowy screen so the image was in better focus.

"Kissing. They're kissing." Bill felt his cock twitch and sweat break out on his skin.

"That's the cable guy." Ted pointed. "He signed in at the front desk. What the hell was his name?"

"Wow."

Ted spun around. "Did you say, 'wow'?"

Bill gulped audibly. "No. I meant, ew." Shaking his head in denial, Bill scoffed, "I didn't say 'wow'."

They both focused back on the screen. "Oh boy."

"What?" Bill dragged over the second chair so they were side by side.

"They're getting hot and heavy."

Trying not to blink, Bill stared at the hazy picture tube

as clothing began dropping off the men's bodies. "Are they insane?"

"Horny! Billy, they're damn horny!"

Bill rubbed his own crotch at the comment. Ted caught it and asked, "Are you getting off on this?"

"No! Come on, Ted. Getting off? On two guys?"

"Then why are you rubbing yourself?"

"Just an itch. Lay off." Bill died of embarrassment. The last thing he needed was for Ted to hate him. Not when he was crazy about him.

Ted turned back to the screen. "Here we go. They're top-less now, Billy. My, oh my, what are they going to do?"

"They've got balls, Ted. I mean, what if the lights pop back on and they're in the middle of something."

"They already are in the middle of something, and we're going to see very soon if they have balls!" Ted laughed.

Bill licked his lip as the action intensified. "You think they know one another?"

"I have no idea. What do you think? Is this just two horny guys taking the opportunity for some exploration?"

Bill paused as he considered the comment. "Exploration?"

"Yeah. Some man on man shit."

Another throbbing pulse rattled Bill's cock.

"They're going sixty-nine!" Ted gasped. "Sweet mother of God!"

"Holy crap." Bill squeezed his knees together tightly as his dick grew harder.

They were both glued to the screen. "That thing have audio?"

Ted spun around quickly. "You want to hear their grunts?"

"No. I just figured in case someone needed help."

As he turned up the volume, Ted replied, "By the look of it, they don't need anyone's help."

"Ah! Oh!"

"There. Is that what you wanted to hear?" Ted laughed.

"Jesus. They're really going at it." Bill stuffed his hands between his knees as the urge to come became stronger.

"Amazing what people will do in the dark."

As he leaned closer to the screen, Bill got a whiff of Ted's cologne or aftershave. All he could see from the camera angle was the man on top, rocking his hips wildly. "He's got to be about to blow."

"Son of a bitch. I wonder if they know the lights will be out a while, or they're just taking a crazy chance."

"Humping like dogs in heat."

A noise of one of the men climaxing, whimpering, came through the speaker. "One's gone." Ted laughed.

"So's the other," Bill added once they heard the second man moaning.

"Wow. Crazy shit."

Bill's eyes watered as he watched the man on top spin around and lie on the man on the bottom. Bet that felt good. So good.

Sitting back in his chair, Bill rubbed his eyes tiredly. "Lucky fuckers."

"You say something?"

"No." Bill stared at Ted. They'd been working the late shift for two months together. Five to one am. He'd been drooling over Ted's amazing good looks and massive physique that whole time but had no idea if Ted would ever be interested in experimenting. He was scared to death that if he even suggested it, Ted would pound him. And a punch from a man as big as Ted would hurt. Badly. Not to mention, it could jeopardize their working relationship. And Bill would not do that. He adored Ted.

He knew Ted wasn't married, but they didn't talk much about their social lives. Mostly just sports, politics, and current events. Bill assumed Ted was a very private man since he never offered information about his social life, so Bill never prodded him to answer personal questions. There was no wedding band on Ted's finger. Ted was an ex-cop. That was all he knew about the attractive black man.

"What should we do? Maybe walk around and see if anyone needs us?" Bill asked, trying to tame his erection and not look at the screen any longer. Just the sight of those men naked and lying prone made him both insane and jealous.

"Probably."

As Ted was about to stand, Bill stopped him. "Look.

They're at it again." Yeah so what. I peeked.

"No!" Ted sat back down to stare at the screen. "What are they doing this time?"

Knowing it would make him crazy, Bill couldn't resist watching this erotic show. He leaned closer. "Screwing. Holy cow."

"You got to be kidding! Anal sex in the elevator? I thought that shit only happened on HBO."

"Who's topping?" Bill chewed his bottom lip in excitement.

"Who's what?" Ted spun around, his face a mask of curiosity. "What the hell's 'topping'?"

"Uh." Bill's face went red and hot as if he had just given away the fact that he was a lewd fan of gay porn. "Did I say that? I think I said, stopping. Who's going to stop it?"

"If you asked me what I think you asked me," Ted narrowed his eyes at Bill, "the cable guy's doin' the screwin'."

Hoping he didn't just give away his sexual preference, Bill continued to chew his lip nervously and stared at the action in the lift. The cable man had the second man's legs pressed backwards and spread wide. Oh yes! Why can't I get fucked like that?

More animalistic grunts came through the speakers.

"Look at them go." Ted shook his head. "Unreal. Like they haven't a care in the world. Fucking like that on the floor of a dark elevator. I swear no one will believe me if I told them."

"Is that video camera recording the action?"

"No, it's just surveillance. It's on a continuous loop. Why?"

"No reason." Bill imagined stealing a copy to view later. Oh well.

Knowing everything he was saying sounded suspect, Bill stuffed his hand in his pocket and tried to appear casual. A tiny package of lube was crushed at the bottom of it. He'd placed it in there the first week he worked with Ted. Wishful thinking. There was a condom in his wallet. Always be prepared. Not only was that motto for the Boy Scouts but for the security department as well. He touched his own hard-on through the pocket material. He was literally going mad watching these two men screwing.

"Yeah! Oh, yeah!"

"Christ, I don't believe this." Ted shook his head.

"It's really hot."

"What?" Ted spun around. "Did you just say it's hot?"

Bill tugged at his collar. "It is a little stuffy in here."

"Geez! I love fucking you!"

"Ha!" Ted chuckled. "You hear that? The cable guy just said he loved fucking the other guy. Looks like they liked it."

"I suppose there's no need to call the fire department. My guess is they won't want to be saved." Bill nudged his dick from under the material of his pocket. Lucky bastards.

"I agree. They'll be wanting a nap after that. You watch."

"Yeah. Good point." Bill moved closer to the screen. "Yup. All tuckered out."

"I'm amazed. Really. I mean, Billy, what if the lights came on quick? You know? What if it wasn't the whole city and those doors opened to show off their bare white asses?" Ted laughed. "I'd be so damn embarrassed."

Frowning, Bill asked softly, "You don't like gay guys?"

"Huh?" Ted spun around to see Bill's face. "Gay guys? I don't have a problem with gay men, Billy. Why should I?"

"I don't know. It's nothing we've ever discussed."

"Why would we discuss gay men?"

Bill was very glad it was dim in the room because he knew his face was bright red. "You want to make the rounds?"

"We should at least have a look and see if everything's okay."

Nodding, Bill stood and moved his chair out of the way for Ted. Ted found his flashlight and keys. "You ready, man?"

"Yeah." Bill sighed in disappointment. Hey, you can't always get what you want. Big deal.

He followed Ted out of their office, locking it behind them. The emergency floodlights were on in the hallways but they were still too dim to be able to see well. Everything appeared shadowy and dark.

"What do you want to check out first?" Bill paused.

"We can start in the basement and work our way up."

"The basement." Bill shivered. "I hate that place in the

light."

When Ted squeezed his shoulder, Bill froze at his touch. "I'm here. No need to be scared, Billy."

"I'm not scared. It's just that it's creepy down there."

"When I was twenty I was scared of the dark too." Ted rubbed Bill's back softly. "But when you're thirty? And been a cop on the streets? Nuthin' scares you anymore."

Closing his eyes at the nice caressing, Bill asked, "I bet you wish you were still a cop."

"No. No way." Ted opened the door to the cellar, turning on his flashlight. "I had enough of being shot at. No thank you."

Bill walked behind Ted down the narrow stairs. "What's to check down here?"

"Just let me make sure the generators are working all right. We don't need a fire."

"Oh. Good point." Bill was always comforted by Ted's common sense.

As they rounded a corner in the dingy, cement claustrophobic space, the whining of the generators grew louder. Hating the atmosphere of the cellar, getting goose bumps, Bill stood back as Ted inspected them. He didn't think he'd know the signs if one wasn't working, other than smelling smoke.

"Are they okay?" Bill shouted over the noise. He'd watched too many slasher movies to be comfortable down here. Images of some man with a hatchet and a goalie mask jumping out at them petrified him. It made the urge to grab hold of Ted even stronger.

"Yeah. Let me just switch this last one on." Ted pressed a button and the whirring noise grew louder. "Three should be better than two."

"I don't smell smoke or anything." Bill wanted to go. He was getting the creeps.

"No. They're pretty new. Should be okay."

Glad for the signal from Ted to go back up the stairs, Bill took the steps two at a time. Once they were on the main floor with the door closed, Bill could hear normally again. "Hate it down there. I know there's rats. Or worse." He shivered. "It's the stuff of nightmares down there."

Ted chuckled and nudged Bill to keep walking. "You've got too good of an imagination. There ain't nuthin' down there to be afraid of, Billy. Come on. Let's check the stairwells."

"Okay." Bill opened the door as a few stragglers were leaving.

"Everything all right?" Ted asked.

"The elevators aren't working," one woman said. "I have no idea if anyone's in there."

"We got that covered," Ted replied.

Bill could see his sly smile.

"I came from the fifth floor. Everyone's pretty much out of their offices."

"Great. Thank you, ma'am." Ted nodded to her.

They began ascending the cement staircase.

Bill was behind Ted, lost on his powerful legs and round ass cheeks.

"Still with me, Billy?"

"Yup."

"Good. If you lose me, shout."

"I'll keep up with you, big guy. I'm in good shape."

"I know you are, Billy. You're in excellent shape."

A proud smile found Bill's lips. He was pleased to know Ted noticed.

At each landing Ted opened the door and shined his light down the hall, once he cleared the floor, they headed up a level.

After ten flights, even Ted was panting a little. Once they got to the top, they paused to take a break. "It's just about vacant."

"Yes," Bill agreed. "I suppose it's a good thing it came at closing time on a Friday. It's just those poor guys left stuck in the elevator."

"Poor guys? You mean the two having the time of their lives?" Ted chuckled. "I wish I knew where that thing stopped so I could let them know they have all night to play."

Bill started laughing. "You are so cool."

"I'm cool. I'm cool." Ted laughed and did a little victory dance.

The amount Bill was enamored by Ted only grew at his playful antics. "I'm so glad we work together. I mean that."

Ted paused in his dance and met Bill's eyes with a serious expression. "I like working with you too, Billy. You're very easy going. You never make a fuss about anything. No whining, no complaining."

"Why should I complain?" I have you.

"Most men do." Ted opened the stairwell door and began their descent. "It's just human nature."

"But I'm happy with you." Bill trotted down the stairwell behind him. When Ted paused, Bill plowed into him at the unscheduled stop. After he collided with Ted, which was like hitting a wall, Bill asked, "What? Why did you stop?"

It appeared Ted wanted to say something, but didn't. After an intense stare into Bill's eyes, Ted resumed their downward path. Bill could only wonder if he was opening his mouth too much about his feelings. After all, two guys screwing in an elevator had him worked up sexually. And he had always been hot for Ted Green.

When they hit the ground floor, Ted once again paused to catch his breath. "I feel like we're doing wind-sprints."

Bill laughed. "I know. Maybe we should slow down. I mean, we have until one in the morning to check the place, and other than the two lovebirds in the elevator, the building is almost empty."

"I bet the wind is howling out there on the street."

"Want to go back to the office and check the radio again?"

"We should. Get another peek at the outside world."

Bill followed him back to their office. Waiting as Ted used his key, they entered the dim room, and Ted turned on the tiny portable. Bill returned to look at the monitor. Both men were dressed, standing, kissing in the corner. "Nice."

"Hm?"

"Nothing. Anything new happening outside?"

"Still wind gusts up to ninety miles an hour. Sounds bad."

"Anyone you need to call? You know, to make sure they're all right?"

"No. I'm the only one here in LA." Ted set the small transistor on the table and sat down, resting his flashlight on the counter. "What are our boys doing?"

"Necking."

"Naked?"

"No. Dressed. I assume they thought they'd be out soon. We really should try to tell them what's going on."

"Give em another minute." Ted winked. "They're in no rush."

Scratching his chin lazily, Bill gazed at the two men as they kissed and stroked each other. "Must be nice to be touched like that."

"Uh huh."

"Been a while for me." Bill sighed.

"Why? You're good looking. Why has it been a while?"

Bill shrugged, not turning away from the two men on the monitor, enthralled by them.

"Billy?"

At the soft tone, Bill looked over at Ted.

"Why are you alone?"

"I'm shy I guess." Bill yawned, stretching his back. "And I have unsociable hours here. You know. Not a lot of chances to meet anyone." Seeing Ted's own expression droop, Bill asked, "What about you? You seeing anyone?"

"Not at the moment."

"Then we're both lonesome losers." Bill turned back to the screen. "They seem so in love."

"In lust more like."

"I wouldn't mind that either."

"Yeah? Just into a sex thing? No strings attached?"

Bill paused to think about Ted's comment. Slowly turning to face him, he examined the expression on Ted's face carefully. "Are you asking me if I would have a sexual fling with no strings attached?"

Ted seemed to get nervous, shifting his weight from one leg to the other.

Bill lost his eye contact. "Ted?"

"I don't know what I'm askin'. Those men have me feeling very strange at the moment."

A rush of chills flooded Bill's body. "Strange how?"

"I don't know. Strange." Ted peered back at the screen.

Bill glanced at it again. "Christ. They're going for number three."

Chuckling, Ted added, "They better pace themselves. They got a long night ahead."

Closing his eyes to try and get his body under control, Bill sighed deeply. Watching the two men in the elevator was driving him insane. He had to stop.

"You all right, Billy?"

At Ted's concerned voice, Bill peered over his shoulder at him. "It's making me feel strange too, Ted."

"We should shut it off. Stop watching. It's private." Ted reached for the switch.

Bill grasped his wrist. "Don't. They may need help. Leave it on." Expecting Ted to jerk back from his touch, Bill was surprised when he didn't.

"You're right. Just in case. I'll leave it on."

The soft tone surprised Bill. Still holding Ted's arm, he pivoted to face Ted again. "It must be the crazy night..."

"What must be?"

Bill drew closer, placing Ted's hand on his hips as he did. Immediately Ted lowered his eyes shyly, but still did not retract his hand.

"I'm expecting a punch here, Ted." Bill panted, losing his breath as his nerves kicked in.

"I'm not going to punch you."

"Why not?" Bill was almost near enough to press his body against Ted's. A hair closer and they were going to be connecting more than just a hand on a hip. Clasped to Ted's wrist, Bill inched Ted's fingers to reach behind him, over his ass. Still Ted did not pull back or react angrily. "You beautiful motherfucker," Bill sighed as he realized Ted was not going to strike him.

A low rumbling laugh came from deep within Ted's chest.

"You want sex without strings?" Bill breathed in short bursts. "I can do that."

"I don't know what I want."

When Ted's dark eyes finally met his gaze, Bill melted at the power. Inhaling for the courage it would take to say his next line, Bill took a chance. Petrified he'd lose everything, but he had so much to gain if he didn't. He said what he never thought he would say to his handsome co-worker. "I've been attracted to you since the first day I set eyes on you."

A little shake of Ted's head, maybe in amazement, followed. After a long pause, as if Ted was considering the comment carefully, Ted whispered, "You like black men, Billy?"

"Fuck yeah. And you in particular."

"Are you gay?"

"That's a stupid question at the moment, Mr. Green."

"I'll shut up now." Ted laughed nervously.

A second later, Ted's fingers squeezed Bill's ass as Ted's hand still rested on him. It sent a rush of pleasure shooting to Bill's cock. "It's dark. No one's in the building but two guys humping in the elevator."

"And?" Ted appeared amused.

"And." Bill boldly reached to cup Ted's crotch. A large hard-on was under his uniform pants. "Holy Christ."

"What are we supposed to do, Billy? You know this is insane."

"Is it?" Bill traced his fingers along the length of Ted's cock, feeling it pulsate. He pressed his body against Ted's muscular chest, moving closer to his lips.

"I don't believe this."

Bill froze. "You want me to stop?"

"No. Yes. No."

Bill laughed at his indecision. "Our secret."

"Jesus. Billy..."

Slowly Bill opened the top button of Ted's trousers. He heard Ted's breathing accelerate. "Stop me whenever you want to." Bill paused. Ted was not stopping him. He pinched the zipper pull and drew it downwards. The grasp on his ass tightened almost in reflex. Bill was so excited he was about to blow.

Once Ted's slacks were open, Bill dipped his fingers into his briefs. When he made contact with his cock, Ted closed his eyes and hissed out a breath of air. "Ted...you fantastic motherfucker."

Ted moaned softly, closing his eyes.

Moving painfully slow, Bill exposed Ted's dick from his clothing and looked down to admire it. It was thick, long, dark and rock hard. Licking his lips, Bill began to sink to his knees.

Ted's breathing became so audible it filled the room, he gasped for air as his nerves and excitement kicked in.

Once he was eye level with Ted's cock, Bill rested his face against it, inhaling his scent and brushing his lips over his pubic hair.

"Billy...Jesus, Billy."

Ted's fingers dug into Bill's hair, encouraging him. About to swoon from living this dream, Bill opened his lips and wrapped them around the head of Ted's cock.

"Oh, my fucking God..." Ted whimpered.

Going wild at his taste and warmth, Bill moaned in delirium, allowing Ted's length to press deeper into his mouth.

Ted's fingertips burrowed strongly into Bill's hair as if Ted's pleasure increased.

Savoring it, wondering if this was some trick of the night in the dark, Bill sucked leisurely from base to tip, finding Ted's balls to caress gently. From his partner, only gasps and whimpers were heard.

Ted drew Bill tighter to his body, deepening the penetration. Bill tasted a drop of pre-cum on his tongue.

"Baby, that feels real good."

Bill moaned at the thought of giving Ted pleasure. Holding Ted's ass, Bill allowed him to fuck his mouth for a few moments.

Widening his stance, Ted took advantage of it and thrust into Bill's mouth with stronger strokes. "That's it. That's it."

The tingles in Bill's body were making him swoon. Hearing Ted growing closer to orgasm, feeling his organ ripple and throb, Bill's own dick was going crazy behind his zipper.

A grunting gasp reached his ears. Ted plunged deeply and gripped Bill's head like a vice. Bill closed his eyes and sucked harder, faster. Ted's cock quivered and shot out his load. Bill moaned and swallowed him down, milking him for more.

"Oh, Jesus Christ!" Ted's knees gave out and he reached back for the counter.

Bill gripped him tightly around his thighs, keeping him upright. Slowing his pace, Bill lapped gently at the tip of Ted's cock, caressing it in adoration, letting him recover.

Allowing Ted's cock to slip away from his mouth, Bill

gazed up at him. Ted was braced on the counter, his eyes staring at the ceiling unblinking.

Having no idea where this act would leave their friendship or their working relationship, Bill sat back, wiped his mouth with his hand and waited.

As if in a dream, Ted tucked himself in, closing his pants.

"Ted?" Bill had no idea how he was feeling.

Ted reached down and gripped both of Bill's shoulders, urging him to stand. When he brought Bill to his lips, Bill melted in Ted's strong embrace. He wrapped his arm around Ted's neck, sucking and lapping at his tongue hungrily. "I adore you," Bill hissed, completely lovesick.

Parting from their kiss, Ted petted back Bill's hair gently. "We just got carried away, that's all."

Trying to get back to himself again, knowing it was indeed only one night, no strings attached, nothing more, Bill nodded, parting from Ted to stand on his own. "Yes." He fought with the pain of longing in his chest.

"We just got out of hand, you know, watching those two men." Ted tilted his head at the elevator monitor.

"Right." Bill ran his hand through his hair, avoiding Ted's eyes as his pleasure changed to humiliation.

"Let's check the parking garage. We didn't get that far on our rounds."

"Okay." Bill tried not to feel too let down. After all, he got to suck Ted's cock. Never in a million years did he think that would ever happen. He should be satisfied with that. It was amazing and he'd relive the fantasy over and over again while he fisted himself in his own bed.

Ted picked up his flashlight. "You ready, Billy?"

"Yes." Slightly dizzy from the manic mood of a thrill immediately followed by a depression, Bill knew it would pass.

Following Ted out, waiting as he locked the office door, they moved through the dimly lit hallway to the parking garage. Bill wasn't sure what to feel at the moment. He was glad to have given Ted a blowjob, but hated the feeling of being let down by it at the same time. Expectations. They were a trap, a bottomless pit.

"Oh shit," Ted muttered.

"What?" Bill woke from his stupor.

"The damn gate's not open."

Bill looked from behind Ted's broad shoulders at a few parked cars near the exit. Silhouettes of two men were back lighted by the emergency exit light.

They approached the men and Bill noticed one was ranting on his mobile phone to someone.

"'Bout time!" the man shouted.

Ted set his flashlight down and grabbed hold of the metal gate tugging at it.

"Does it have a release switch?" Bill whispered.

"It should. Point my light at it."

Rushing to help, Bill aimed Ted's flashlight at the box attached to the electric gate.

The second man stood close. "Will it open?"

"I don't know." Ted tried to feel around the mechanism in the dark.

Bill bit his lip, looking back into the garage. "Are you the only two here?"

"Yes. Everyone else got fed up and left their cars," the second, calmer man answered.

The first man snorted in annoyance, speaking into the phone, "I have no idea. He's looking at it now."

Bill crouched down so he could whisper. "Any luck?"

"No." Ted stood, got a hold of the iron gate and tried to muscle it back. The other three men joined in, grunting to get it open.

"We tried that," the calm man said, giving up. "It won't budge."

Ted rose to his full height, brushing off his hands. "Right. I have two ideas. One: let me go get my toolbox and see if I can open the damn thing up. There has to be an emergency release. The other is to call my supervisor and see if he knows where the release switch is. You got another minute?"

The calm man smiled. "There's no power anywhere and it's blowing like a hurricane out here. Where the hell do I have to go?"

Bill heard the wind whipping past the open cement driveway watching branches of palm trees skid by.

"Hold on." The first man cupped the tiny phone. "Well?"

"Give me a minute." Ted tilted his head to Bill, gesturing for them to leave.

Bill shut off the flashlight and followed Ted, returning to the building door. "Ted."

Ted paused before he left the garage, spinning back to him.

"I'm sorry about before."

When Ted wrapped his arm around him and pinned him against a parked car, Bill gasped in shock.

"I'm not." Ted pushed his hips into Bill's seductively.

"Shit! Really?" Bill's pulse raced.

Ted reached between Bill's legs and massaged his cock. "It just took me a moment to think about it."

Shivering with erotic chills, Bill went limp in Ted's arms.

"And I liked it." Ted kissed Bill's neck.

"God. I'm going to explode." Bill moaned in agony.

Ted peered over his shoulder quickly before he knelt down and opened Bill's slacks.

"Holy shit!" Bill was on fire. The minute he felt Ted's hot, wet mouth he almost fainted. "Ted...ohmyGod, Ted."

Hearing Ted's moans of pleasure, the sucking, powerful and strong, Bill went limp against the car behind him. It was pure fantasy. Never in a million years had Bill expected Ted to reciprocate. Love him! Oh yes! I love him so much!

The churning in his balls became a rocket launch. The pleasure began at the root deep inside him and expanded like an exploding stick of dynamite.

Bill gripped tightly to Ted as if he would be launched off the cement floor of the parking garage. The intensity of the sensation was like nothing Bill had ever felt before in his life. Peering down, seeing the fantastic Ted Green going down on him, giving him head, Bill was near passing out with a swoon. I must be dreaming! Hallucinating! This can't be real!

But it was, and it washed over Bill like a tidal wave. Biting his lip to prevent a scream of bliss that would alert the entire city of his climax, Bill came, grunting as quietly as he could in ecstasy. "Oh, man...Ted..." He gripped the solid muscle of Ted's shoulder, sated and completely in love.

Parking Blues

"What the hell is taking them so long?" The man on the cell phone checked his watch.

The second man leaned against his car and sighed. "Give it a rest. Where the hell do you have to go in this storm?"

"Anywhere but a freezing garage." The man pocketed his phone and sighed. "Did they even go in?"

"Go in what?" the second man asked.

"Those security guys. I didn't see them enter the building."

"They had to. They were getting tools and calling someone."

The first man walked closer to the lobby door.

The second man watched him, following curiously. When the first man stopped short the second one caught up. "What?"

Without a word, the first man grabbed the second one's arm and pointed.

The second man peered into the dimness to see the big black security guard crouching in front of the young white one. "Holy fuck!"

The first man shoved the second one back from the other two men, so they could speak and not be overheard.

"I don't believe this." The first man shook his head.

"Any port in the storm?" The second man chuckled.

"I don't think we're getting out of here for a little while more."

"Uh, no. Me neither."

"I'm fucking freezing." The first man rubbed his suit jacket over his arms.

"Come on. Let's sit in my car." The second man chirped his key fob and unlocked the doors to a Mercedes. He climbed into the driver's seat and waited as the second man did the same next to him. "I'm Pete."

"David." He reached to shake Pete's hand.

"Are you warm enough or do you want me to turn on the engine?" Pete asked, putting the key in the ignition.

"Why waste the gas? We could be here a while. I just felt as if the garage was a wind tunnel. It was whipping through there." David looked back in the direction of the security men. "Do you believe that?" He gestured.

Pete slouched down in the seat, smiling. "Yeah, why not? Maybe they're lovers."

"Come on. Sucking in the stupid parking lot? Give me a break. That building must be vacant by now. They could have found an office or something."

"Maybe some guys like the excitement of being caught. Or watched." Pete grinned wickedly.

David didn't reply.

In the pause, Pete glanced over at him in annoyance. "What's the deal?" Pete asked, "You're not a homophobe, are you?"

"No. Are you?"

"No." Pete chuckled. "Are you gay?"

"That's awfully forward of you." David appeared indignant. "I don't know you other than you're the guy who's stuck in the parking garage with me in the middle of LA during a windstorm."

Pete shrugged. "Then you know me."

David flipped open his phone.

"Wife waiting?" Pete asked flippantly.

"No. Fucking thing's going dead anyway." He closed it and pocketed it. "Your wife waiting?" David asked in the same sarcastic tone.

"No."

"Are you gay?"

"Nosy fucker." Pete thought the question was tinged with nastiness. He didn't like the attitude one bit.

"Ha. Now you know how it feels. I don't suppose we need

to ask our security team that."

"Nope. Moot point." Pete relaxed his arm on the seat back.

"Which office is it you work in?" David pressed his back against the passenger's door so he was facing him.

"A law office. Larsen, Knight, Bernstein and Associates."

"Huh. Me too. Ladden and Pugg."

"Which floor?"

"Eighth. You?"

"Ninth." Pete smiled smugly. "We must be better than you."

"Ha ha." Under his breath David mumbled, "Jerk-off," before he added, "What branch of law?"

Pete heard the insult but chose to ignore it. "Civil litigation."

David nodded. "Same here."

"No shit?"

"No shit!" David teased in an exaggerated tone of excitement.

The wind blew something big past the iron gate.

"What the hell was that?" David asked.

"Looked like a roof."

"Holy crap." David shifted uncomfortably in his seat.

"We're probably in the best spot to sit this thing out. It's a massive concrete and brick building. Not some thatched hut."

"Thatched hut? Who the hell are you? Gilligan?"

"Why are you being such an uptight ass?" Pete sneered.

As if it was David's turn to ignore the demeaning comment, he asked Pete, "Did they predict the storm to be like this? I don't remember anyone saying it was going to be this bad? I heard thundershowers. That was it."

"Do you want me to turn on the radio?"

"Yeah, just for a minute."

Pete turned the key to auxiliary and searched for a news channel.

"...gusts up to eighty miles an hour continue to pummel the area...rainfall of up to six inches expected by morning... power is out to more than six hundred thousand homes..."

"Holy shit." David shook his head.

"Hope my place survives." Pete scrubbed his rough jaw.

"Why? Are you on the coast?"

"No. Bel Air."

"Me too."

"Shut up." Pete laughed as if David suddenly had to compete with everything he said.

"Why shut up?" David tilted his head and glared at him.

"How much more are we supposed to have in common? Are you making it up as you go along simply because my law firm is one floor higher than yours?"

"No, you stupid idiot." David laughed. "I don't know why we have things in common. But if you keep asking me questions I'll keep telling you the answers. If you don't want me to tell you shit, then shut up."

Turning the car off so the radio quieted, Pete was beginning to enjoy the playful banter this blackout had caused very much. "Fine. I'll keep asking you just to see how bad it is." Pete paused before he added, "How old are you?"

"Twenty-seven." David replied snootily, his nose up in the air.

Pete choked in surprise. "When's your birthday?"

"May fifteenth."

"Jesus!"

"What?"

"I'm twenty-seven and my birthday is May first."

"Old fart," David teased, "You're older than me by fourteen days, nyah, nyah."

"Shut up, ya baby." Pete laughed at his silly expression. "Fuck. This is getting weird." Pete rubbed his hand over his own thigh nervously.

"Weird? No shit! Our two security guys are probably still sucking each other off. That is fucking weird." David twisted back in their direction. "And I'm stuck with Gilligan who lives in a straw hut." David peered back to the lobby door. "How long could it take for them to get back here and open the stupid gate? You don't think they're still there doing each other, do you?"

"I could think of worse things to do," Pete muttered, touching his jaw.

"Huh?" David asked.

"Nothing."

"You are gay. You are so gay." David laughed at him, pointing rudely.

"Oh, shut up. You don't know what I am."

"I'm surprised you don't live in West Hollywood...gay man. Gay man," David taunted.

"Are you looking for a belt in the mouth?" Pete bristled. "Because you're coming close."

"Are you going to punch me because you're gay or not gay?"

"None of your fucking business."

That reply only made David laugh harder.

"What is the big deal about everyone's sexual preference anyway?" Pete ran his hand over the steering wheel absently. "Whose business is it who I fuck?"

"Uh, let's see. The government?" David scoffed. "The fucking bible-thumpers are pressuring the government all the time. They seem to think they need to decide if we have the right to marry."

Pete blinked. "We? You said 'we'. Then you are gay?"

"I didn't say that."

"You fucking did."

"Did not."

"Did!" Pete pointed at him. "You just said 'they need to decide if we have the right to marry'. 'We'. And that pronoun indicated you were including yourself. You can't fool me. I'm a lawyer."

"A dumb lawyer. You heard wrong. You have a screw loose."

"Gay man! Gay man!" Pete tormented him.

"Shut up." David shoved him playfully.

At the contact, Pete dove on him, pinning him to the passenger door. David gasped and his eyes blinked wide in shock.

"I know you're fucking gay," Pete hissed, close to David's mouth. "You're fucking gorgeous and giving off gay sparks all over the place. And my gaydar never fails me."

"I'm...I'm..." David shook his head in denial.

"You're what?" Pete ran his hand between David's legs over a nice package of male flesh.

"Fuck it. I'm gay."

"Knew it." Pete went for his mouth. At the touch of their tongues he felt David squirm under him. The semi-erection went rock hard. "Delicious." Pete moaned. "Holy shit, you feel nice."

"Now I don't want the security guys to come back." David panted. "Christ, what if they catch us?"

Pete shook his head at him. "Catch us? They were just sucking cock. Are you sure you're a lawyer? Because you sound like a dumb jock."

"Hey! You won't get any if you keep that up."

"Won't I?" Pete snaked his hand under David's dress shirt to his chest.

"You're molesting me."

"You can't molest the willing." Pete pinched David's nipple making him gasp.

"That's a man's argument."

"And?" Pete laughed. "What are you, a woman?"

"In some respects." David blinked his eyelashes shyly.

"A bottom. Ah! Fucking perfect." Pete wriggled his hard dick against David's thigh. That knowledge sent him wild for a good hard fuck.

"You're calling me a bottom? Are you implying you plan on screwing me in your car?"

"It's too cold and windy to fuck you out there." Pete pushed David's shirt high on his chest. The excitement in him was beginning to make him feel uninhibited and out of control. A feeling he liked very much. Leaning upright, Pete took a moment to see what exactly he had in his car with him. He was very pleasantly surprised. "Wow! Look at you. Jesus, David. Nice!"

David's naked chest shimmered like silk in the dim light of the emergency beacon.

Unable to resist, Pete lowered to lick his nipple. David moaned and began to writhe on the seat. Turned on by David's cologne and the scent of his pits, Pete lapped his way to the hair under David's arm shoving his clothing back and going for a deep inhale. "Intoxicating." He licked at him hungrily.

"Oh! Ah!" David arched his back and shivered. "Yes. I

love it when men lick me there."

"How did I know?" Pete chuckled, continuing to lap under his arm and digging his fingers into David's slacks beneath his belt.

"If you make me come in my suit trousers I'll be pissed off."

"Hold on."

"With you licking me and teasing me? Are you insane?" David bucked his hips.

"I'll get there. Be patient."

David let out a pathetic moan.

"The power's going to be out forever and we're stuck here at the moment. Let's just take our time and play." Pete lapped his way to David's nipple again. "I need you naked."

"Naked? In a car? In the parking garage of our office? Man, you have lost your mind."

Pete leaned up and unbuttoned David's shirt, loosening his necktie. "In the dark, in the storm, in a power outage. Stop whining. You do sound like a woman."

"Brute." David pouted out his bottom lip in exaggeration.

"I haven't even started my conquest of your fantastic body yet." Pete slid David's tie out of his collar and parted his open shirt over his chest. "Better." Just the sight of David's spectacular physique made Pete crazy for him.

"Am I the only one expected to be exposed here?"

"Nope." Pete took off his suit jacket in the tight space and tossed it onto the back seat. His tie and shirt disappeared next. "Okay?" He sat up and gestured to his nakedness.

"More than okay." David smoothed his hands over Pete's chest in excitement.

Dying to get down and dirty with a man as pretty as David, Pete kicked off his shoes, reaching for David's next. They were dropped to the floor of the car with a thud.

"I'm freaking." David panted anxiously.

"Don't worry. I'm here to protect you from the storm, baby." Thinking David was adorable in his damsel in distress act, Pete petted David's dark hair.

"No, not that, you dildo! I mean, what if someone sees us."

"No one will see. Besides, what's wrong with giving someone a little show? Huh? Guys pay good money to see live sex acts." Pete went back to licking David's armpit.

"Ah! I love that!" David squirmed.

Happy to get his mind off his paranoia and back on their sex, Pete crooned, "Mm you smell good," and rubbed his face into David's pit, sniffing deeply.

"New deodorant. Supposed to turn the women on." David moaned and pushed his hips up into Pete's.

"Ha." Pete laughed at the irony. "It's turning me on." He opened David's belt with one hand. "Can't wait to feel your cock. Cut?"

"Yeah. You?"

"Yup."

"Good."

"Ditto." Pete dipped his hand into David's briefs. It was already damp with his pre-cum. As Pete ran his fingers over his prick, he was impressed. "Nice! Man! Eight inches?"

"Just over," David purred proudly.

"You hot motherfucker!" Pete slid his palm over and around David's length suddenly going wild for him.

"You're making my ass pucker. You better have condoms and lube."

"I do. In the glove. But I ain't ready yet, lawyer." Pete exposed the head of David's cock from his dark briefs. "Gorgeous! What a cock." Pete felt his own pulsating like mad.

"Christ, I'm so fucking horny." David worked his hips up and down into Pete's hand.

"I want to savor you all night." Pete licked David's lips teasingly. David moaned and opened his mouth.

While he stroked David's cock, Pete devoured David's tongue, sucking it like it was his prick. Under him David began thrusting like mad. So he wouldn't come yet, Pete released his cock.

David whimpered in agony making Pete smile against his lips.

With his elbow on the seat to prop him up next to David, Pete paused to see his face again in the poor lighting. "Fucking gorgeous." He petted back his hair from his forehead.

"I need to spurt."

"You need my cock up your ass."

"Yes, please."

"I have so much I want to do to you first."

"I need to spurt," David whined in anguish.

"If you hold out, I'll get a bigger load out of you."

"Yeah! On your car seat."

"Uh uh. In my mouth." Pete chewed on David's earlobe.

"You better start sucking, because I'm about to shoot my wad from all this teasing."

"Hold on," Pete whispered seductively.

David moaned and grabbed Pete's face, connecting to his lips again.

When they parted mouths, Pete whispered, "I'm gonna fuck you, fuck you, fuck you..."

"Ohhhh..." David closed his eyes and shivered.

Kissing his way down David's rippled chest and abs, Pete paused to lick and taste his skin down to his treasure trail of hair leading to his pubes. His chin bumped into the head of David's cock and a sticky drop coated it. Wiping under his jaw with the back of his hand, Pete licked it off and hummed in delight. He scooted lower on the seat, wedged tightly against the driver's door and took his first lap of the oozing slit of David's cock. "Holy shit you taste good." Pete's own cock throbbed hotly and he knew he most likely spurted out a nice drop of pre-cum himself.

David whimpered and thrust his hips up into the air.

Pete yanked David's trousers and briefs down, struggling to get them off and toss them on the backseat.

Naked except for his black socks, David suddenly seemed to lose his inhibitions, straddled his knees and smoothed his hand down his own thighs, begging, "Suck me. Suck me."

"Hold on, pretty boy." Pete laughed softly. He urged David's legs backwards and exposed his ass. "Shaved balls. You son of a bitch!" Pete went completely crazy at the sight.

David just moaned in lustful agony.

Cramped against the side of the car, Pete burrowed into David's sack, licking at his root and his rim like mad. David went berserk underneath him, whimpering, moaning and gripping the leather upholstery as if he were holding on for dear life. Pete tongue fucked him and David cried out, squeez-ing his own cock, obviously preventing himself from coming.

Loving it, Pete was going just as insane as David was at the moment, dying to fuck him, and fuck him hard.

"I can't take it. I can't take it." David shook his head side to side imploringly. "I'm gonna come. I can't hold back."

Pete sucked on one testicle, then the next, rolling them in-side his mouth. Sitting up, staring down at David in the sparse light, Pete licked his lips hungrily. "Jesus, David. What a bod!"

"Fuck me! I can't take it!" David fumbled to open the glove compartment. The door fell open and he blindly began dumping things out onto the floor. "Where're the rubbers, where's the lube? If I don't get your dick in my ass I'm going to scream."

Smiling at David's desperation, Pete felt around the items on the floor and located what they needed. "I got it. Hang on."

"I can't hang on!" David yelled. "You get it? I'm done hanging on!"

That only made Pete laugh more. "Yes dear." He rolled a condom on his cock and opened the bottle of lube. Lowering back down again, he used two fingers to penetrate David's tight ring, loosening it up.

"Augh!" David cried, arching his back. "I'm there, you motherfucker! Augh!"

Seeing David was unable to stop the surge this time, Pete took all of David's dick into his mouth and finger fucked him gently. David was so pent up, it took nothing to make him climax. The minute Pete's lips sealed around his head, David exploded.

"Aahfffuck!" David screamed, shooting his wad into Pete's mouth as he almost flew off the bench seat with the convulsions.

In pleasure Pete massaged David well inside and out, swallowing the huge load of cum that had been waiting im-patiently for him. Continuing to suck and finger David, Pete moaned contentedly at giving David an orgasm to remember.

Coming up for air, Pete gasped, and caught his breath. The coolness of the evening air wasn't enough. Inside the car they were boiling hot and the windows even began to steam, coating with dew.

Once he had recovered slightly, and his breathing soft-ened, Pete got into position and pushed his dick into David's slick hole. "That's it." Pete inched closer, deeper.

"Yes. Finally." David relaxed against the supple leather.

When he was up to the hilt, Pete paused to savor the tight penetration. "Dee-lightful."

"Unreal. Give me a good one, Pete."

"I will. Don't you worry." Pete braced himself on David's torso and began thrusting. Instantly chills raced over his skin. When he peeked open his eyes, he caught David, his head propped up by the passenger door, biting his lip as he stared down at the connection of their bodies.

"You doing okay, handsome?" Pete asked.

"More than okay, stud."

"Good." Pete quickened his pace, their balls slapping against each other's bodies as they began to sweat. "Oh yeah. Oh yeah..." Pete began to rise to the heavens. Ogling David's amazing chest and abs, Pete felt his nuts tighten up for the blast. "That's it! That's it!" He jammed as hard as he could inside and upwards and came, opening his mouth to gasp as his cock pumped sperm out in rapid blasts. "Holy shit." Pete gulped for air. "That was so intense!" He could still feel the reverberating echoes racing through his crotch.

"Tell me about it." David pressed his ass as tight as he could to Pete's body before Pete pulled out.

After Pete disconnected and dropped the used condom on the floor mat, he collapsed on top of David to recuperate. "Damn..."

"Yeah. Damn." David panted in time with Pete.

"Now I'm wiped." Pete yawned, nestling into David's neck and hair.

"Me too. Complete sated and exhausted." David echoed his yawn.

Pete cupped David's jaw and kissed him tenderly, clos-ing his eyes as the urge to nap overwhelmed them. It felt so nice. So cozy.

≈≈≈

David stroked Pete's shoulders affectionately. Now that

they were calm and quiet he could hear the wind still howling past the parking garage's gate. Sirens sounded in the distance but nothing seemed to concern them at the moment. David embraced Pete, loving the sweat between them and the scent of sex in the air. Caressing the back of Pete's head gently, David closed his eyes and inhaled a deep satisfied breath knowing they were falling asleep. He asked himself if he cared.

It's late, it's dark, there's a storm. We can be together for a moment in time. It's no one's business but our own.

He never intended on anything like this to happen. Never. The security men would return, the gate would be released and David would make his way home. This was madness. Should he be responsible for the insanity of the act of two men, horny and alone in the middle of a blackout? Yes. No. I don't know.

David tried not to think too deeply about it. Shit happened. Sometimes shit you never expected in a million years happened. And if Pete wasn't gay, or gorgeous, or right there at that moment in time, then no, nothing would have happened. Odds were it could have been anyone else trapped in the parking garage with him. Not Pete.

But it was Pete. And why did Pete have to be gorgeous, gay, and willing?

Fate. Nothing he could do about it. Don't beat yourself up, David. It's done. You had sex with another man. Oh well. Life happens.

He'd worry about it later. After. Some other time. Not now. Now he was sated, exhausted, and had a sleeping man lying on top of him. A naked, utterly fabulous sleeping man, by the way. He was only human. I'm human! Not a goddamn robot! Keep telling yourself that, David. Keep telling yourself that.

Hearing Pete's deep restful breaths, feeling the softness of it brush past his hair by his ear, David couldn't be upset. In fact he was delirious. It was a living fantasy. The stuff of gay wet dreams. What was he supposed to feel? Angry? Upset? Uh uh. He didn't. Not now anyway. Now he was in the arms of a dreamboat.

Smiling happily, David snuggled against him, and felt their soft, moist cocks press together. He sighed in bliss and fell asleep.

VOYEUR

His motorcycle helmet in his hand, Miguel had finally made it to the ground floor after being locked in his office for two hours. Mumbling profanity under his breath, he descended the ten floors down the stairwell in the horribly dim lighting and made it to the parking garage. So many cars were left abandoned he got a bad feeling in the pit of his stomach that the gates would not open because of the power failure. Walking to the iron rail, seeing it sealed shut, he swore in Spanish under his breath. Waving his hands in exasperation, Miguel kept muttering in frustration. A noise woke him from his anger.

"Hola?" He listened. No one replied. Walking closer to where he thought the sound had originated, Miguel paused and noticed one of the cars near the gate was occupied. About to approach them and ask if they knew when the gate would open, he stopped short as one of the men vanished below the dashboard and the other began undressing.

"Aye!" Miguel looked around in paranoia. "What are you doing, my friends?" he whispered to himself. Tiptoeing backwards, moving to a dark shadow near the car parked beside the Mercedes, Miguel had a look inside the front seat. "Mi dios," he gasped.

Trying to keep back from their view, Miguel could not believe what these two handsome men were doing inside the front seat of a car at seven o'clock in the stormy night during a black out.

"Oh, mi amigos, I wish I was you," he sighed silently.

Afraid to blink, Miguel crept closer when one of the men pushed open the legs of the other and began lapping between his thighs.

"Aye! Qué están haciendo? What are they doing?" he asked himself. "They are making love! Why do I ask a stupid question?"

Setting his helmet down quietly, Miguel positioned himself behind the front door so the man on top could not see him. Yet Miguel had a spectacular view of the action inside. A very dim sliver of light from one of the emergency floods was aimed perfectly into the passenger window illuminating the carnal action.

Chewing his lip as the events inside the car heated him up to a level of excitement he hadn't felt in weeks, Miguel rubbed his own cock through his slacks and moaned softly.

One man sprung to his mind instantly. "Stuart Jones. Aye, Stuart. En caso de que sólo podría ser nosotros, mi bellezo. If only that could be us, my beauty." Miguel had lusted after his straight friend Stuart for a year. They played racquetball, worked out, dined, watched sports on television, did everything together. Everything but. Pero el sexo. And Miguel wanted to seduce him so badly he ached at night, preventing any sleep. But losing Stuart as a friend would kill him. "Why can't you see how beautiful our love could be?" Miguel witnessed the orgasm wash over the face of the handsome man on the bottom and closed his own eyes. Massaging his cock as it throbbed, Miguel felt pain from the longing in his heart.

I should try. I need to try. Maybe he is open? How do I know? He does not date. He goes with no one. Why? I ask myself why? He is muy guapo. A beauty. Why won't Stuart date a woman? Eh? Why? He no date women, and he no date men. He sees me every night. He will love me. He will.

Miguel peeked in. The man on top was rolling on a condom. My love. My Stuart. Why not this? Hmm? Why not? Look at the two of them. Bliss. Look at their faces. Lovers! They are fulfilling the sexual needs of each other.

Dabbing at his eye as it filled, Miguel knew watching those men was an imposition on their privacy. But? In a car? In the garage? Fair game.

"Mi amante, you will love me too." Miguel moved around the other side of the car so he could see the man on top as he humped the one underneath. "Beautiful. Look at them."

Soon the man doing the fucking was awash with an orgasm, his handsome face appearing like Eros himself.

Rubbing his jaw in agony, Miguel moaned as frustration took hold of him to the extreme. "I will go. I will see you tonight. I must."

Peering back at the horrible storm and the debris whipping past the gate, Miguel knew riding his bike in this weather was suicidal. And that was even if he was able to get that gate open, which he had an idea he couldn't.

Looking back into the car, the two men naked and resting after their exertion, Miguel retrieved his helmet and made a useless tug at the gate. "Nada." It was as he suspected. Locked.

The urge to see Stuart raged in him. Placing his helmet on his head, Miguel rolled his bike to the lobby door and propped it open, narrowly squeezing his Kawasaki into the foyer to wheel through to the main entrance doors. The lighting was so poor Miguel could barely make anything out. Awkwardly wedging the glass front door open, he scraped the handlebars against the pane and prayed nothing shattered. The wind instantly pressed him and his bike back against the building front. Using all his strength, he righted the heavy bike and set it on its kickstand for a minute.

"I am crazy! Loco!" He fastened the strap of his helmet, lowered the visor and took a good look at the slanting rain, the swaying blacked-out streetlights and bending palm trees. Debris and branches whipped through the pitch black streets.

Determined to see the man he loved, Miguel hiked the bike back off its stand, rolled it down the few concrete steps and straddled the seat. After a deep inhale for courage, he started the motorcycle up and revved the engine. The headlight seemed to be the only thing giving him any illumination in the horrible blackness. The streets were vacant except for a distant emergency vehicle screaming by with red and blue lights flashing and screeching sirens.

He touched his chest in the sign of the cross, muttered a prayer to the Virgin and sped off hoping nothing would hit him and knock him off the bike.

∽∾

Stuart lit a few candles and paused every time it sounded like something hit the house. "Jesus!" He set out a few hurricane lamps with glass domes covering tiny flickering wicks and curled on the sofa with the only thing he had to contact the outside world; his CD player with an am/fm radio. The station was static ridden but he could at least hear it enough to gauge the storm's severity.

"...winds expected to continue well past midnight with gusts of up to seventy miles per hour...power outages are far reaching all the way up the western coastline. High wind advisories continue in counties; Kern, Los Angeles, Orange, Santa Barbara, Ventura..."

Stuart jumped at a noise. Shutting off the radio and hopping off the sofa, he pushed back the curtain to look out his front window. "What the fuck!" he gasped, racing to the door and swinging it open. "Miguel? Are you insane?"

"I am! I am!" Miguel appeared pale as he tugged the helmet off his head. "It is a nightmare outside! Terrible!"

"Where's your bike?" Stuart searched the dark.

"Out in front of your garage."

"Get it in!" Stuart slipped on his shoes.

"No! Too much trouble!"

"Not for your brand new bike it isn't." Stuart raced outside and opened the garage door as rain and wind pelted them both with debris.

He helped Miguel push it next to his Viper, closed the garage again, and grabbed Miguel to hurry back inside.

Once they were in the living room with the door locked, Stuart gaped at him. "What the fuck are you doing riding in the fucking storm?"

Miguel set his helmet down, unzipping the leather jacket he wore that was running with rainwater. "I need see you."

"You risked your life to come here? Are you insane?" Stuart helped him off with his jacket, holding it out as it dripped. "You're soaking wet."

"Si. Soaking."

"Come upstairs. Let me give you some dry clothes." He

picked up a candle to take with him. After he bounded up the staircase, Stuart hung Miguel's jacket over the bathtub to allow it to drip dry. Setting the candle on his dresser he dug for a pair of jeans and a t-shirt. "Why didn't you stay home?"

"I was no home. I was trapped at work for two hours. I only now get free."

Stuart dropped the clothing on his bed and stared at Miguel. "Trapped? What happened?"

As he took off his boots and socks, Miguel snarled, "Some idiot lock me in. Everyone leave early on Fridays. Is normal. But I still in the office trying to finish my paperwork. The lights go out. Everyone goes home but this I did not know. I no think nothing. Not until I have to leave. Then! Aye! I have to pry open the door with a letter opener. I so angry. No phones working, nada!"

"Okay, buddy. Calm down." Stuart touched the ends of Miguel's long black hair feeling how wet it was where it had poked out from the motorcycle helmet in back. "You must have frozen your ass off."

"Not too bad. Just wet and cold now."

"I wish I could make you up a cup of coffee. Sorry."

"No. I no need coffee." Miguel struggled to drag his wet jeans down his thighs. He dropped onto the bed and yanked at them in frustration to get them off.

"Why did you come here and not go home?" Stuart held the bottoms of the pant legs and pulled, helping Miguel.

Once Miguel removed his shirt and was sitting still with only his briefs on, he seemed to pause to catch his breath. "I need see you."

Stuart relaxed next to him. "Why? Are you okay?"

Combing his fingers back through his long hair to get it out of his eyes, Miguel shook his head. "No. I no okay."

In the flickering light of a single candle, Stuart took in the sight of his best friend. Miguel's dark black hair was wavy and wild from his ride as it surrounded his square, dark coarse jaw. His brown eyes were smoldering under his arched eyebrows and the long lashes surrounding them made them appear painted. The sight caused the breath to catch in Stuart's throat. Trying not to look at Miguel's fantastic physique,

Stuart was embarrassed to be lusting after his best friend. It was the last thing he wanted to do. To insult him, to lose him.

"Did something happen at work? Other than getting locked in?" Stuart had to touch him. Gently he pushed the long, wild hair back from Miguel's eyes. "Get dressed, you must be freezing. I can't believe you rode your bike in seventy mile an hour winds—"

When Miguel grabbed his jaw and kissed him, Stuart choked in shock. "What are you doing?" He stumbled off the bed and fell to the carpeted floor, astonished.

"Sorry!" Miguel cried out. "Perdon. Oh, Stu...I not know what I am doing. Please forgive me." Miguel covered his face and hunched over.

Stuart tried to analyze the situation. Touching his mouth and still feeling the reverberations of Miguel's lips on his, Stuart began to pant. "Miguel?"

"I must leave. I must. I humiliate myself. What have I done?" He rose up, pacing, rubbing his face in agony. "I not want to lose you. No. You are mi mejor amigo. I insult you."

Slowly getting to his feet, Stuart gaped at Miguel in awe. "You? You?"

"Sorry. No. So sorry. I go." Miguel grabbed his wet jeans and struggled to get them on.

Stuart clasped his arm. "You're not going anywhere."

Holding up his hands in surrender, Miguel assented, "Yes. Hit me. I deserve. Go. Hit me."

Stuart ripped the wet clothing out of Miguel's hand and felt him flinch, gearing up for a belt. Instead, Stuart hugged him in bliss and rocked him, squeezing him tight.

"Aye? What?" Miguel asked in surprise. "What? No! You feel this way for me? All this time?"

Stuart dug his hands through Miguel's hair. "You told me you were straight. Why?"

"Why? You ask me why? You say you are. What can I do? I no want to make you hate me. So? We both are straight."

Stuart inhaled Miguel's fragrant hair. The wind howled outside and rattled the windows as things hit the house, battering it. "You know how long I have loved you?" Stuart ran his hands over Miguel's shoulders and down his arms.

When he met Miguel's eyes, he found them glistening in the candlelight.

"You say love?"

"Yes." Stuart urged Miguel to sit on the bed.

"I no can believe. No. I no believe what I hear. You love me?"

"Yes." Stuart began to unbuttoned his shirt, staring down at his handsome friend.

"I must be dreaming. Estoy soñando, si."

Laughing softly, Stuart whispered, "No, Miguel, you aren't dreaming." He tossed his shirt down on the floor, unzipping his jeans.

"We make love?" Miguel asked innocently.

"Would you like to?"

"It is my wish. Yes." Miguel reached out for Stuart's hand.

Once he was down to his briefs, Stuart crawled with Miguel to lie face to face on the bed with him.

"Is chilly. We cuddle under covers?"

"Yes. Good idea." Stuart drew the blankets down and they scrambled to get beneath them. Once they were under the bedding, they embraced, wrapping their arms around each other. "I don't believe it. I can't believe you want me this way."

"Why you no say before? Why you wait so long?"

"I could ask you the same thing." Stuart pushed Miguel's hair back from his eyes so he could gaze into them. "What happened today? Why did you risk life and limb on your bike in hurricane winds to come here to me and seduce me? Why tonight?"

A shy smile first appeared and Miguel averted his eyes before he answered. "Two men. In the parking garage. They were locked in, no?"

"Yes?" Stuart wrapped his legs around Miguel's.

"They get very sexy on each other in the front seat of one of their cars. I can no help myself."

"Did you watch them?" Stuart grew excited at the thought.

"I did. So bad. I watch them. Oh, the love they made..." Miguel inhaled deeply. "It make me loco for you. I think, why not me and my Stuart do that? Why not?"

"Wow. That's really hot."

"You think so? You no think I terrible?"

"No. I'm glad. Maybe it was the push we both needed."

"What now? What do we do?"

"Have you ever been with a man, Miguel?"

"Si. I have. You?"

"Once. In college."

Miguel smiled and cupped the back of Stuart's head gently. "Then we already know what to do. No?"

"Yes." Stuart closed his eyes and met Miguel's lips. At the touch of his tongue, Stuart felt his body heat up to a slow burn morphing to a boiling caldron. Digging his fingers into Miguel's long hair, running them through the damp ends, Stuart couldn't be more excited to be holding a man he adored for so long from afar.

"Touch me. Me toque."

Miguel urged Stuart's hand downwards. As he found Miguel's stiff length, Stuart moaned and smoothed his palm over it from base to tip. Though he'd caught a glimpse of this part of Miguel's body in the shower at the club once, it was soft at the time and too brief of a glance to savor. To be holding it in his hand when it was erect and hot, Stuart thought he would die from the thrill.

"So good. Oh. So good, Stu. You touch me like an angel."

Sweating suddenly from his excitement, Stuart tossed off the blankets dramatically and stared at Miguel's handsome face, lowering his gaze to take in the beauty of his body. When he caught sight of that huge cock poking out of his briefs, Stuart began dragging the underwear off Miguel's legs. When they were both nude, Stuart kissed his way down Miguel's chest to his crotch.

"Es bueno, muy bueno."

"Good." Stuart licked Miguel's belly button, kissing his way through his pubic hair to his cock. Rubbing his face against the silky skin of his engorged shaft, Stuart moaned in ecstasy.

An unseen breeze flickered the lone candle flame, making Miguel's flesh appear to shimmer.

"You are fantastic." Stuart lapped at his slit. "I can't believe we waited so long."

"No wait now. You do what you please. I am yours to enjoy."

A shiver rushed over Stuart's body at the delightful offer. "Can I make love to you?"

"Yes. You must." Miguel spread his legs in invitation.

Stuart maneuvered between Miguel's thighs and began running his tongue up the underside of Miguel's cock. Miguel's quadriceps tightened and he whimpered softly.

"I am going to enjoy sucking you off," Stuart hissed seductively.

"Aye! Me as well." Miguel laughed.

Stuart propped himself up between Miguel's thighs and took his time licking his mushroom-shaped head, enjoying the scent and salty flavor. Tiny moans of pleasure met his ears like music in the wild wind.

The number of nights Stuart had dreamed of having beautiful Miguel Rodriguez this way were too many to count. Holding himself under the sheets, Stuart had fisted himself with the thought of doing just what he was doing at that moment. He groaned loudly at his own pleasure and deepened his sucking.

Miguel responded, raising his hips and caressing Stuart's blond hair.

Tasting a drop of pre-cum on his tongue, Stuart paused and stared at Miguel whose gaze was riveted to him. Stuart made a move for the drawer of his nightstand and removed a condom and a bottle of lubrication.

A low laugh came from Miguel. "I no know you have these. Maybe I should look in that drawer sooner."

"Yes. Maybe you should have." Stuart knelt up and rolled a condom on himself. "We would have made up for lost time."

"No lost time no more. I am so glad I come. Stu...you make love to me and I will be yours. I want to be yours."

A chill rushed up Stuart's spine at the loving compliment. "Miguel, you are so fantastic. I'm glad you risked your neck to come here as well. But don't do that again!" Stuart chided playfully.

"No. No again. Now is for loving, no talk."

"Yes." Stuart squeezed the gel onto his fingers and tried

to see between Miguel's legs in the shadowy glow of the single candle. Feeling first, he located his tight hole and began sliding his fingers around and inside it. Miguel hissed out a breath of air and his body relaxed, splaying out on the bed.

Moving two fingers in and out slowly, Stuart felt Miguel let go of his tight muscles and soften up for him. Placing the head of his cock against Miguel's rim, Stuart met his eyes in the dark room. "This means everything to me."

"Me too." Miguel reached to touch him.

Pushing in, feeling the heat and tightness of Miguel's body around him, Stuart inhaled a quick breath.

"Si. Mas!"

At Miguel's request, Stuart penetrated deeper. His balls clenched as their connection united their bodies as one. "Miguel," Stuart moaned adoringly, "Lover..."

"Te quiero con toda mi alma."

Stuart thrilled at the sound of Miguel's Spanish crooning to him as they made love. He didn't have to know the translation, he already got the meaning.

Hearing Miguel's breathing quicken, seeing his chest rising and falling rapidly, Stuart gripped Miguel's cock and worked it as he fucked him.

"Si! Si!" Miguel bucked his hips underneath Stuart.

The sensations rose to their climax. Stuart felt the churning in his nuts and his cock go rigid. Miguel's hands covered over Stuart's and he fisted himself frantically as, he too, was ready.

Feeling Miguel's dick throb as he came, Stuart opened his eyes to see Miguel in orgasmic bliss. Cream spurted out of his cock as he watched Miguel clamp his eyes shut and opened his soft full lips. Just the sight of Miguel in climax put Stuart into a tailspin of passion. He gripped both his hands behind Miguel's neck and drew him towards his mouth, still glued together at the hip. Miguel wrapped his arms around Stuart to bring their lips together. When they kissed, Stuart whimpered in agony at the affection he was feeling for his best friend. His heart exploded in his chest, he was so satisfied they had connected sexually.

Gently pulling out so he could rest more comfortably

on top of Miguel, Stuart covered his face in kisses making Miguel laugh.

"Te quiero con toda mi alma."

Hearing it again, Stuart asked, "What does that mean?"

"It mean, I love you...with my soul."

Chills washed down Stuart's back. He squeezed Miguel as tightly as he could and held back a sob of relief. "I love you too. So much."

"Bien...muy bien."

The sound of a loud crack startled them both.

"What was that?" Staurt sat up.

"I no know. We must see. It was very loud."

Stuart took a candle to the bathroom to remove the rubber and clean up quickly. When he returned to the bedroom, Miguel had dressed in the spare jeans and t-shirt Stuart had provided. Stuart slid on his pants and shirt, held the candle aloft and they hurried down the stairs.

"What you plan to do?" Miguel asked.

"I have to go outside and look."

"No. No go out. Is terrible out."

Stuart pushed back the curtains. It was still blowing hard and the rain was moving horizontally. "Jesus. I think a tree came down. I can barely see it but something huge is blocking the road. Can you see?"

Miguel leaned against the window. "No. Is too dark. I see nothing."

"Let me just call Chris. He lives right on the coast and I'm really worried about him." Stuart located his mobile phone.

"The phone works? The phones in the building no work."

"Let me try my mobile." Stuart turned the tiny cell phone on and it appeared to get a signal. He dialed a number and put it to his ear. "It's ringing," he relayed to Miguel.

"Hello?"

"Chris?"

"Stu?"

"Yeah. I was worried about you. Are you all right? I know you have a place right on the beach."

"You're not going to believe this."

"What?" Stuart glanced at Miguel who was listening

curiously.

"I'm stuck in a department store at the moment."

"You're joking."

"No. I wish I knew how my house was doing. Let me go, Stu. I'll call you in the morning when I know the score."

"Okay, Chris. Just tell me if you need help with the clean up or anything."

"I will. Thanks."

Stuart hung up and gaped at Miguel. "Chris is stuck at a department store."

Miguel covered his laugh. "I should not think funny. Sorry."

Seeing his impish grin, Stuart embraced him. "Get over here."

"I here." Miguel hugged him tight.

Rocking him side to side, Stuart wondered if the wind had brought something magical with it. Though it should have been a horrible evening, the chaos, the blackout, the damage, it wasn't. It was the best night of his life.

MALL MEN

Chris stood in the dressing room of Nordstrom's in the Glendale Galleria. A pair of slacks on his hips, he modeled for himself in the mirror trying to decide on making a purchase or not. The lights flickered. Chris paused and looked up at the ceiling where florescent bulbs were covered by plastic shields. He checked the time. It was nearing five.

Sliding the black dress slacks off his legs to hang back on the hanger, Chris froze as the entire area went pitch black. "You have to be kidding me."

"Oh shit."

Chris heard the exclamation in the next dressing room stall.

"They coming back on?" Chris asked the stranger.

"I hope so. I'm standing here in my underwear and I can't see a fricken thing."

Chris laughed. "Ditto."

"Shouldn't there be emergency lighting? I can't see my hand in front of my face."

Setting the slacks he had in his hand down on a ledge he knew was to his left. Chris began feeling around the area for his own trousers. "This sucks!"

"Jesus! Where's my fucking pants?"

Hearing the same panic in the second man's voice, Chris actually laughed. "If I leave wearing the wrong clothes, they can't arrest me for shoplifting. I can't see shit."

"There has to be emergency lights. This is insane!"

"I don't even have a book of matches," Chris muttered.

"Me neither. Don't smoke."

"Hello?" Chris called out. "Anyone have a flashlight?" He heard the second man chuckle. "What are you laughing at?"

"You. This place was almost empty when I came into the dressing room. Who exactly are you shouting for?"

Chris thought he located his pants. "Anyone?"

"Fuck. Where's my fucking jeans?"

Managing to get his slacks on, at least thinking they were his own pair, Chris touched the pockets and did indeed feel his wallet, phone, and keys in them. He lowered to the floor and began reaching around for his shoes. He touched a hand and jumped.

"Is that you?" the second man asked nervously.

"Yes. You're reaching under the stall to my spot. You didn't find my shoes did you?"

The man laughed. "Still looking for my fricken jeans."

"Well, they're not in here."

"They have to have a generator. This is really unbelievable."

"It is. I hate the sense of blindness. It's making me crazy."

"Finally."

"Found something?" Chris knocked into a shoe as he groped blindly.

"I think. Hopefully."

Imagining the man to be in his twenties, Chris smiled. "I think I have a shoe."

"Is it mine or yours?" the man laughed.

"What size do you wear?" Chris joked.

"Ten and a half."

"Well then. It could be either of ours."

"Stealing my shoes?"

"Yeah, that's me. Shoe fetish." Chris sat on the floor and put one shoe on, reaching around for the other.

"How can they not have emergency lights?"

"You can write a letter complaining about it when you get home. How's that?" Chris began searching for shoe number two. He ran into a hand again. "Are you crawling in here with me?" he asked jokingly.

"Depends. What the hell do you look like?" came an impish reply.

Chris broke up with laughter. "I can lie. I can say I look like George Clooney. You wouldn't know."

"Yeah? Clooney?"

"No. Sorry. Not that good." Chris enjoyed this insanity though being sightless was maddening. He pitied the blind instantly.

"You sound good."

"Did you take my shoe?" Chris couldn't locate the second one.

"No. I swear I didn't take your shoe. I'm still working on finding my pants."

A pause followed as Chris continued to feel the floor for his second loafer.

"You'd think they'd send someone around with a flashlight and make sure everyone is all right."

"You certainly have high expectations for a shopping mall store." Chris grew frustrated. "You sure you didn't steal my shoe?"

"Hang on. Let me see how many I have in here."

Waiting patiently, Chris chuckled at the comedy of the situation.

"The floor is really gross."

"I know. I'm loath to touch it. Seems its been a while since they swept." Chris brushed off his hands.

In the pause Chris listened. Other than the man next to him, he couldn't hear another human voice. "You don't think they'd lock us in here?"

"They have to do a sweep of the place. Wait...is this your shoe?"

As he sat on the floor of his stall, Chris reached under the wall towards the next one. "Where are you?"

Cracking up, the man said, "I haven't moved. Where am I?"

"Hang on." Slowly, so he wouldn't bang into anything, Chris made it to his feet and felt around the walls.

"Where are you?" the man asked curiously.

"I'm trying to get to you." Chris smoothed his fingers along the painted wooden divider.

"Yeah? That sounds inviting."

Chris grinned broadly. "Really?"

"You getting close? I'm afraid to move and slam into you."

"Where are you in the stall?"

"Still sitting on my ass on the floor searching for my clothing."

"Okay." Anticipating the man being low, Chris crouched down and found the entrance of his dressing room right beside his own. "Where's the shoe?" He reached into the space and felt skin. "Sorry." He imagined it was a leg but couldn't be certain.

"No problem. Where's your hand?" He laughed.

"Believe it or not, I'm holding it out for the shoe."

"I believe it, but I can't see a fucking thing!"

Chris inched closer. He definitely felt a leg covered in soft hair. "I found you."

"Sweet. What did you say you looked like?"

"Why? Is the pitch darkness giving you lurid ideas?"

"If I say yes, will you hit me? Or worse, abandon me?"

"I could describe myself but it's useless." Chris kept his fingertips in contact with what he was imagining was a shin.

"Try."

Assuming he knew where the second man was now, Chris sat down so he wouldn't step on him. "I'm Chris. I'm twenty-eight, six foot tall and weigh two hundred pounds."

"Nice. Don't stop touching my leg. At least I know where you are, sort of."

"All right," Chris replied, smiling, resting his hand on that warm limb. He tried to imagine what this man looked like solely based on his voice. "Your turn?"

"I'm Phil. I'm twenty-five, six foot three, and around two hundred and twenty pounds."

"Christ, you're big. I won't screw with you."

"Too bad."

At that sexual invitation, Chris chuckled. "What color are your hair and eyes?" He knew he should move his hand but hell the guy said to keep it there.

"Brown and brown. You?"

"Brown and blue."

"I love that. Brown and blue." After a deep inhale, Phil

asked. "Any face hair?"

"No. Clean shaven."

"Me too. Ah...married?"

"No." Chris laughed shyly.

"This keeps getting better."

"Does it?" Chris wished he had a pack of matches. He'd love a quick glimpse of Phil.

"Where the hell are you?"

Chris felt a wash of air as if Phil was feeling around for him. "Why? What will you do if you find me?" Chris released Phil's leg to defend against an accidental swipe at his face.

"What do you want me to do to you?" Phil responded wickedly.

"In the pitch dark on the floor of a dirty fitting room? Are you serious?"

"What are we supposed to do? I can't see for shit. I still can't find my pants and if you think it's scary in here, I'll bet if we try fumbling our way out of the dressing room and into uncharted territory we'll get killed out there."

"There has to be an emergency lighting system. Maybe not in here, but out there." Chris pointed over his shoulder but he knew it wasn't seen in the complete blackness.

"Yeah huh? Don't count on it. Crap. Help me find my fucking jeans, will ya?"

"Where did you leave them, Phil?"

"I thought I left them on the ledge, but when I checked they weren't there. They must have slid off when I put the slacks I was trying on over them."

Chris knelt up and began reaching out to the same side of the stall as where he was crouching. His knuckles hit a solid object. "Ouch."

"That sucked."

"I'm afraid to move. My luck I'll smack my face against the wall." Chris ran into Phil again, touching warm, naked skin. His thigh? He had no idea and didn't know if he should investigate. "We have to stop meeting like this."

Phil laughed. "Man! I want to know what you look like."

"Where is your hand?" Chris asked.

"Why? What are you going to do with it?" Phil responded

seductively.

"Brush it off and try to find my hand." Chris heard some rustling.

"Clean now. Where are you?"

Chris waved his arms around and found Phil's fingers reaching towards him. He held Phil's wrist and brought it to his face. "Here I am."

"Cool. Hang on. Let me brush my other hand off."

Feeling the warmth of Phil's palm on his cheek, Chris waited patiently. More rustling sounds followed. A second hand slowly touched the other side of his face. Now Phil was cupping Chris's jaw.

"Braille me." Chris laughed.

"If you're cute, I'll fucking nail you."

Chris laughed. "You're gay?"

"I am now!" Phil chuckled. "Jesus, Chris, you sound like a hot motherfucker."

Closing his eyes, Chris kept quiet as Phil touched his face lightly. As gently as possible, Phil tickled Chris's forehead, ran his fingers over his eyebrows, down his eyelids to his cheekbones, his jaw line, his lips, his nose, and finally his hair, running both hands into it sensually.

"This isn't helping me picture what you look like, but it's getting me hotter than hell."

It was getting Chris 'hotter than hell' as well. "No. I suppose it was a stupid idea." Chris caught a whiff of Phil's cologne and inhaled. Phil's hands lowered slowly down Chris's neck. "Going exploring?"

"I was planning on it. Do you mind?"

"I don't have any idea if I do or not." Chris smiled. "I've never been in a situation like this in my life."

"I can't decide if it's driving me crazy because it's so frustrating, or so incredibly sexy."

"Our luck the lights will go on and we'll cringe at the sight of each other."

"Why do I have a feeling that's not going to happen?" Phil ran his palms over Chris's shoulders.

Tingling at the caress from his unseen stranger, Chris prayed Phil was as good looking as he was imagining. "Who do you look like?" Chris asked, "Like anyone I would know?"

"You mean like in a movie star? Or someone famous?"

"Yes. Like that. Who do you resemble?"

"Uh...Rock Hudson?"

"Shut up!" Chris laughed. "Rock Hudson."

When Phil didn't reply, Chris whispered, "For real?"

"I've been told I look a little like him. But I don't have his or your blue eyes."

Boldly Phil's fingers touched the skin on Chris's chest near his open top shirt button. A flash of fire hit Chris instantly. "Rock Hudson?" Chris began panting at the excitement, wanting Phil's hands to continue their little voyage.

"Yes. A little...what about you? Please tell me someone good."

Chris laughed softly. "I don't know. I've certainly not been compared to Rock Hudson."

"Well, you're not bald. I know that." Phil smoothed his hand over Chris's head, combing through his mane.

Laughing, Chris replied, "No. Full head of hair."

"Tell me...come on. You must resemble someone."

Dealing with the chills Phil was causing as he continued to caress and fondle him in the dark, Chris racked his brains to think. "Fine. Did you watch the Olympics on TV?"

"Yes..." Phil replied tentatively, his hands pausing as they rested on Chris's shoulders.

Though Chris had the urge to reach out and touch Phil, he kept his own hands on his lap at the moment. "Did you see the javelin competition?"

"Yes..." Phil answered.

"You take a good look at the gold medalist?"

"Andreas Thorkildsen?" Phil gasped. "You look like Andreas Thokildsen?"

"Well, I—" About to add a disclaimer that he only resembled the gorgeous Norwegian, Chris was grabbed by the jaw and yanked down to the floor on top of Phil. The zinging sensation of being on top of a hot male body in the pitch dark had Chris's head spinning.

"No! Tell me you're lying!"

Hearing Phil panting in excitement, Chris felt badly. "I've

been told I look a little like him." Chris wasn't the kind of guy to boast about his charm or appeal. He was modest and hoped he wasn't setting Phil up for a disappointment when the lights came on.

As if the image of having a man as spectacular as Andreas Thorkildsen pressing down on him heavily was lighting Phil on fire, he shouted, "Holy fuck," and connected to Chris's mouth, sucking at his lips and tongue wildly.

Astonished, Chris's eyes sprang open even though it did nothing to help his blindness. Phil was going crazy under him, wrapping around him with his bare hairy legs and gripping his head tightly for a deep, passionate open mouth kiss. Parting for a breath of air, Chris gasped, "Jesus! Phil!"

"Is it true?" Phil ran his hand over Chris's face in excitement. "Are you telling the truth or just saying that to drive me insane?"

Unable to catch his breath at the sensory overload of Phil's fondling, gasping and writhing under him, Chris felt dizzy. "How could I say it to drive you insane? You think I had intuitive knowledge you had the hots for that man? Christ, I'm surprised you even know who he is."

Phil's fingers smoothed down Chris's back to his ass, squeezing a cheek in each hand ardently. "I know. You kidding me? I know every gorgeous stud who participated in those games. I make it my business to know."

The heavy petting from Phil had gotten Chris into a heightened state of arousal. It was time he became an active participant and stopped limply accepting all of Phil's advances.

After wiping his hands off on his own slacks to get the floor grit off, Chris found Phil's head and touched his hair and the side of his face. "Do you really look like Rock Hudson?"

"Yes."

"Are you a model?"

"I am."

"Damn." Wriggling his hips on Phil, Chris tried to imagine Phil's features as he ran his fingertips along his forehead, down his nose to his mouth, just as Phil had done to him previously.

Phil's hand clamped onto Chris's ass urging his crotch harder down on top of his own. "It's making me crazy that I can't see you," Phil snarled seductively.

"Me too. It's very disorienting." Chris gave up on trying to 'read' Phil's features.

"Why don't they have floodlights? Isn't it required?"

"I don't know, Phil. I have no idea what's going on in the outside world at the moment. I only know what's going on in this dressing room. And that, barely." Chris laughed.

"I think I remember them talking about a thunderstorm, but not one that would blackout the city, if it has."

Chris dug his fingers into Phil's thick hair wishing he could visualize his face, but now all he could picture was Rock Hudson. But that wasn't a bad thing. "I really have no clue what's going on. Do you want to try and find your clothing and go see?"

"No."

Chris smiled. "No?"

"Screw the outside world. I have Andreas Thorkildsen lying on top of me. With a fucking erection, I may add."

"Man, I hope I don't regret telling you that and when the lights come on you're disappointed."

"Did you lie?"

Chris's smile dropped. "No. I didn't lie. I have been told I resemble him." Instantly, he was embraced and rolled. Chris flinched as if he would get smashed into a wall. He knew these rooms weren't known for their size. Now Phil was on top of him, his weight impressive as he pressed Chris to the floor. "You're a big fella, aren't you?" Chris whispered.

"Yes. Wanna feel how big?"

As Chris swallowed nervously his hand was led to Phil's hard-on over his briefs. "Wow."

"You like?" Phil asked, using Chris's hand to massage himself.

"Jesus. You're huge. Who on earth do you model for? Gay porn?" A low chuckle found its way to Chris's ears. "No. Do you?"

"I dabble."

"Dabble?" Moaning softly at the feel of such a wonderful appendage, Chris ran his fingers up and down the length of Phil's imposing dick.

"I do a little dancing in West Hollywood on the side as well."

"No shit?" Chris felt a shiver of excitement wash over him. He loved go-go boys. Fucking loved them!

"Yeah. You hang around WeHo at all?"

"A bit. Yes. Not as much as I'd like." But I will now! Growl!

Phil whimpered softly. "That feels good. You can go into my briefs you know."

"You think this blackout is just temporary?" Chris felt a pang of nerves as the action grew more heated in this pitch dark environment. "You know, and the lights will come on and..."

"How am I supposed to answer that question?"

"No. You can't. I suppose I was just looking for an opinion."

"If you want my opinion..."

"I do."

"We should get naked."

Chris started laughing. "Bad boy! Naked on the floor of Nordstrom's fitting room. How romantic."

As if the idea was perfectly reasonable to him, Phil began kissing Chris's neck sending tingles all over his skin.

The caressing was making Chris crazy. "Holy shit. You weren't kidding." One by one the buttons of his shirt were popped open. When Chris was exposed to the cool air, he felt Phil's fingers exploring his chest and nipples, all the while Phil licked at his jaw and cheek. In reflex Chris squeezed Phil's cock, pumping it in his palm. It obviously was driving Phil crazy because he groaned in longing and began tearing off Chris's clothing.

Fearing the walls of the tiny space hitting him in the head, Chris reached out just to get a notion for how much room they had in case they began flailing around from passion. The back wall with the mirror was located, and one side wall. It appeared there was a little space to their right.

"You still with me?" Phil asked between kisses and gasps.

"You'd know if I vanished."

"It just felt like you were doing something."

"I was trying to locate the walls so we wouldn't smash

into one."

"Got it."

It felt as if Phil sat up and Chris's pants were dragged down his hips by unseen hands.

"You realize we'll never find anything once we're naked."

"We will. Let's worry about that later."

The sense of disorientation at being stripped in such darkness was almost too intimidating for him. Chris fought the feeling of anxiety with the image of a man as gorgeous as Rock Hudson making love to him. How bad could that be? A go-go boy as big and beautiful as Rock? Mama mia, that sounded fantastic.

"I wish I'd have gotten a peek at you when you came in here." Chris chided himself for being a gentleman and not leering into the next stall while the light was on.

"Me too. You kidding me?"

Chris jolted as a hot mouth wrapped around the head of his dick. "Holy Christ!" He had no idea where Phil was in the small space. He did now.

"Mm!"

Closing his eyes to fight the sense of claustrophobia the darkness was causing, Chris reached out to find Phil and touched his thick head of hair as his head bobbed up and down over his crotch. Chris ran his fingers through it, judging its length, imaging the dark color. "So nice..." He felt a rush of sexual euphoria when Phil paused to lap at the head of his dick. That exploring mouth moved on to his balls.

"I can't believe this," Chris sighed, moaning and losing contact with Phil's hair as Phil lowered down his body. Chris heard him hit a something. "You okay?"

"Ouch. Yes. Found the back wall. Scoot up."

"Scoot up?" Chris reached over his head and touched the mirror. "I have nowhere to scoot."

"Never mind. I'll do this."

Both of Chris's legs were hoisted backwards so he was almost kissing his own knees. "That'll work. Shit, good thing I'm flexible." A tongue ran over his ass. "OhmyGod."

"I can't believe I'm licking a guy as good looking as Andreas Thorkildsen."

"Phil. Please. I'm not him nor am I his fucking double. You just asked—" A tongue penetrated his ring. "Oh, my fucking God." When Phil's mouth returned to Chris's cock, a finger replaced his tongue. Instantly the urge to climax rose over Chris. "I hope you're ready because I'm fucking close."

As if that excited Phil, he sucked deeper, harder, probed with more zeal.

"That's it...Rock, baby, I'm coming," Chris teased. He tensed his muscles and spun into an amazing climax. Phil kept sucking him, milking every last drop from his dick. "Geez, Phil, you sure know how to suck cock." Chris gulped for air as he recovered.

"Love it," Phil purred, continuing to lap and stroke Chris hotly.

Chris rested his hands over his chest and felt his own heart thumping under his ribs. "That was fucking amazing. I never imagined Rock Hudson giving me head before."

Phil chuckled softly. "My turn to imagine the famous Norwegian sucking my dick?"

"Yeah, why not? I wish I had his accent. I can't even begin to figure out how to sound Norwegian." Chris reached for him. "Go slow so we don't give each other a black eye."

"Right. Where's your other hand?"

"Here." Chris waved it until Phil attached to it with his. "Roll?"

"Roll slow. I know there's a wall around here."

"We have more space right than left."

"If you say so."

Phil wrapped his body around Chris tightly. They flipped over so Chris was on top. Once he sat up, Chris oriented himself with the walls again. "We're good."

"I'm about to be very good."

"Where the hell are you?" Chris reached down and contacted skin. As he smoothed his hands upwards, he realized he was at Phil's waist. "Mind if I check out your chest?"

"Be my guest."

Chris felt the soft material of a cotton shirt and pushed it higher.

"You want me to take it off?"

"You'll never find it. I can move it up." Chris could tell Phil was helping him, hearing and sensing his movement. The t-shirt was raised so it was no longer covering Phil's chest. Chris imagined Phil had actually taken it over his head and the shirt was tucked behind his neck. As he explored, Chris realized he was correct in that assumption.

Phil's rippling, solid curved abs and massive rounded pectoral muscles with hard nipples excited Chris so much he was hard again. "Wow!"

"I lift weights."

"I can tell. Holy shit."

"Wish you could see me."

"Me too." Chris made his way to a nipple, chewing on it happily. Phil moaned and exhaled a deep breath.

Licking and gnawing his way to Phil's second nipple, Chris could easily imagine how big and buff he was by his feel. "You're fucking Atlas."

Phil chuckled.

Running his tongue down the middle of Phil's chest to his abs, Chris's chin brushed against Phil's treasure trail and then his pubes. Inhaling him, rubbing his face into his patch, Chris moaned in pleasure. "Christ you smell good."

"Just showered. Came here after the gym."

"Yes. Yes, indeed." Chris nuzzled Phil's hard shaft, impressed with his size. "Go-go boy," he purred.

"Grrr..." Phil teased.

Chris bypassed Phil's cock, holding it in his fingers, while he enjoyed what Phil had enjoyed on him. A little taste of his sack and bottom.

"Yes...perfect." Phil sighed.

Chris felt Phil bend his knees to widen his straddle for him, giving him access. Reaching behind him, making sure he didn't collide with anything, Chris backed up another inch and burrowed between Phil's legs.

"Ah! Yes, fantastic!" Phil crooned.

The scent of masculine musky soap and cleansed skin was making Chris go crazy. His own cock kept brushing against his arms as he crouched on his knees and sticky drops had begun oozing out of his dick once again.

Licking his way to the base of Phil's cock, Chris gave a long loving lap to the tip and slipped it inside his mouth. Instantly Phil's hips elevated and he whimpered loudly.

Phil's hands combed through Chris's hair, encouraging him to suck deeper. Chris closed his eyes and sank into a dream. I'm sucking Rock Hudson on a beach in Malibu. Wow.

Lost, hearing Phil's pleasure escalate to loud grunts and moans, Chris sat up higher, gripped the base of that magnificent cock and went for it. His hands working in tandem with his lips, he sucked and jerked at Phil's length, hearing it work magic on the big man under him.

"Ah! Ah!"

The noise echoed in the hollow room.

A blast of cum hit Chris's tongue. He moaned in delight and swallowed as a second surge followed. Writhing as Phil's exclamation of ecstasy made his skin cover with goose bumps, Chris sat up and began jacking off over Phil.

"Chris?"

Clamping his eyes closed, Chris came, milking his cock in bliss.

"Shit! You just creamed all over me."

Blinking, still completely blind and now slightly disoriented, Chris muttered, "Sorry."

After a minute, Chris heard Phil laughing.

"You want me to try and wipe it up with something?"

"Yeah. Use one of Nordy's things. They owe us for not having a floodlight."

"And where will I find one of their items of clothing?" Chris humored him.

"It'll have tags. Just feel around."

Chris felt all over Phil playfully.

"Ah! Tickling! No fair!" Phil curled up in a ball.

"You are too cute." Chris felt the spatter he'd made with his fingers as he brushed his hands over Phil's torso.

"Fuck the spunk. Get your mouth where I can taste it."

Locating him again, Chris climbed over Phil's body and connected to his lips. Humming happily as they kissed, Chris sighed deeply and caressed Phil's cheek.

After a long leisurely bout of kissing, Phil suggested, "We

should try and get dressed and see what the hell's going on out there."

"We should. If we don't I'm about to nap on your chest." Chris yawned.

"How the hell are we going to find our clothes now?"

"Slowly. I don't want an elbow breaking my nose."

"You move first. I'll stay still."

"You're a gentleman." Chris began buttoning his shirt, which was still on him but hanging open. "You have any idea where my pants are?"

"No."

Chris heard the smile in Phil's voice. "I didn't think so." He began scanning the floor for them, deliberately brushing over Phil's crotch in a tease, making him laugh and wriggle.

Finally Chris found something that felt familiar. Running his hand down the fabric, he touched his wallet, mobile phone, and keys that were thankfully still in the pockets. "I think I've got them. Do you have your wallet and keys in your pants?"

"Yes. Did you find my jeans finally?"

"Oh, right. Denim. No, these must be my slacks." Still sitting on the floor, Chris slid them up his legs. "I'm standing to zip them up," he warned.

"Okay."

He rose to his feet, fastening them and tucking in his shirt. "Ah..."

"What? Playing with yourself?" Chris chuckled.

"Funny. No. I found my jeans."

"Good."

"Are you upright?"

"I am. Why? Are you joining me?"

"Yes. Don't move."

Chris waited. He could hear and imagine what Phil was doing. A jingle of either keys or pocket change sounded.

"Thank fuck. Now I just need my shoes."

"Don't both of us bend down at the same time. We'll bonk heads."

"I'm crouching. Stay there. I'll look for all of them for us."

"What a guy." Chris sighed happily.

"One."

Chris felt a shoe being handed to him, brushing his leg. As he touched it he could tell it was his.

"Two?"

"Good man! Where the hell was it?" Chris leaned back against the wall and slipped them on.

"Over there."

"Wherever that is."

"Thank fuck. Got mine."

"I'm not moving until you stand up. I don't want to kick you."

"Thank you."

"No problem."

"I'm standing up."

"Okay." Chris touched his pockets to make sure he did indeed have everything he came in with. "Got your keys? Wallet?"

After hearing shuffling, Phil replied, "Yes. I have everything."

"Right. Let's see what the hell's going on outside of this room." He reached for Phil's hand, brushing against him until it was clasped tightly.

Using his free hand, Chris kept swinging it out front of him so he wouldn't smack into anything. When they exited the dressing room, a very dim red light shone way out in the distance, other than that, the entire store was vacant and dark.

"Motherfucker! They didn't even look for us?" Chris complained.

"We better not be locked in." Holding hands, they walked towards the only scant source of light on the entire floor, a red sign that read 'exit'.

As they neared that ambient crimson glow, Chris tried to prepare himself for the sight of a man he had just had sex with. He flinched hoping he wasn't going to be disappointed.

The moment they stood under the dim red light, Chris spun around to see his partner in the flesh. A big smile found his face. "You weren't lying."

"Neither were you." Phil beamed at him. "You fucking do look like him."

"Do I?" Chris was bursting with excitement to be able

to see Phil's details.

Phil cupped his jaw and drew him to his lips. The kiss was toe curling in its passion.

"Wow!" Chris panted.

"I don't want to go anywhere. I want to hang out here and play with you," Phil purred, stroking Chris's face.

Chris tugged on the door. "You got your wish."

"No! Locked? Really?" Phil yanked on the doors. "How could they do this to us?"

"Listen to it blowing out there." Chris gazed out into the blackness. When his mobile phone rang he jumped in surprise that it was working.

≈≈

Phil paused, watching Chris answer it. He was hoping Chris didn't already have a boyfriend. He wanted more of him, especially now that he could see him.

"Stu?"

As Chris spoke on the phone, Phil caressed his arm lightly.

"You're not going to believe this." Chris grinned at Phil. "I'm stuck in a department store."

Phil kissed his cheek, tenderly. He could just make out a man's voice coming through the other end of the phone.

"No. I wish I knew how my house was doing. Let me go, Stu. I'll call you in the morning when I know the score. I will. Thanks." Chris hung up. "That was a friend of mine checking on me. I have a house on the beach and God knows what shape it's in at the moment."

"Shit. That sucks." Phil tugged on the doors again. "How could they lock us in? I don't get it, Chris. You would think someone would have had the intelligence to look in the dressing room first."

"Do you wish they had?" Chris caressed Phil's face gently.

"No. I'm glad they didn't." Phil accepted Chris's kiss. "We could go up to house wares and screw on some sheets and pillows." Phil wanted to make love to him. Especially now that he could see how beautiful Chris was. He liked everything about him, including his sense of humor and his ability to play in a very awkward situation.

"I love it." Chris laughed. "Screwing in the house wares department. I don't know about you, but that's always been a secret fantasy of mine."

Enjoying Chris's smile and his kindness, Phil melted in the grip of Chris's endearing gaze. Holding Chris's jaw in his hands so he could stare into his light eyes, Phil whispered, "I'm glad we did what we did. And that you look like my javelin thrower."

"Me too, Rock." Chris laughed. "I don't want to go back into the darkness. I like being able to see your face."

Phil combed Chris's hair back from his forehead, just barely making out the blueness of his eyes in the strange red glow. "Stay here. We'll call someone to get us out."

"Yeah. In a minute."

"In a minute." Phil wrapped around Chris and pulled him closer to kiss. In an hour...later. Maybe never?

FLAT OUT

Michael jogged from the blacked out restaurant to his car in the mall parking lot. Once the lights went out, he and the rest of the restaurant staff cleared the patrons from their establishment and locked up for the night. The wind and rain were brutal, stinging his face with pellets of water and litter being blown around violently. Using his key fob, he chirped his lock and opened his door, stopping short. "No way!"

His left rear tire was flat, right to the rim, sitting on the pavement. "I don't believe this!" He sat down behind the steering wheel and took out his mobile phone. Pushing the tiny button to turn it on, he remembered it was running low on battery power and opened his glove compartment, illuminating the overhead dome light to see if he had his adapter for the cigarette lighter. "Great." It wasn't there.

"Fuck!" He sat a moment and removed his wallet, thumbing through the selection of credit cards for his Triple-A membership card.

Not seeing it, he grew angry and stuffed his wallet back in his pocket, shutting the overhead light. It was pitch black outside. Rubbing his face, trying to psych himself up for the soaking he was going to get while he changed the tire, he noticed two men in the distance standing inside the entrance to Nordstrom's. He could just make out their forms in what appeared to be a very dim red light. "Maybe they have a working cell phone."

Taking a breath for courage, he withstood the blasting wind and rain, and exited his car. Jogging up to the storefront he stopped short at seeing the two men making out.

"Ah! Holy shit!" Pausing, feeling the gusts blowing him sideways, he stood gawking at the two men as they appeared completely enamored with each other and deep in a swoon. "Er, okay, maybe not right now." He retreated and stopped when he stood at his car. "Fuck!" he shouted in vain. Popping open his trunk, he could barely see a thing in the total darkness. "Jesus, this is going to be fucking impossible without light."

Looking back at the two men again, Michael gave up being shy and ran to the front entrance. As he drew closer he could see them really going at it hot and heavy. "Wow." And they were both amazing looking to boot.

The rain instantly soaking him, Michael cleared his throat awkwardly and rapped on the glass door to get their attention.

They jolted in surprise and spun to look at him with wild eyes.

"Can you help me?" Michael shouted through the thick glass.

"Locked!" one yelled back, jerking the door.

"My car has a flat. Can you call someone for me?" Michael huddled against the storefront for some protection.

One man held out his phone. "What number?" he asked.

"Shit!" Michael took his wallet out again and searched the stack of business cards in vain.

"You want me to call 911?" the man asked.

"No. It's only a flat tire. I just need a tow truck. I can't see for shit."

They both nodded.

"Which tow company?"

Michael became frustrated. "I don't have a clue." He was getting drenched and now cold as well.

The bigger man of the two jerked at the doors violently.

"They locked you guys in there?" Michael asked in shock.

"Yes! Morons!" the big one growled.

"Never mind. Thanks anyway guys! I'll just change it myself somehow."

They waved as he walked away. When he turned back they were kissing again. "Wow. That is a trip."

Cursing under his breath, Michael dug under the carpet mat in the trunk and felt metal. With his fingers growing numb and wet, he tried to unscrew the jack and release the small spare tire. Skinning his knuckles a few times as his hand skidded off the tight screw, he peered back up at the front of the store to those two men. "It's like some kind of romance movie. Two guys, locked inside a mall...meet...kiss. Wonder if they'll fuck." He bit his lip. "Bet they do. Two gorgeous hunks..."

Finally the wing nut of the jack loosened up to his twisting. He was completely saturated from the rain and occasionally pelted with something harder than water drops but ignored it.

Sirens were wailing in the distance and Michael couldn't even imagine calling anyone for help for a simple flat tire under these circumstances. The cops were busy with real emergencies. Not a stupid flat.

Another peek up at the front of the store and the men had vanished. "Uh huh. Gone to play. Lucky fuckers."

He set the jack down beside his tire and fought with the next screw to release the tiny temporary spare. His hands were raw and clumsy.

The sound of a car and the flicker of headlights made him spin around. He waved in hope that the person would see him. When the car veered towards him he sighed with relief.

The tires cracked on the wet tarmac and the window rolled down an inch. "You need help?"

"Yes. Just some light. I can't see a thing. I'm trying to change my flat."

The car backed up and the front headlights of it aimed directly towards his driver side fender, right where he needed it.

My hero. He sighed with relief. With the help of the light, Michael was able to see into his trunk and remove the spare. He set it on the ground.

A moment later the man was standing next to him, a rain slicker with an upturned hood on his back. "Let me give you a hand."

"You'll get soaked. Go back in the car. I just needed the light."

"It's okay." The man knelt down by the jack and felt under the car for a place to set it up.

Michael crouched next to him. "You don't have to do this."

"Look, let me just get you fixed up. Okay?"

A glimpse at the man's handsome face convinced Michael he should let the man help him. Peering back at the storefront where the lovebirds had been, Michael wondered if it was his turn to get lucky. He could use a good screw to warm him up after this.

The man began cranking the lever on the jack.

Michael stood by with the tire iron until the man got the car raised up slightly.

"Pop the hub off."

Nodding, Michael pried the hubcap off and set it upside down on the wet pavement.

The car shook as it raised up off the axel.

"Let me loosen the bolts." Michael waited for the man to move back. He cracked the five lug nuts loose and nodded. "Okay."

The man went back to cranking the lever and the tire elevated off the water soaked tarmac.

"Perfect." Michael removed all the nuts, placing them into the upturned hubcap.

The man pulled off the flat tire, setting it against the side of the car. Michael tried to get the small temporary spare lined up and struggled.

"Here." The man leaned against his side and helped him get it on the five protruding bolts. At the brush of his shoulder, Michael felt a rush to his loins. "It's really great of you to help me out."

"Look, the whole town is gone to hell. It's the least a person can do."

They both began threading the nuts back on. "Were you shopping at the mall when the power went out?" Michael asked.

"No. I work at one of the stores inside."

"Which one?"

"Bailey, Banks and Biddle."

"Jewellery?" Michael smiled.

"Yeah. I'm the store manager. What the hell are you doing here so late? I thought they cleared out the shoppers the minute the lights went out."

"I work for Cleo and Cucci."

"Ah. Gotcha."

"My name is Michael."

"Greg."

Michael shook his wet hand.

"Let me lower the jack so you can tighten those up."

Leaning back, Michael bit his lip as Greg lowered the car so the tire touched pavement. Once he did, he went to work tightening up the lug nuts.

A loud crackle and bang scared Michael. He jumped out of his skin as one of the enormous power poles started sparking near the entrance of the parking lot and tilted at an odd angle.

"Holy fuck!" Michael gasped.

"This is not a very good spot to be in at the moment."

"Go! I'll finish." Michael nudged him.

"No. I'll wait until I'm sure you're okay."

"Wow. You're really nice. Thank you." Michael continued cranking on the lug nuts until he couldn't move them anymore.

Sirens were heard once again all over the city.

"This is one of the worst storms I can remember." Greg started loading Michael's trunk with the jack and flat tire.

"Me too. I still have no idea how bad it is. I haven't gotten a chance to listen to the radio."

"I have. The power's out in ten counties."

"Motherfucker." Michael tossed the tire iron into the trunk as Greg removed the jack and set it in the back with the rest of the items.

Michael was soaking wet. He closed the trunk of his car and reached out his hand. "Greg, I wish there was a way I could thank you."

"Were you headed home?"

"Yes. I live close by so I know my power is out."

"Me too."

"You want to come over? You know, keep me company? I have a well stocked liquor cabinet."

Greg laughed sweetly. "You serious?"

"Yeah. As my way of thanking you."

Checking his watch, Greg seemed to be undecided.

Michael felt badly for placing him in an awkward position. "Never mind. You must have family to see to."

"No. It's okay."

"Up to you. But decide soon, I'm freezing."

"Go. I'll follow you."

Michael's skin lit on fire through the chill of being soaked. "Stay close to me in case the spare tire screws up."

"I'll be right at your back door."

Meeting Greg's gaze for a moment, seeing his handsome smile, Michael hoped he was indeed going to be at his back door.

After a smile and a nod at Greg first, Michael climbed into his car and started it in excitement. "Yes! This is too cool!"

As he drove to his apartment in West Hollywood, the traffic signals and streetlights were out, swaying in the strong gusts. Making sure Greg stayed behind him, Michael made his way slowly to his place. He parked on the street out front and Greg was able to pull in behind him. Racing through the teeming rain, taking out his house keys from his pocket, Michael waved him on to his front door. Once inside, Michael lit three large pillar candles and kicked off his shoes. "Are you wet?"

Greg met his eye as he took off his raincoat.

"I mean, do you need something to change into?" Michael blushed. Was that a controversial thing to say? Greg wasn't a woman.

"I'm okay. This rain coat is very efficient."

"Give me two secs. I just want to change my things."

"I'll be here."

Well if Greg didn't know I was gay before, he must know now. Posters of Bette Midler on the wall? A collection of gay porn in the DVD cabinet and gay erotic novels in the bookcase. WeHo? Hello?

Michael washed his hands, scrubbing the greasy dirt off them, then rubbed a towel over his black hair and brushed it to stop it from standing straight up from the wild wind. Next he changed into a pair of soft worn jeans and a long-sleeved black cotton jersey shirt.

When he returned, Greg was washing his own hands at the kitchen sink. Able to see him better in the candlelight, Michael estimated his age to be late thirties. Good. He preferred older men.

"Bourbon? Scotch? Vodka? Name your poison."

Chuckling as he dried his hands, Greg requested, "Bourbon."

"My favorite." Michael removed two glasses from the cupboard. "Thanks again, Greg. It was so dark I couldn't even see into the back of my trunk. I really would have struggled without your help."

"It was my pleasure, Michael."

"Sit. Don't be so formal."

Greg relaxed on the velour sofa. He had taken his shoes off at the door.

"Here. Enjoy." Michael handed him a glass.

They paused prior to taking a sip as the wind howled outside.

"It's really bad out there." Michael sat next to him on the sofa. Holding up the glass in a toast, he said, "To kindness."

"To kindness." Greg tapped his glass.

"Are you hungry?"

"Don't open your fridge. You have no idea how long the power will be out. Best to keep it closed." Greg sipped the alcohol.

"I have snacks. Pretzels? Chips?"

"I'm okay for now."

Michael set his glass on the coffee table and folded his leg under him. "Want to hear something funny?"

"Sure. I can always use a good laugh."

"When I first realized I had a flat tire..." Michael studied Greg's expression closely for his reaction to his little ditty. "I noticed two guys behind the entrance of the doors up at Nordy's."

"Security?"

"No. Two customers locked in."

"No kidding? That is funny."

"That's not the funny part." Michael placed his drink on the coffee table and rested his arm behind Greg's head on the sofa.

"I'm listening."

"They were making out."

Greg's eyes widened.

Michael went for the kill. "Kissing, sucking face. Two men, locked in the store alone, going mad on each other."

Greg choked on his booze and set the glass down to cover his mouth as he coughed.

Thought so. Straight as they come. Oh well. "You okay?" Michael went to pat Greg's back.

He nodded, holding up his hand. "Sorry."

"No problem. Sorry for making you choke."

Shaking his head no, Greg replied, "I was just surprised."

"Yeah. So was I. They were a couple of hunks. God only knows what they'll be up to in that place alone overnight."

Once he cleared his throat, Greg gestured to wall hangings. "Can I assume you're gay?"

"You 'assumed' correctly." Michael picked up his drink casually. "Time to run away?"

"What makes you think I want to run from you simply because you prefer men?"

Blinking at him, Michael felt his skin tingle. "Uh, because you look like a straight happily married man with kids?"

Greg held up his left hand showing an empty ring finger. "Do you see a ring?"

"Single? Separated? Divorced?"

Greg grimaced in reply.

Wondering if he was going to get any verbal answers, Michael added, "Any kids?"

"Two."

The plot thickens. Michael scooted closer. "Curious?"

"Curious?" Greg tilted his head. "About gay men?"

"Mm?"

"I've been with men, Michael."

It was Michael's turn to choke. He set his glass aside and coughed as he inhaled the bourbon down the wind side of his piping. Seeing Greg's wry smile, Michael gazed at him in expectation. Been with men? You? Really? He wanted to shout that, but bit his lip.

After a deep exhale, Greg replied, "Let's just say the marriage was my experimentation with the straight side of life."

"Holy shit. I take it, it didn't work?"

Greg finished his drink and placed the glass down. "It didn't work."

"So?"

"So?"

"Back to men?" Michael gulped the rest of the contents of his glass and twisted to face Greg.

"I haven't gotten that far yet. I suppose I was slightly apprehensive diving back into the gay pool."

Michael smiled sweetly and opened his arms. "Dive with me."

Again Greg seemed surprised. "A handsome young man like you wants me?"

His jaw dropping in exaggeration, Michael gasped, "Are you kidding me?"

"I'm thirty-five, Michael. I must have ten years on you."

"And your point?" Michael scooted closer, the candlelight reflected off of Greg's square jaw and high cheekbones. He touched Greg's knee.

"You find me attractive?"

"Greg!" Michael laughed at the joke. "You're very handsome. Not only that, you're my knight in shining armor. Do you have any idea what it would have been like to change that tire in the storm without light while power lines fell and sparked around me? What planet are you from?"

"Then it's just a way to say thank you. With sex."

"No! Duh! I'm hot for you. Do you own a mirror?"

"A young man as pretty as you? Hot for me?" Greg seemed astonished.

"You have been out of the gay pool too long."

"I don't find it conceivable. You're very attractive. You can get any young man you want."

"I like older men." Michael leaned against him. "They have their shit together. Older men appreciate young ones. You know?"

"I come with a big load of baggage, Michael. You can do better than me."

"And? You don't have to move in. We can have some nice times together. Dinners out? Long sessions in the bedroom after a show or a movie?"

They paused as the sound of sirens raced by and the wind rattled the walls.

Greg gave Michael his attention once more. "That does sound nice."

Michael leaned over Greg's lap, closer to his lips. "How long were you married and without male touch?"

"A decade."

"You must miss it."

"I do. Very much."

Reaching for Greg's hand, Michael used it to caress his own face. "You can touch me, Greg." Michael felt Greg shiver and watched the expression of longing cross his handsome face. "Kiss me."

As kindly and as gently as possible, Greg cupped Michael's face and drew him to his lips. Michael let out a long low moan and wrapped his arms around Greg's neck. After they had kissed for a few moments, swirling tongues and sucking them gently, Michael asked, "As good as you remember?"

"Yes." Greg ran his hands up Michael's arms to his shoulders.

"Come to bed." Michael stood, picking up a candle to take with him. Using the tiny wick to illuminate his small bedroom, Michael set the candle on his dresser, spinning back to stare at Greg as Michael undressed himself.

Greg's eyes appeared luminous as he watched.

Michael revealed his narrow, lithe figure, dropping his clothing in a pile on the floor. Once he was naked he posed. "Suitable for a fuck?"

"Very suitable."

Floating over to Greg, Michael began undressing him, kissing his skin as it was revealed. Peeling back Greg's dress shirt, seeing a solid chest covered in dark hair, Michael shivered with delight. "Nice." He ran his fingers through the soft brown curls that were between Greg's pectoral muscles. "Just the right amount."

"You really know how to make a man feel desirable, Michael."

"Do you think I'm making it up as I go along? You are desirable, Greg. You're what I love to call 'distinguished'.

You're glorious."

Michael helped him step out of his trousers and briefs, lastly his socks. When Greg was naked, Michael led him to his bed. "I take requests," Michael teased. "Anything you've been craving for the last decade?"

"Everything."

"I have all you need in my bag of tricks." Michael sealed their bodies together, admiring Greg's good looks in the flattering candlelight.

"I'll let you guide me." Greg caressed Michael's hair affectionately.

"I'm a bottom, Greg. Do you recall what that means?"

Smiling shyly, Greg replied, "I recall."

"Good. Then let's play a little while, and then you can shove that fantastic cock up my butt. Sound good to you?"

As if he were holding back his laughter, Greg's eyes glistened. "Sounds perfect."

"Mm. Good. Come here, my hero." Michael draped his arms around Greg's neck and urged him closer. Michael opened his mouth and pressed his lips against Greg's moaning happily.

∼∾

Greg cherished Michael's considerate pace and delicate touch. Though he'd yearned for a man to enjoy, Greg hadn't found the courage to venture out. He felt out of practice and too old for the young crowds at the local gay bars. Besides, bars were never his scene.

Seeing the poor man out in the blackness changing a tire on his own, Greg couldn't ignore him. He wasn't the type. Any person's misery was his own. Perhaps he was too soft, had too much empathy.

But he was being rewarded for his good deed. Maybe fate was smiling at him finally.

Michael's youth and freshness were arousing Greg intensely. As they licked the flavor of bourbon off each other's tongues, Greg felt his skin sizzle with passion.

He smoothed his fingers down Michael's arm to his hip pausing to feel the firmness of his flesh. Unable to help himself, Greg ran his hand over Michael's perfect backside. And he was very happy indeed Michael preferred to bottom.

As Greg gently traced the line of Michael's crack from the top down, Michael shivered and his kissing intensified.

The whimper from Michael caused Greg's craving to escalate. While the wind pelted the apartment from the outside, they were lighting an inferno on the interior.

Running his palm over the globe of Michael's ass cheek, making Michael squirm and moan, Greg dipped his fingers between those firm muscles and brushed against Michael's rim lightly.

Michael broke the kiss to take a deep breath and wriggle. "Greg!"

Greg met Michael's wild eyes.

"Touch me again!" Michael urged Greg's hand to grow bolder.

Shifting on the bed, Greg rolled to his side so they were facing each other. He caressed Michael's low back, once again making his way between his tight cheeks.

Michael thrust out his hips in response and began stroking Greg's cock.

At the first touch of Michael's hands on his dick, Greg quivered and closed his eyes. The stroke was so exciting it sent shivers along his spine. Inhaling Michael's skin, Greg grew more aggressive as his needs urged him on. Using hard pressure with his index finger, he massaged Michael's anus, slipping in and around it until Michael was gasping and squirming on the bed.

Michael's mournful cries were driving Greg insane.

In an abrupt movement, Michael jumped on top of Greg, collapsing Greg to his back against the mattress. They were both panting in time with the howling wind.

Michael dug in a night table and produced a condom and lubrication.

Greg watched as the rubber was rolled onto his cock, which was standing upright from his body like a pole. Michael massaged lubrication all over it, and Greg actually had to hold back and not come at the handling.

Blinking in the flickering candlelight, Greg witnessed Michael squirt the bottle into his own anus quickly. Greg remembered anal sex with men, but nothing like the simplicity and compliance he was enjoying with Michael. Michael obviously knew exactly what he wanted and had the experience to get it.

The lube set aside, Michael proceeded to impale himself on Greg's protruding cock. To help Michael ease down, Greg held Michael's waist, assisting him in gradually allowing penetration while gravity took care of the rest.

Studying Michael's expression, Greg held his breath at the bliss washing across the young man's face.

It took a moment, but Michael was finally seated on Greg's pelvis with his knees bent and straddling Greg's hips.

The connection was sending Greg to the moon.

Opening his eyes, not realizing he had closed them, Greg stared at Michael as he rose and fell up and down on him, his cock bobbing and the head glistening with pre-cum.

Awed by Michael as he proceeded to fuck him, not the opposite, Greg felt his own body rising, preparing for climax.

The sight of this handsome willowy young male screwing him, Michael's face a mask of pure pleasure, Greg felt a rush to his crotch and couldn't prevent the groan from escaping his mouth.

When Michael heard it, he quickened the pace and depth of his thrusts.

Greg couldn't believe the sensation of pleasure washing over his dick. He gasped and bit his lip, holding back a scream and an expletive of shock. His entire body tensed and his back elevated up off the mattress. Greg jerked upwards into Michael and pumped cum out of him and into the condom, deep inside this adorable man.

The sensation of something spattering on his skin caused Greg to open his eyes. Without anything touching Michael's cock, it had erupted and sprayed cum onto Greg's chest.

Looking at Michael's face in the candlelight's flickering flame, he found his teeth bared and his eyes sealed shut in orgasmic pleasure.

Greg reached both his hands towards Michael's lovely narrow cock and stroked it for him since Michael was using both his arms to brace himself on Greg's thighs.

Moaning sensuously, Michael's head rolled heavily to the

side and his breathing softened.

As they recovered, Greg felt his own cock throbbing in that tight hole. Very slowly Michael raised himself off Greg's body, disconnecting them.

"Be back." Michael removed the spent condom from Greg's length.

Nodding, too amazed to do much else, Greg waited as Michael took a candle with him to what Greg assumed was the bathroom.

Catching his breath, listening to the eternal wail of sirens and wind gusts still carrying on outside, Greg felt pleasantly weary.

A flickering light emerged into the room. Michael had a wet washcloth and proceeded to clean Greg up considerably.

"Thank you."

"My pleasure." Michael kissed his chest.

Once that task was complete, they crawled under the blankets together.

"Oh! Let me just make sure the doors are locked and I didn't leave any candles lit in the other room."

"Okay." Greg smiled adoringly at him and watched as he climbed out of bed.

≈≈

Michael put the security chain on the front door and checked that it was bolted. Before he blew out the single candle lit in the room he placed their empty glasses in the sink, paused and looked back to smile at his bedroom as he thought of the man occupying his bed. Biting his lip, he picked up the telephone and dialed, hoping the wind gusts blowing outside would mask the sound of his conversation.

"Doug?"

"Mickey?"

"Yeah, it's me!" Michael giggled. Doug was the only friend that called him Mickey. "How are you coping with the storm?"

"I got stuck in a movie theater. It was weird!"

"I had a flat tire in the parking lot at the mall." Michael looked back at his bedroom. "Met an awesome guy who helped me change it in the pouring rain. He's in my bed!" Michael tried not to shout and pump his arms in excitement, but he had to tell his best friend the good news.

"I've got my own story to tell, believe me. Let me go. Call me in the morning."

"I will, Doug. Can't wait to get back to my man."

"I'm glad some good has come out of this crazy storm."

"Me too! See ya." Michael hung up, thrilled to hear his best friend's voice and share his fun. Carrying the last lit candle with him to the bedroom, Michael found Greg waiting for him, a soft contented smile on his face.

"Everything all right?"

"Perfect." Michael crawled between the sheets and blew out the candles. In the pitch blackness he cuddled around Greg and held him tight as the storm lashed out with all its fury.

MOVIE HOUSE

Doug had heard about this theater ever since he'd moved to the area from the mid-west. The TomKat was where you went to see gay porn twenty-four hours a day.

Well, he wasn't a porn addict, but the place had such a notorious history with straight porn first, converting to gay porn later, Doug felt obligated to check it out.

And with the weather prediction of rain and wind, he decided there was no better night than tonight to huddle in the dark and watch some good hot sex.

After paying for his ticket, Doug was slightly disappointed with the interior décor and appeal but raised his head bravely and walked down the aisle. His shoes stuck to the floor as he scooted down one of the rows to a handful of empty chairs. It was between flicks so a series of trailers and advertisements were rolling on the big screen.

Couples and even triples, were already taking advantage of the dim lighting and sexual ambiance. Doug could smell sex in the air, or something similar. He didn't inhale too deeply.

Keeping his leather jacket on, he slumped in the seat and slouched low, his hands buried in his pockets. Last minute he made sure his cell phone was off. He would have preferred coming to the movie with his good friend Michael, but Michael was busy working at the mall. He was a sous-chef at Cleo and Cucci. It was a shame. Michael would have gotten a good laugh out of hanging out with him here. Maybe he should have waited for Michael to have a night off.

The sense of being ogled by some lecherous fiend grew in him. Running his hand through his hair nervously, Doug actually imagined bailing out, but fifteen bucks was too much of an investment to blow off lightly. He'd hangout and at least see some of the porn he'd paid to view.

"This seat taken?"

Doug jolted out of his daydream to see a hottie with blond hair and blue eyes gesturing to the seat next to him.

"No." Doug shifted nervously as the man sat down right next to him, not leaving a gap seat as people normally did in mainstream theaters. He sat right next to him.

"Carl." The handsome man actually reached out for his introduction.

"Doug." Doug took his warm hand and shook it.

"Looks like it's going to be a shitty night out. The wind is already picking up."

"I heard they were predicting thunderstorms. They don't expect it to be too bad do they?" Doug checked out Carl's long legs in his tight faded jeans. Yum. Nice.

"I don't know. I got bored after they repeated the stupid news story ten times. I just figured I'd get out of the house for a few hours. There's nothing on the television."

"Never is." Doug nodded in agreement. He moved his foot and it made a sound as his rubber sole stuck to the floor. "Ew." Doug curled his nose in revulsion.

Covering his laughter, Carl asked, "I take it this is your first time here."

"Yes. I'm a virgin to the illustrious TomKat." Doug peered backwards at three men still doing lurid things behind them.

"I'm not a regular but I do think the place has its...uh... err... charm." Carl shifted in the seat, as if carefully not using his hands to touch the armrests. "But you do have to be sensible."

"Man, why don't they give it a good scrubbing?"

"Can't. Twenty-four hour schedule."

"Ah. Right. But still." Doug made a face in exaggeration of disgust, making Carl laugh.

The lights flickered and Doug assumed that meant the movie was beginning. He heard some rustling of people finding their seats around him and felt Carl's arm lean against his pleasantly.

The film began and as Doug had predicted the movie was pretty typical of the gay porn he had rented himself previously.

The room became almost pitch black but for the screen giving off a shadowy glow. The minute cocks were in holes in the motion picture, Doug assumed the same action was going on around him.

"Ah, oh, yes. Ah, oh, yes..."

The dialogue always made Doug laugh. At least the actors could remember their lines.

Carl's hand rested softly on his knee. Doug stared at it in the ambient light. The heat of Carl's palm sent Doug's cock moving instantly. Doug returned his attention to the action in the movie. Macho men wearing only work boots, socks, and yellow hard hats were sucking and fucking with wild abandon. "Ah, oh, yes. Ah, oh, yes..."

The sensation of Carl's fingers stroking inside his thigh was lighting Doug up. Beginning to enjoy this little adventure, Doug allowed his legs to splay out in a wider straddle. Stroke me, baby, stroke me.

The handling was modest, yet tantalizing. If Carl meant to drive him crazy, he was. The man didn't go near his cock. Carl just seemed content to massage Doug's inner thigh muscle and kneecap all the while staring enthralled at the action. Though Doug thought the redundant acts were beginning to get monotonous and slightly boring, he was happy to endure them if it meant Carl petting his leg.

Jesus! Touch my cock! Doug didn't know how to send out that message without actually verbalizing it or physically drawing Carl's hand to where he wanted it. And not knowing Carl, Doug had no idea what he had in mind.

Fine! Two can play this game. Doug removed one of his hands from his jacket pocket and wrapped around Carl's arm to do the same to him, stroke his thigh and knee.

Carl shifted his position.

That made Doug smile. He stayed away from Carl's cock and squeezed the meaty muscle of Carl's inner thigh.

The two of them began to squirm in their seats at the frustrating little ploy.

A shift in scenes brought more naked men doing more

intimate things to each other. This time, outdoors on a picnic, a young twink was servicing an older man.

Carl's hand didn't grow any bolder. It massaged and rubbed Doug's leg, and only his leg. Doug was about to scream in frustration and grab Carl's cock hard in his hand when the screen went black and the room became pitch dark.

Pausing, Doug whispered, "Okay..." softly, as if waiting for the next sign.

A dim exit light lit, that was it.

"Power's out," Carl said.

Around them it seemed the blackness was urging the men in the room to new heights. Grunts and rustling of garments echoed in the silence.

They waited, holding each other's leg, no longer stroking.

"What the hell are we supposed to do?" Doug asked, looking over his shoulder.

"I guess if it doesn't come on soon, someone will kick us out."

They sat in silence while the sound of someone grunting during climax echoed behind them. The pause became protracted.

"I don't think the power's coming on again any time soon," Doug whispered.

"Hello?" a man's voice echoed in the large room. "The power has gone out. Can you all exit the theater?"

"Unreal." Carl released his hold on Doug's leg. "I don't suppose we'll get a refund."

Doug chuckled softly, standing up with him and scooting out of the aisle. The man who had made the announcement was shining a flashlight on a group of guys who were in the middle of their own porn scene.

"Wow." Doug gaped in shock.

"Good luck disconnecting that group," Carl quipped.

Doug found his way to the lobby in the darkness. Zipping his jacket as he stood at the glass entrance, he peered out. "Not a light on anywhere."

"The wind's really whipping," Carl observed.

"How far away do you live?" Doug wanted to hang out with him. Get to know him.

"About a fifteen minute drive. You?"

"Walking distance. My apartment is only about ten blocks away."

Carl nodded but didn't make any suggestion of them staying together. Exiting the theater, they bent over to defend against the wet gusting wind.

Doug removed his mobile phone from his pocket and turned it on.

"Holy shit!"

Doug stopped short and spun around. Carl was gaping at a car.

About to ask him what was wrong, Doug noticed a wire resting on top of the car's hood, sparking. "Agh!" He grabbed Carl's arm and drew him back from it instinctively.

"That's my fucking car!"

"Don't go anywhere near it." Doug gripped him tighter, keeping him from touching it.

"What the fuck!" Carl said in anger and removed his mobile phone from his pocket.

"Who are you calling?"

"911. I have to get my car out of this."

When the wire whipped and sparks shot out of it in a spray, Doug wrapped his arm around Carl and dragged him a few more yards away.

In fury Carl said, "A recorded message? Do you believe this? 911 has a recorded message that all emergency services are already strained and I should hold on only if it's a 'real emergency' of life threatening proportions."

"Forget it."

"What the hell am I supposed to do?"

They were both getting drenched from the sideways rain.

"Come home with me. Come on."

Growling in anger, Carl disconnected the line and shoved his phone into his pocket. Doug held his waist and upped their pace so they wouldn't be too soaked by the time they got to his place, but they were already dripping wet.

Branches of palm trees rattled around the parked cars and an occasional blast from a transformer exploding in the distance and wailing sirens echoed in the black night.

"Fuck." Doug shivered in anxiety. "I had no idea it was this bad out here."

"Did they say it was going to be a hurricane?" Carl tightened his grip on Doug's waist as they began jogging.

"I can't remember." Doug's mobile phone rang. As they kept moving quickly, he took it out of his pocket and popped it open.

"Doug?"

"Mickey?" Doug peeked over at Carl's curious eyes.

"Yeah, it's me!" Michael giggled. "How are you coping with the storm?"

"I got stuck in a movie theater. It was weird!"

"I had a flat tire in the parking lot at the mall. Met an awesome guy who helped me change it in the pouring rain. He's in my bed!"

Smiling at Carl excitedly, Doug replied, "I've got my own story to tell, believe me. Let me go. Call me in the morning."

"I will, Doug. Can't wait to get back to my man."

"I'm glad some good has come out of this crazy storm."

"Me too! See ya."

Doug hung up and resumed their pace, now running to get out of the terrible wind. "That was my friend, Mick."

Carl nodded. "Boyfriend?"

"No. Just a good friend." As they came up to his apartment house, Doug released his hold on Carl and removed his key from his soaked jean pocket.

A loud bang and the sound of a thump scared them both, making them jump. A palm tree had collapsed and fallen across the road a few feet away from them.

"OhmyGod!" Doug gasped.

"Get in. Come on."

His hands shaking from the fright, Doug opened his door to a pitch black unit. After they were both inside, he closed the door and stood still, taking off his wet jacket and shoes. "Flashlight, flashlight..." he muttered to himself as he thought.

"Candles?"

"Yes. I have candles." Reaching out in the blackness, slowly moving around his furniture, Doug made it to the kitchen and felt inside the drawers. "This is maddening."

"It's fucking dark."

Doug found a book of matches and lit one. With the sparse light he located a small glass with a scented candle in it. He lit it and gave them a little glimpse of light. Doug noticed Carl still standing at the doorway obviously waiting to be able to see before venturing into an unfamiliar room.

"Take off your wet things." Doug set the candle down on the coffee table. He heard a wicked, "Heh, heh," laugh come from Carl.

Doug chuckled. "Yes, it's my excuse to see you naked."

"Sure it is." Carl laid his jacket across the arm of the sofa.

"I'll get you something to change into." Doug didn't want to be accused of anything lascivious.

"I'm joking."

Doug paused, staring back at Carl in the weak lighting. Carl had stepped out his shoes and was dragging his wet blue jeans down his thighs. At the sight of those long powerful legs, Doug felt his own spark of electricity. "Nice."

Posturing when he was in just his briefs and shirt, Carl put his hands on his hips and pushed out his pelvis. "Wanna make our own gay porno movie?"

Doug rubbed his palm over his own crotch as it filled his damp jeans. "Hell yeah."

Carl sauntered over seductively. He smoothed both hands down Doug's thighs. "You're wet too. Take them off."

They both went for the zipper simultaneously. Carl helped Doug drag his sticking jeans down his legs. While Carl was kneeling before Doug, he kissed his cock through his cotton briefs.

Sirens screamed in the distance. They both paused to listen.

"I must have a flashlight somewhere."

"Forget it. Take the candle with us." Carl rose to his feet. "Which way to your bedroom?" He picked up the tiny flame and held it aloft as Doug led the way.

In reflex Doug turned on the light switch. "Duh. That was smart."

"Creature of habit."

"Yes, I am." Doug peeled back the blanket and bedspread

on his bed. When he spun around Carl had rested the candle on the dresser.

"You mind if I just wash my hands?" Carl held them up.

"I suppose after being in that theater we should scrub up good."

"Hey!" Carl brightened. "Wanna take a shower?"

"You think there'll be hot water?"

"There should be some in the tank. We can wash up until it goes cold."

"Sounds fun!" Doug yanked his shirt over his head.

"Excellent!" Carl stripped off the rest of his clothing. "I've never showered in a blackout."

"Better take our little candle with us." Doug picked it up and brought it with him.

"Our tiny lifeline." Carl followed him.

"I really should be better prepared for this kind of thing."

"Forget it now." Carl leaned back against the doorframe.

After Doug placed the candle on the sink, he spun around. The seductive pose of Carl's was irresistible. "Look at you..."

"You like?"

"What's not to like?" Doug reached into the shower blindly feeling for the taps while his gaze was riveted to Carl's naked body.

The sound of water spraying drowned out the whistling wind and sirens. "Better get in while it's hot."

"Get it, while it's hot!" Carl echoed, laughing.

They hustled into the tub quickly, closing the sliding door. The moment they had wet down under the warm spray, Carl held Doug and kissed him.

The romance was not lost on Doug. A power outage, in the dark, in a candlelit shower with a hunk. Wow.

Carl reached for the soap and as he kissed Doug, he lathered his hands and began washing Doug's chest.

Doug was in heaven. His stiff, wet cock brushed against Carl's. As Doug was woozy from Carl's tongue action, Carl began soaping up his cock. The feel of Carl's slippery fingers made Doug moan and shiver. He parted from the kiss to watch. Carl's hands were working him to a frenzy. "So nice..."

"You gorgeous fucker," Carl hissed.

Doug took the soap and worked it up to foam in his hands. He reached between Carl's legs and returned the favor.

"You want to come now? Or in bed?" Carl asked, his chest beginning to heave.

"What a choice." Doug wanted both.

"Now." Carl made the command decision.

As Carl increased the speed of his hand, fisting Doug's cock like crazy, Carl massaged his balls at the same time making his body surge with pleasure from the fondling.

Forcing himself to reciprocate, Doug jerked Carl's cock with as much vigor as he was receiving. Hearing Carl's gasp, Doug shivered and announced, "I'm there..."

"Me too."

Doug felt Carl squeeze his dick tighter and jerk faster. He climaxed and pulled on Carl's cock frantically so they could spurt together. Carl's deep grunts echoed on the wet tiles, making Doug shiver with pleasure.

As they recuperated Carl whispered, "Is it getting cold or is it just me?"

"It's getting cold." After making sure they rinsed the soap off, Doug shut the water and drew back the sliding door. He handed Carl a towel.

"Thanks." Carl took it and wiped his face and hair.

As Doug dried off he couldn't stop staring at Carl in the flickering light. "Why are you single?"

Carl's light eyes darted to Doug's instantly.

"Why are you?" Carl asked sharply.

Regretting his query, Doug turned aside. "Never mind."

"Good idea."

Once they stepped out of the tub, Doug wondered if he just soured the mood. Perhaps Carl wasn't single, or he had just ended a bad relationship. Who knew? This night wasn't meant for heavy talk. It was a fantasy night.

≫≪

Carl dried his legs and back, draping the towel over the shower door. He raised the lid of the toilet and urinated, knowing Doug was watching.

He finished, moving to the sink to wash his hands, seeing

his dim reflection in the mirror above the basin.

"I'd love a drink. You want something to warm you up inside?"

Carl smiled. "Yeah, your cock."

Doug touched Carl's back and found Carl's reflection in the looking glass. "Definitely. But...I still need something strong. Join me?"

"I'd love it."

"Get in bed. I need the candle and you shouldn't be stumbling around here blindly."

Carl followed behind Doug's raised hand with the only source of light in the unit. He climbed onto the bed and under the blankets.

"I'll be back."

"I know." Carl smiled.

After a flirtatious wink, Doug left the room in blackness.

Sliding down, getting comfy, Carl listened to the sounds around him since he couldn't see an inch in front of his face. More sirens blasted in the distance, the wind rattled everything surrounding the apartment house and things kept battering the exterior walls. He tried not to think about his car, knowing everything would be better in the light of day.

Hearing Doug in the next room, Carl bit his lip as he waited. He thought about Doug's question. Why was he single? Carl wasn't. He was in a bad relationship and wanted out. But that was his business at the moment. He didn't know if this thing with Carl was just a one-night event, or more.

A light approached. In one hand Doug held two shot glasses by the lips, and the candle in the other. He set the candle on the dresser and handed Carl one of the shot glasses, joining Carl in the bed.

"To the calm after the storm."

Carl tapped Doug's glass. "Here, here." He sipped the warming brandy and sighed. "Nice."

"Heats the guts up when it's chilly."

"It never gets very chilly here. Where are you from originally?"

"The mid-west. Man, do I have an accent or something?" Doug grinned.

"Not really." Carl shot the entire contents down his throat and set the glass on a night table. He wanted his hands free. Rolling to his side, he moved the blanket down Doug's torso so he could touch his silky skin.

"That feels nice." Doug emptied the brandy into his mouth and slid his glass next to Carl's.

"You feel nice." Carl ran his fingers over Doug's chest and nipples. It occurred to Carl he didn't know anything about Doug. Not his last name, his occupation, his age, nothing. He wasn't a big fan of stranger sex, but the circumstances guided their acts as far as he was concerned. And in the theater? He wouldn't have done anything more than what he was doing, caressing Doug's leg. He intended on them being companions for that brief moment, not sex partners. The film was supposed to give him a break from his arguing boyfriend and not complicate his life further. But that didn't happen. Doug was cute. And from what he could gather from their encounter so far, pretty wonderful.

Carl smoothed his hand up Doug's throat to his jaw, gazing into his dark eyes. Feeling stubble scratching his palm, Carl scrubbed against it, enjoying its roughness. As Doug closed his eyes, Carl couldn't resist drawing him into a kiss. When their mouths connected, both men pressed their bodies together.

Carl felt Doug's re-hardened cock resting against his own. Why was love always so tantalizing in the beginning and soon wore out into mundane routine and weariness? Couldn't relationships stay fresh and new? Did they always have to deteriorate into arguments?

Pushing those intruding thoughts from his mind, Carl savored Doug completely. His taste, scent, feel, and freshness. Carl didn't realize how badly he missed those things until he was in the arms of another man.

He nudged Doug to lay back and went for his cock, kneading it in his fingers. Doug moaned and closed his eyes. The wind seemed to pick up, howling past their small space inside the apartment house. Carl closed out the outside world. He had Doug here to play with, let everything that was troubling him go away. What if the universe came to a halt tomorrow? What if tonight was his last night on earth?

"Enjoy," Carl whispered his thoughts out loud.

"I am," Doug replied softly.

That made Carl smile. He kissed his way down Doug's clean body and positioned himself between his thighs.

"Why can't they make porn movies like this?"

"Hmm?" Carl leaned up on his elbows to see Doug's face.

"Movies. Why can't they be like this? You know, romantic?"

Carl laughed softly, stroking Doug's cock. "I don't know."

"With plots, storylines, happy endings."

"Gay movies like that? Dream on." Carl licked underneath Doug's engorged cock.

"I'd go see them. I'd like them better than sticky porn."

Carl started laughing. "You mind? I'm trying to suck dick here."

"Sorry. Carry on."

"Thank you." Carl gave Doug a wicked look. "We have to shoot the sex scene, you know."

"True."

Carl nudged Doug's cock towards his mouth and gave it good long suck. Doug wriggled and opened his thighs wider. Fondling Doug's balls as he enjoyed his length in his mouth, Carl wondered if Doug would bottom. He was hoping for it.

To test the water a little, Carl wet his finger and went for Doug's rim. Doug moaned and splayed his legs even farther apart. Good. *I need a fucking bottom, exclusive. Is that you, my lovely man?*

Carl continued to work Doug's dick with long strong sucks from the base to his head. "Got lube?"

Doug paused, then roared with laughter.

"What'd I say?" Carl chuckled.

"Got lube? Got milk?"

"Oh." Carl laughed with him. "Sorry. It did come out that way."

Doug rolled over and stretched for his nightstand drawer.

Another loud crackle of thunder sounded outside.

"Shit!" Doug gasped.

"Forget it. There's nothing we can do about it. Let's concentrate on inside this room."

"Right." Doug exhaled. "Here's the lube. You want a rubber?"

"That depends," Carl replied, taking the bottle. "Can I fuck you?"

"Uh, I'm hoping you will. Any objections?"

"Do you enjoy bottoming?"

"I do." Doug's eyes grew wicked.

Bingo! "I struck fucking gold." Carl sat up and tore open a condom. "Mother fucking gold."

"You got it, top man," Doug teased, fisting his own cock in excitement.

"Yes. Perfect. Where the hell have you been all my life, Douglas?" Carl rolled the rubber on excitedly.

"My mother calls me that."

"Sorry." Carl glanced at Doug and gave him a devilish grin.

"I've been here. Where the hell have you been?"

In a shitty relationship. "Here. I'm here now." Carl knelt upright and urged Doug to fold his legs backwards. Making Doug comfortable, Carl rested Doug's calves on his shoulders.

Once he was in position Carl massaged Doug's ring with the slick gel. Using two fingers, Carl entered Doug's back passage. Doug moaned and closed his eyes.

"Nice?" Carl grew harder.

"Love a good hard fuck."

"Wow. You do sound like a porn film now."

"Will that turn you on?" Doug grinned. "Ah, oh, yes. Ah, oh, yes."

Carl roared with laughter. "Stop! Not now. Joke after!"

Doug replaced the bottle of lube on the nightstand and stared at Carl intensely.

In the weakening candle's glow, Carl could make out Doug's handsome masculine features and cut chest and abs. Glorious. Just how he liked his men, young and fit. After giving Doug's prostate a nice massage, he removed his fingers and placed his cock against him. "Ready for our action scene?"

"Go for it."

With pleasure Carl entered Doug's body, slowly, deeply, to the hilt. Watching the euphoria on Doug's face, thrilled he loved to bottom, Carl was about to spurt. "Perfect. Fucking perfect."

"That feels so fucking good."

"Excellent." Carl began pumping gently. "So tight. Doug, you are amazing."

"Wow. You too. Geez, Carl, don't be afraid to go for it."

A rush of chills cascaded over Carl's skin at those words. "Sweet!" It was all he wanted a partner to say. Go for it, Carl. Not, Stop, I don't like it when you top, Carl!

He went wild. Bracing himself on his hands on the bed, Carl thrust deep and quick into Doug. Doug howled with the wind, fisting his own cock in a blur of movement.

Just the sight of Doug's orgasmic pleasure was all Carl needed. "I'm coming! I'm spurting. Ohfuckkk!"

Doug's ass tightened around Carl's cock. As Carl looked on in awe, Doug clamped shut his eyes, parted his lips to gasp and sprayed cum all over his own chest.

"Fantastic!" Carl announced, gaping down at that beautiful sight. "I want you! Doug, I have to have you!"

"You fucking just did!" Doug laughed, catching his breath.

"No. I mean, I want you." Carl felt possessive. Good, handsome, giving men were so hard to find. He had to get out of his present relationship and into this one. Now!

Suddenly the light in the room grew almost non-existent.

"That scented candle is either gone or drowning in its own wax. Let's clean up before it's out completely." Doug disconnected their bodies, climbing off the bed.

They washed up quickly and dove back under the blankets. The timing appeared perfect as the candle smothered itself, leaving the room in complete blackness.

Carl wrapped his arms and legs around Doug tightly, kissing his chest and neck. "I mean it. I would like us to be a couple."

"I know what you mean." Doug caressed Carl's hair lovingly.

"What do you say?"

"I say you need to get free of the relationship you're in first."

Carl choked in shock and wished he could see Doug's

eyes. "How the hell did you know?"

"I can just tell."

"Jesus!" Carl shivered and drew Doug closer. "Am I giving off some weird vibes?"

"Sort of."

"Don't worry. I'll be out quick."

Doug kissed Carl's head. "I'm tired. Let's try and sleep. Everything will be better in the light of day."

Carl snuggled against him, closing his eyes as the wind continued to blast the walls outside. Yes. Tomorrow. Everything will change come the morning.

In the Light of Day

ELEVATOR MEN

Coming around from a deep dream, Brad felt the earth jolt under him. Opening his eyes wearily, he found Kent sound asleep on top of him on the floor of the elevator. He checked his watch. Suddenly the lights came on and the elevator moved.

"Agh! Kent! Wake up!"

"What?" Kent's eyes slit open.

"The power's on!"

"Shit!" Kent jumped to his feet, tucked in his shirt, zipped his slacks and ran his hand through his hair anxiously.

The door slid open at the next floor. No one was there. As they scrambled to put their shoes on and make themselves presentable, Brad said, "It's morning. Do you believe this? We were stuck in this thing all night?"

"I was fucking out of it. I slept like a rock." Kent hoisted his toolbox and they both waited for the elevator to get to the lobby.

"It's Saturday. I wonder if anyone is even left in the building."

"I hope we're not locked in."

At the ground floor the doors slid open again. Several men were waiting.

A sensation of guilt and being overwhelmed by the four security men hit Brad instantly.

"Are you guys all right?" a man in a uniform asked.

"Yes. Just a little dazed," Kent replied, rubbing his face.

"Either of you need any medical care?"

"No." Brad shook his head, "We're fine. Just exhausted from being in that thing all night." He caught the eye of a handsome black fellow. A slightly devilish smile was aimed his way. Instantly Brad remembered the surveillance camera. So, it was on. Oh my!

"The doors are open. Just let us know if there's anything you need after your ordeal."

Laughing, Kent answered, "A shower, a piss, a shave, and a cup of coffee."

"Not necessarily in that order!" Brad laughed heartily.

"Toilet is that way."

Brad nodded and followed Kent to it, pushing back the door. Setting his briefcase down, he stood next to Kent at the urinal. "Man!"

"Christ, I had to piss."

"Me too, babe." Brad felt relief finally after he was able to urinate.

They stood side by side at the washbasin. "I look like crap." Brad ran his hand over his coarse jaw and wild hair.

Kent leaned against him purring, "You look damn sexy."

Brad licked his cheek in appreciation. "Come to my place. We can shower and have breakfast."

"I need to change my clothes. I'm not wearing this uniform all day."

"Where do you live? I'll follow you."

"Cool."

Before they left the men's room, Brad held Kent back. "It was a really great night, all things considered."

"It was." Kent set his toolbox down and embraced Brad, rocking him gently.

"I mean it. I'm thrilled we met."

Checking behind him quickly, Kent drew Brad to his lips. Brad moaned in pleasure knowing that even in the light of day, Kent was still interested. How cool was that?

When they parted mouths, Kent whispered, "Let me just grab a pair of jeans and a shirt at my place so we can get to your place and have a nice day together."

"Perfect." Brad waited as Kent picked up his toolbox.

"Oh. Hang on."

Brad paused.

Opening the box, Kent gingerly removed the spent condom and tossed it in the trash.

At the expression of revulsion on Kent's face, Brad began laughing.

"Yeah, ha ha. It should have been in your briefcase on your paperwork." Kent rinsed his hands.

"Spunk on your hammer. I love it."

Kent nudged him playfully. "Get going before I make you suck my hammer."

"Mm!" Brad lit up.

"Go. You're bad. Very bad. You look normal but you're not are you?"

"No. I'm a sexual deviant. Just ask my parents."

"Let's not go there." Kent opened the door for him.

"Good idea. Where are you parked?"

"Out front."

They exited the building and paused looking at the damage that was all around them.

"Oh, my God." Brad gasped at the downed trees and missing roof tiles.

"I had no idea it was this bad." Kent walked slowly to his pickup truck. It was covered in leaves and debris.

"I think some of the power is still out. Look." Brad pointed. "That traffic light isn't working."

In the brilliant sunlight, Kent narrowed his gaze to where he was gesturing. "Just take your time. I'll wait for you to pull your car around."

"Okay." Brad pecked his cheek.

Kent smiled sweetly at him.

≈≈

When Brad walked back through the lobby to get to the parking garage, Kent set his toolbox in his truck and began brushing off the palm fronds and litter from his hood. A few cars were on the road but not many. Mostly police and cleanup crews. "Wow." Kent took his phone out of his pocket and dialed.

"Hello?"

"Hey, Mom. It's me."

"Kent! I was worried sick."

"I got stuck in an elevator all night."

"How horrible."

Kent smiled. "No. It wasn't. It was awesome."

"Do I want to hear this story?"

"No. You don't. I just wanted to let you know I'm okay."

"Thank you, sweetheart."

"Any damage to your home?"

"No. We did fine. How about you?"

"I'm just headed back to my apartment now. I'll let you know."

"Okay. I'm glad you're okay, Kent. Thanks for the call."

"No problem, Mom." He hung up and climbed into his truck. When he started it, he noticed a car slowing down near him. Seeing Brad behind the wheel, he pulled onto the roadway and made his way cautiously to his apartment. As he drove, he kept muttering under his breath in awe at how bad everything looked. Damage was everywhere. "My God. What a fucking night."

In a few minutes he was parked in his apartment building lot and climbing out of the truck. Seeing Brad still in his business suit made Kent smile. Blue collar mixing with white? Would that work? Time would tell.

"Hey." Brad met him at the door to his modest abode.

"It's not much. Don't have high expectations." Kent pushed back the door.

"I'm not your judge. Why should I care?"

Kent tried a light switch. "Still out."

"I hope mine is back."

"Let me just get out of these work clothes."

"Take a few things you'll need to spend the weekend. I have no intention of letting you out of my sight."

Kent grinned at him wickedly. "What's your place like?"

"Decent. You'll like it."

Having a feeling Brad was being very modest, Kent nodded and hurried to grab a handful of overnight items.

∽∾

Though Brad had the urge to follow Kent into his bedroom and get down and dirty, he knew once they had showered and had a bite to eat they would feel much more inclined to love making.

Looking around the small one bedroom unit, Brad smiled wistfully and admired a few things Kent had set around the room: family photos and some sports memorabilia.

In a short time Kent returned wearing tight faded blue denim and a t-shirt.

"I can drive." Brad twirled his key.

"Fine."

They locked up the apartment and walked to Brad's car. "Is this weird? Us two meeting this way?"

Once Kent had climbed into the passenger's seat, he set his backpack down on the floor and answered, "Yes. Very weird."

Brad waited for Kent to fasten his seatbelt. "Good. I think it's cool."

Kent laughed softly.

As he made his way through the fallen trees, downed power lines and black traffic lights, Brad wondered what Kent would think of his home. He was about to find out.

He pulled into the driveway of his four bedroom house in Sherman Oaks.

"Fuck!"

Brad smiled. He assumed that meant Kent was impressed.

"Man, what do you want with me?"

"Everything." Brad shut off the car and said, "Come on. Let's see if my power is on."

They headed to the front door, unlocked it and pushed it back. Brad tried a light switch. "Yea!" he cheered. "Hot coffee and a good breakfast it is!"

"Perfect. Wow. What a fucking place."

"Thanks. Come on. We both need a shower and shave."

Brad led him to his master bedroom, undressing as he went. Once down to his briefs, he gestured to the bathroom and made sure he had plenty of towels.

"Brad..." Kent took off his clothing.

"Yes?" Brad turned on the shower, heating up the water.

"It's okay."

"What's okay?"

"It's okay if it was just a storm thing."

Brad tilted his head in confusion. "Storm thing?"

Suddenly Kent looked shy and averted his gaze.

"Come on. Let's wash." Brad slipped his briefs off and reached out his hand. He escorted Kent into the marble tiled stall and they alternated wetting and scrubbing.

"Are you okay?" Brad thought Kent had become very quiet.

Kent glanced only quickly at him but didn't answer.

Brad embraced him, pulling him to rest against his body under the shower spray. "I don't care how much money you make. I don't give a crap what you do for a living."

"Come on," Kent replied sarcastically. "Everyone does."

"No. Not me." He hugged Kent tight, moaning at his feel as they connected under the hot spraying water. "I think you're wonderful."

"I'm not. I'm just a cable guy."

"Hopefully 'my' cable guy."

Kent leaned back to stare into Brad's eyes as if judging his sincerity.

"Are you done?"

"Yes."

Brad shut the taps and pushed back the sliding doors. After drying off, they stood side by side at twin basins, shaving and brushing their teeth. Once that was done, though Brad knew they were both dying for a cup of coffee and some food, he picked Kent up into his arms and awkwardly carried him to his bed, tossing him on it.

Kent laughed in amusement as he spun around to look at him. "Heavier than I look huh?"

"No. I'm weaker than I look." Brad shook his head. "I tried to impress you with my brute strength."

"Uh, try your good looks next time."

Enjoying Kent's humor, Brad pinned him to the bed and made sure they were connecting everywhere. "I want us to give this a try."

"It's useless, isn't it? We come from different back-grounds."

"Opposites attract."

"Bull shit."

"Kent!" Brad was stunned at the negativity.

"How can it work?" Kent began to battle for release. "I'll always envy what you have, your income, your house."

A squeezing sensation from his emotions filled Brad's throat. "So? That's it? We come from different backgrounds and you made the decision it can't happen?"

Kent covered his face in humiliation.

Feeling sick over Kent's admission, Brad dug his arms under Kent's body and held onto him. To him it wasn't just one crazy night stuck in an elevator. It was the beginning of something special.

Resting his cheek on Kent's chest to hear his heartbeat, Brad closed his eyes, wanting this man, unhappy Kent wasn't willing to even try.

After a few minutes Brad felt Kent's arms settle down to rest around his back. Inhaling and exhaling a deep sigh, Brad allowed them to just lie naked on each other, and he savored it wondering if it would ever happen again.

Finally Brad leaned up on his elbows look at Kent. "No matter what you decide, Kent, I still think you are an amazing man."

A smile flickered on Kent's face, and vanished.

Pouting, Brad echoed softly, "An amazing man."

"I want you, Brad. Don't think I don't."

"The what the fuck's the problem? Seriously. What I own I'll share with you and vice versa."

"Yeah, I'll bet you were just salivating over a chance to hang out on my used furniture."

"Stop it." Brad covered Kent's mouth. "Don't put barriers up between us already. Do you have any idea how hard it is to find a compatible partner around here? One that you desire, crave? And one that craves you back?" Brad paused to see if his words had any effect. "If you begin placing economic walls between people, don't you narrow our choices down substantially?"

"And you're too smart for me."

"Kent!" Brad breathed in exasperation. "All I'm asking is for a test run. Okay? A week? A day at a time? Is that such a difficult thing to do?"

Kent's expression softened.

Kissing his chin, his cheek, his ear, Brad breathed into Kent's ear, "Try. Please."

"You really like me that much?"

Brad shook his head in amazement. "Yes. I do. You're beautiful inside and out."

"You got that from one wicked night in an elevator?"

"Didn't you?" Brad gaped at him. "Didn't you feel something intense in there? And I don't mean just from the power outage."

A long moment past. They just stared into each other's eyes. Finally Kent whispered, "Yes."

Brad crushed him in an embrace and feathered kisses all over his face. The amount he wanted Kent was already strong. Overpowering. He didn't want to let him go to get a cup of coffee, he certainly had no intention of having him walk out of his life for all the wrong reasons.

"Come get it, top man." Brad wriggled on him seductively. He was glad it made Kent laugh.

As Kent's smile faded, he cupped Brad's jaw and drew him to his lips. On contact, Brad combusted. Kent tasted so good, felt so right. "Take me," he hissed against Kent's lips. "Take what I have and make it yours."

"Wow!" Kent shivered visibly.

"I mean it."

"I'm astounded."

"Why?" Brad reached into his nightstand and found what they needed. "Why are you astounded I find you desirable? Delicious? Incredible? Why are you surprised I want you in my bed, in my life?"

"I...I..." Kent shook his head, his eyes wide.

"You what?" Brad sat back and stroked Kent between his legs. "You want in? Huh?" he teased. "Give me a good fucking?"

A light shone in Kent's blue eyes. He lunged at Brad and muscled him down under him.

"That's better!" Brad was thrilled.

"Give me that thing." Kent reached for a condom.

Excited, Brad touched Kent all over as Kent rolled the

rubber on his cock.

"Roll over," Kent purred wickedly.

"Yes!" Brad ignited and spun around so he was face down on the bed, his ass up in the air in invitation. As Kent's warm hands tugged at his balls, rubbed lube in all the right places, Brad crushed his face into his pillows and moaned.

"You ready, lover?"

"I'm ready, babe." Brad smiled. Heat filled him. He inhaled a hiss of air and shivered at the penetration. "So nice. Kent, so very nice."

"Jesus, you feel good."

Once Kent sank in deep, he held Brad's cock and worked him in time with his gentle thrusting. Brad wanted him. He had no doubt this man was perfect for him. "That's it, baby. Take what's yours. You own it."

His words obviously setting Kent alight, Brad felt him increase his speed and depth, grunting as he neared his peak.

And with it, Kent's hand quickened on Brad's length. As they both soared into the stratosphere of a strong climax, Brad lavished in the throbbing and heat that fulfilled him.

Kent attempted to cup the sperm as it pumped out of Brad's body, trying to keep the sheets clean under them. Brad had to smile at the consideration.

A moment to pant and sweat together past before Kent separated their connection and said, "I'll be right back."

Rolling over to his side, Brad smiled adoringly at him. "Hurry."

Kent winked and jumped into the air as he sprinted to the bathroom.

Feeling an enormous amount of affection towards Kent already, Brad was hoping Kent at least would give them the opportunity to try.

～～

Once he cleaned up, Kent smiled at his reflection in the mirror. "Yeah. Why not?" He shut off the light, bounded out of the bathroom to leap on the bed, pinning Brad under him. "Okay."

"Okay?" Brad laughed.

"I'm game."

"I'm so glad."

Warm kisses covered his face and neck. Kent hummed contentedly. Why not? Anything is possible. Even finding true love in a power outage.

Surveillance

Both men were dozing in their chairs when the lights blinked on in the office. Billy sputtered awake and sat up. Next to him, Ted did the same.

"Power's back."

"Yup. Come on. Let's see how those guys in the elevator are doing."

Nodding, rubbing his rough face to wake up, Bill followed Ted down the hall and through another corridor to the front lobby. When they emerged into the wide light space, two other security men were there, just coming in.

"Hello, Ted, Bill."

"Bout time!" Ted laughed, shaking his head. "I'm exhausted."

"It's hell out there at the moment. Most streets are either blocked by trees or emergency crews. Sorry it took so long to get you relief."

"It's all right, John, Al." Bill tried to smile. It was more than all right in his opinion.

The elevator door opened and two very frazzled-looking men stepped out. Bill knew they had screwed all night but kept his face a mask.

"Are you guys all right?" John asked them.

"Yes. Just a little dazed," the man in the blue uniform replied, rubbing his face.

"Either of you need any medical care?"

"No." The man in the suit shook his head. "We're fine. Just exhausted from being in that thing all night."

Bill noticed the businessman and Ted exchange curious

glances. He knew what Ted was thinking. Then wondered if the men realized there was a security camera in that elevator.

John informed the two exhausted men, "The doors are open. Just let us know if there's anything you need after your ordeal."

Laughing, the uniformed man with the toolbox answered, "A shower, a piss, a shave, and a cup of coffee."

"Not necessarily in that order!" the man in the suit laughed heartily.

"Toilet is that way," John said as he pointed.

When the two men walked towards it, Ted smiled know-ingly at Bill.

At the tender look, Bill's chest burned with adoration for him.

"Go home." John waved at them. "You're off until Mon-day. Get some rest."

"Thanks, John." Ted patted his back.

Bill waved at the men and walked with Ted to where they had parked their cars on the street. They were silent as they went. Bill wished he had the guts to say something. It would be great to see Ted socially, outside work. And they had two days off in a row now to play. He just had to get up the nerve to open his mouth.

Ted took out his car keys and spun around. "Have a nice weekend, Billy."

"You too." About to walk away, Bill called out, "Ted?"

Ted paused, waiting.

Trying to find some courage, Bill closed the gap between them. "So? That's it? Just a no strings attached sex thing?"

"I don't know. Can we take some time to just think about it? I'm not so sure I want a full-fledged romance at the mo-ment, Billy."

"No. And not with another guy. I get it." Bill laughed but he felt crushed.

"That's not the issue."

It took a second but Bill caught the comment. "Really? Being with a man isn't the issue?"

Ted took a glance around the area before he whispered, "I had a male partner when I was in the police."

Bill shrugged, "So?"

"A male sexual partner," Ted clarified.

Bill choked in surprise. He had no idea Ted had been with a man before their own encounter and was stunned.

"So, let me think about it over the weekend. Okay, Billy?"

Wanting Ted, hoping for more, Bill mumbled, "It's okay with me if it's just physical, Ted. It's better than nothing."

"I won't play that mind game with you. It's either all or nothing."

Bill's gut wrenched figuring it'd be nothing. "Okay."

Ted took a quick peek again at the area, touched Bill on the chin and kissed him.

Bill's toes curled at the heat.

"Go home and rest, Billy. I'll see you Monday evening."

"Okay, Ted. Drive carefully."

Ted gave Bill a wink and got into his car.

As Ted drove off, Billy muttered under his breath, "You are an amazing man, Ted Green. An absolutely amazing man."

∽≈

Ted looked into his rearview mirror for a last glimpse of Billy before he turned the corner. Recalling their night of fervor, Ted smiled broadly. "Well, well, Bill Patton, you surprised me. I had no idea you had so much passion in you."

Turning on the radio to hear the latest update on the aftermath of the storm, Ted was anxious to get home and see if his own place was all right.

As he drove across town, Ted couldn't wipe the grin off his face. Having a man as honest and adorable as Bill in his life could only be a benefit not a detriment.

"Billy, Billy, Billy," Ted sighed, "You amazing man you."

After a long journey through blacked out street signals and fallen trees, Ted arrived home. Kicking some branches off his front path, Ted removed his keys from his pocket and opened his front door. His orange cat curled around his legs instantly.

"You hungry, pudding?" Ted tossed his keys on the side table. "Sorry I'm late." Taking care of his pet first, Ted opened a can of cat food and set it on floor. "There you go."

Walking to his bedroom, Ted began unbuttoning his shirt, intent on a hot shower. Once he was naked, he caught his reflection in the mirror over the dresser. An image of Billy kneeling in front of him flashed through his mind, sending a shock through his body. Closing his eyes to savor it, Ted exhaled and muttered, "What's wrong with me? Am I insane?" He picked up his cordless phone and dialed a number he knew by heart, Billy's mobile phone number.

"Hello?"

"Billy."

"Hi, Ted? Did your house survive?"

"Yes. Everything is fine here." Ted caught another glance at himself in the mirror. "Look...do you have plans this weekend?"

"No. Why?"

He could hear the excitement in Billy's voice. "Why don't you come on by?"

"You mean it? I thought you said—"

"I know what I said. I just think it would be nice to spend time outside work. Get to know you as something other than a security guard."

"Yeah?"

"Yeah." Ted smiled. "Later on, you want to walk along the beach? Sometimes after a storm, all sorts of good things wash up."

"I'd love that! I collect shells and stuff. Is that girly?"

"No. I do too. Good. Why don't you come here at around one? That will give us both a chance to have a nap and freshen up."

"Excellent! Thanks, Ted! I can't wait."

"Me neither. You remember how to get here?"

"I do."

"Good. See you later." Ted hung up, his smile still on his lips. "Why not? He's good fun." As he walked to the shower, he giggled, "Collects shells." After turning on the water in the shower, Ted picked up a spiral seashell he had sitting on his sink basin. Admiring it, Ted sighed. "You better not beat me to the good ones, Billy!" Laughing at himself, he climbed into the steaming water to refresh himself. "My, oh my, whatever have I gotten myself into?"

PARKING BLUES

Pete opened his eyes. The muscles in his neck were aching. Jerking back in surprise, he realized he was naked in his car sleeping on top of David. The morning light shined down on them, exposing them to the world.

"Fuck." He sat up and dug in the back seat for his clothing.

David awoke. "Oh, man..." he moaned, rubbing his face.

Pete checked his watch, it was nine fifteen.

"Fuck!" David seemed to have the same reaction when he became aware of where he was.

They both scrambled for their clothing frantically, tossing things around the interior of the car.

Once Pete had his shirt tucked into his trousers, he sat in the driver's seat and slipped on his shoes. On the floor was a spent condom and wrapper. Shit. Pete rubbed his rough jaw and screwed up hair tiredly. Twisting the rearview mirror, he took a look at his face and tried to tame his hair in vain.

When David had stopped fussing, his clothing on his body to his satisfaction, he paused and gazed at Pete, panting nervously.

Pete held up his hands. "Look. It was just a crazy night."

"I am so dead."

"Why?" Pete asked anxiously.

"I...I have a boyfriend, Pete."

Closing his eyes in relief, Pete replied, "So do I."

"Jesus!" David moaned, "What did we do?"

Shrugging, Pete responded, "We did what we did. It was just a crazy night."

David flipped open his phone. It was obviously drained

of battery power. He closed it and slouched in the seat. "He's going to wonder why I never came home."

"Tell him you were trapped in your office building."

"And that I happen to smell like another man because... why?" David sneered. "I was huddled together for dear life? Come on."

Pete removed his own mobile phone from his pocket and turned it on. It beeped with messages. Biting his lip nervously, he put the phone to his ear to listen to them.

"Babe? It's Danny. Where are you? I'm worried about you. Why aren't you answering your mobile phone? Call me."

Pausing to look at the number of messages Danny left, Pete felt sick inside.

"Your boyfriend?" David asked softly.

"Yes." Pete scrubbed his rough face tiredly.

"Look, Pete," David began, touching his thigh, "No one needs to know. It was just a one off thing to pass the time."

Pete laughed sadly. "Yeah, he'd buy that."

"You don't have to tell him."

"I know. But it'll be our first nasty secret between us."

"How long have you been with him?"

"A week." Pete frowned sadly.

"A week? That's barely a relationship. I've been with John for five years."

Pete whipped is head around to David. "Five years? Five years and you cheated on him?"

"You seduced me!" David pointed at Pete in accusation. "I was sitting here minding my own business when you jumped on me!"

"I did not! Jumped on you? You were begging for my cock up your ass!"

David gathered his suit jacket in his arm and made like he was getting out.

Pete stopped him. "Hang on."

Hesitating, David sighed loudly and closed his eyes.

"Let's not make this any more than it was, okay? We were two horny guys trapped in a parking garage. Seriously, David, that's it."

"Two horny guys who fucked each other." David rubbed

his eyes in anguish. "And what a fantastic fuck it was, Pete."

"It was the situation." Pete rubbed David's arm gently. When David met his eyes with his red ones, Pete stopped touching him. "Do you love this John guy?"

"Yes. Very much."

"Then don't mention it. Just forget it."

"Forget it?" David laughed sadly. "Forget it, forget you?"

"Yes. Look, I'm just getting into a relationship with a great man. I really like Danny. I want to have an exclusive partnership with him."

"After a week of dating you had your dick in another man's ass. Nice beginning, Pete."

Pete's cheeks heated up. "Like I said, it was extenuating circumstances."

"Sure, babe. Whatever excuse gets you there."

"David." Pete held him back from opening the door again. "It meant something to me. Last night. I know it was nuts, but I do feel a strong bond with you."

"Really? Do you intend on sharing that sentiment with Danny?"

"Don't be glib. Is there a need to torment me?"

David's expression dropped. "I feel so guilty."

"Don't." Pete brushed his hair back from his face. "It was just one crazy night in a blackout. Don't beat yourself up."

Pete thought his words were ironic because he was just beginning to agonize over what he had done to his and Danny's budding relationship. He hated secrets. Pete knew eventually he'd have to tell that adorable twin the bad news. It just would fester inside him if he didn't.

Seeing David fret, Pete assumed this had to be harder on him. Five years? That was an eternity as far as Pete was concerned.

That had to be gnawing at David horribly. He felt terrible for him. "Babe." Pete used one knuckle to feel the texture of David's coarse jaw. "Don't wallow in it. It's done."

❧❧

David's eyes watered as he gazed at Pete's handsome face in the morning light. Slowly he touched Pete's jaw and drew him for a light kiss. When they parted, David whispered hoarsely, "It was like a fantasy, Pete."

Pete smiled broadly. "It was."

David shuffled around to get to his wallet. "There's no reason we can't keep in touch or go out for a coffee during the day. I mean we work in the same building." He handed Pete his card.

"Is that wise?" Pete took it, inspecting it.

"I don't know, but I feel it's necessary."

Pete nodded, slipping the card into his pocket.

"Pete."

Pete met his eyes.

"I'll see you around."

"Yes." Pete caressed David's cheek.

Feeling emotional, knowing he was exhausted, David gave him a weak smile and climbed out of his car. As he walked to his own, he watched the electric gate pull back and waited as Pete's car drove off, Pete giving him a last wave.

Sitting in his own car, plugging his phone into the adapter on the dash, David waited for the tiny mobile to light up. Instantly it beeped with messages. He put the phone to his ear reluctantly. John's voice sounded first concerned, turning to furious.

"Where the fuck are you!"

David listened to them all, dialing as he started the car.

"Finally!"

"Sorry, John."

"What the fuck is going on? You realize how worried I was all night? I didn't fucking sleep!"

"I got stuck in the parking garage. My phone wouldn't work until now," he lied. "I slept in the front seat of my car. I feel like hell."

"Are you on your way home now?"

"I am. Just leaving the garage. The gate opened finally." David waited for the iron rail to pull back, freeing him.

"David, I swear I thought you were dead. I don't understand why you couldn't borrow a phone and just tell me you were okay."

"I spoke to you last night about the gate barricading me

in. I did call you. You had to know I was just stuck in the ga-rage." David peered at all the damage as he drove, astonished at the amount of trees down.

"I did. I just didn't know why the communication stopped. How come you can call me now?"

"I kept trying but last night the phone just went out. I don't know. Maybe the storms blew out some tower some-where. I'm on my way home now. I need a shower and some food. I'll be home in soon."

"Good. I miss you."

"You too, babe. See you soon." David set the phone on the seat beside him and rubbed his forehead wondering how the hell he was going to get Pete off his mind. Sniffing his hand, David also had to find a way to get in the shower before John got a good whiff of him.

Keeping his fingers near his nose to remind him of Pete, David drove home with a heavy heart. "What an amazing man you are, Pete. Danny is one lucky guy."

Seeing John standing at the front door of their home, David knew he was a dead man. The minute John embraced him he'd smell Pete's scent on him. "Shit. Shit." David pulled into the driveway behind John's car and tried not to shake nervously. He loved John and the thought that he had cheated was making him nauseated. Seeing John's bright, relieved smile only made David feel worse.

"Babe..." John reached out for him.

Pressing his hand onto John's chest to keep him back, David said, "Let me shower. I know I stink and I feel like crap."

"Since when do I care?" John laughed.

"I have to rinse off. Just give me a minute." Walking past John's suspicious glare, David yanked off his suit and immediately put it into a bag to take to the cleaners. Down to his briefs, standing in the bathroom with his hand under the spraying water, David found John glaring at him from the doorway.

"Who'd you fuck?"

"John," David whined.

"Who'd you fuck?" John roared.

"No one!" David was so overwhelmed with guilt he was

going to cry.

"You're a fucking liar! Why else wouldn't you want me to get close enough to fucking sniff you? You bastard."

Covering his face, David tried to gain control of himself. Meeting his lover's eyes, David sighed. "We just kissed. That was it."

John threw up his hands in exasperation.

"I swear!" David said, "We were locked in together. We sat for a little while in his car to talk. We exchanged a peck or two. That's it."

"That's it?" John approached him. "A peck or two?"

"The guy was married. He wasn't even gay. He just wanted to see what kissing a guy was like. We didn't even use tongues." David wondered why lying came so easy? Why? If he lost John he'd die. That's why. And he never cheated on him before. Never. It was just the crazy storm.

The shower began making the room misty from the heat.

"Can I wash?" David pointed to the tub nervously.

John barely nodded, his arms crossed over his chest. Once David stepped into the torrent, he caught John standing with the door partly open, as if inspecting his body. David prayed he had no unusual marks on him.

"Just a kiss with no tongue? To a straight married guy? Are you telling me the truth?"

Holding up his hand in a vow, David swore, "I am, so help me God."

As it taking a moment to ponder it, John asked wryly, "Did he like it?"

"No. Hated it. He said it sucked."

John chuckled softly. "Was he hot?"

"No. Kind of old and soft. Not hot. I was just bored." David rinsed the shampoo out of his hair.

"And then what happened?"

"I got into my own car, lay down on the seat and slept."

"And the guy?"

David shrugged. "I guess he slept in his car. I don't know. I lost track of him." Finished washing, David shut the water. John handed him a towel. "Thanks. I'm sorry, babe. It was just something that happened in the moment. He was kind of nasty. I certainly didn't enjoy it."

"I'm surprised you did it. You're so picky when it comes to men." John rubbed a towel over David's hair.

"I am." David felt sick.

John hugged him. "I'm just glad you're okay. It was a rough night waiting for you."

"Babe. I'm so sorry. I'll make it up to you."

"You will!" John grabbed David's rump and gave it a squeeze. "Get in bed."

David pecked his lips, tossed his towel over the shower door and walked to their bed. As John undressed for their lovemaking, David did his best to not think of Pete. From then on, Pete couldn't cross his mind.

Easier said than done.

"You ready for me?" John smiled adoringly.

"Yes. I'm ready." David gave him a brave smile and reached out to him. As John filled both their needs, David closed his eyes and hated himself, wishing he could absolve himself of this sin.

Voyeur

Miguel stretched lazily as light flooded into the bedroom. Beside him his best friend Stuart Jones still slept. Staring at him, Miguel leant up on his elbow and gazed down at Stuart's shaggy blond hair and darker brown eyebrows. "So pretty." Miguel smiled adoringly. "How long we wait to do this? Hm?" he breathed.

Caressing Stuart's blond hair back from his forehead, Miguel was greeted with Stuart's crystal blue eyes at his touch.

"Morning."

"Buenos dias."

"Did you sleep well?" Stuart rolled to his side, facing Miguel.

"Like a bebe'."

Stuart sat up. "The power's on."

"Is it?" Miguel twisted around and found Stuart's clock blinking the wrong time. "Muy bien."

Stuart dropped to lay on his back and drew Miguel closer. "It's Saturday. Do you have any plans?"

"Yes. We spend all day Saturday together. So? Why do any different today?" Miguel nudged the sheet down so he could caress Stuart's chest.

"Are we crazy?"

"Who knows? All I know is I wanted you like this. In my arms. For too long. Now? I have you." Miguel squeezed him close.

"You do." Stuart pinched Miguel's jaw. "But you always had me."

Miguel's smile softened. "No. Not like this I no have you."

Miguel ran his hand down Stuart's torso to his pubic hair.

Seeing Stuart's passionate expression and his legs spread under the blankets, Miguel's excitement grew. "You are so pretty, Stuart. You and your blond hair and eyes azul."

A shy chuckle erupted from Stuart. "I feel beautiful when you look at me that way."

"Is because I love you." Miguel caressed Stuart's rough cheek.

"What now, Miguel?"

"Que? What now? How you mean?"

"Can you move in?"

Miguel's heart skipped a beat. "You want me move in? Here?"

"Yes." Stuart tightened his grip on Miguel's body. "Please."

Miguel looked around the huge master bedroom and thought about his tiny place in Inglewood. "You are sure? You no just say that because last night was good sex?"

Laughing, Stuart replied, "No. I'm not just saying that. I would have asked you months ago but I didn't think you'd be interested. Now that we're lovers...are you?"

"Si!" Miguel was thrilled. "I will love living with you. If you are sure. You need think about it. Have you thought about it?"

"Yes. Please live with me."

Miguel crawled across Stuart's body to lie on top of him, his legs spread over Stuart's hips. "I do anything you wish. Anything."

"Good. Then it's settled."

When Stuart dug his fingers into Miguel's hair, Miguel felt tingles rush down his back. "What you want me do to you? Hm?" Miguel purred, nuzzling Stuart's neck.

"First let me piss and brush my teeth, then I want all of you."

Laughing as he scooted back, Miguel agreed, "Yes. After, we will have all."

In all the time he'd known him, after that crazy, heart-stopping ride on his bike last night through the terrible storm, Miguel could never have predicted the outcome of his daring deed to have been him and Stuart together as couple, cohabitating. It was his dream. He only wished he hadn't waited so long. That Stuart had shown him some kind of sign he wanted him for more than just a friend. But even Stuart's light touches and sweet smiles weren't enough. Miguel knew Stuart was good-hearted and gave generously to all his friends. How was he to know he was special?

"You okay?"

Smiling affectionately at his lover, Miguel nodded, "I okay. I more than okay. I am so in love with you."

Pausing, Stuart embraced him in delight. "Wow. You know how to sweep a man off his feet. Is that the Latino in you?"

"Si, yes. You have found your Latin lover." Miguel's dark eyes shined luxuriously.

"Perfect." Stuart pecked his lips.

≈≈

Stuart led the way to his master bathroom, found Miguel a new toothbrush and then stood at the toilet to urinate.

Seeing Miguel peeking at him in the mirror's reflection, Stuart smiled sweetly. "Feels nice. Comfortable. We've known each other a long time."

After rinsing his mouth, Miguel nodded. "Yes. It feels good. Natural."

They swapped places. Miguel let go his stream as Stuart brushed his teeth. After he spat out the toothpaste, Stuart shook his head in admiration. "You have such an amazing body, Miguel."

"Si? You like?" When he was through at the toilet, Miguel modeled for him, holding out his arms before he washed his hands at the sink.

"I like!"

"Vamos. Back to bed." Miguel patted Stuart on his bottom.

Stuart raced back and leapt on the bed with a bounce feeling like a playful kid. And what a toy to play with! Yowza!

As Miguel hurried back under the blankets to snuggle, Stuart moaned and squeezed him tight. "I don't want to get out of bed today."

"Then we no get out of bed." Miguel began running kisses

down Stuart's neck.

Chills washed over Stuart's skin as Miguel set him on fire. "But we usually play racquetball...you know. Have a good lunch afterwards...uh..." Stuart lost his train of thought as Miguel sucked at his throat. "Never mind."

Miguel laughed in a deep seductive purr.

Opening his body up for Miguel to explore, Stuart kept trying to remember this wasn't a dream. Delectable Miguel Rodriguez was really here. Naked. Licking and sucking on his body. "Ohhh..." Stuart howled in pleasure. "I love windstorms, I love windstorms."

"Stop. You making me laugh and I cannot kiss you." Miguel broke up with giggles.

"Kiss me. Take me. Love me."

Miguel held Stuart's face and coaxed him to meet his eyes. The serious expression on Miguel made Stuart's heart pound.

"I do love you. So much." Miguel's dark eyes simmered as he spoke. "Why we wait so long? Why?"

"I don't know." Stuart couldn't believe how sensual Miguel was: his deep voice, his masculine scent, his ethnic looks, like an exotic aphrodisiac. "But we did it. We're here together. Now. Right now."

"Si. Now. Aqui'."

When Miguel closed his eyes and kissed him, Stuart became an animal. He wrapped his arms around Miguel's back and squeezed him as tightly as he could, pressing their crotches together hotly.

Spinning them over so he was on top, Stuart used his knees to part Miguel's thighs and lay between them. Rubbing his erection on Miguel's, thrilling at the friction of his taut mocha skin and dark wiry pubic hair, Stuart moaned in longing. "I have to have you."

"Have me."

Sucking on Miguel's tongue for another minute, Stuart parted breathlessly to grab a condom and the lube. As he fussed to prepare himself, Miguel watched, stroking Stuart's arm gently.

After he was ready, Stuart urged Miguel's legs wide and higher. Seeing him exposed and so willing, Stuart's throat closed up with emotion. "I love you, babe. So much."

"Si. I know. I know you love me long time."

The moment he pushed inside Miguel, Stuart stared at him in awe. "You knew?"

"Yes. I know you love me. But like a friend. Yes?"

Nodding, smiling, Stuart understood. "Like a friend. No. Like a lover, Miguel." He pushed in deeper, the pleasure washing up and over him like a tsunami.

"My lover." Miguel caressed Stuart's cheek. "Stuart with the beautiful golden hair."

Thrusting more aggressively, Stuart closed his eyes as orgasm drew closer. Miguel began to croon in Spanish to him. Giving Stuart all he needed. He gasped, arching his back and pushed in as tightly as he could. His cock throbbed with his racing pulse and shot out cum into the rubber which was buried inside Miguel's ass.

Gasping for air, Stuart opened his eyes and found Miguel's adoring expression. Miguel's beard had grown dark on his square jaw overnight. A more masculine man Stuart had never seen. He pulled out gently, dropped the spent condom on the floor and snuggled in between Miguel's legs. Lapping at his balls, moaning in pleasure, Stuart devoured him from his root to his head.

When Miguel was writhing under him on the bed, Stuart slipped his finger back inside his slick passage and sucked deeper, harder. Miguel's body tensed and his breath quickened. As Miguel's cock gave up its prize, Stuart whimpered in ecstasy. Drawing on him, enjoying every last drop, Stuart slowed down his sucking and finally stopped, allowing Miguel's cock to slip out of his mouth gently.

Seeing the sated expression on his lover's face, Stuart crawled up his body to lie on top of him. "You amazing man. You absolutely fabulous, amazing man."

A low rumbling laugh echoed in Miguel's ribcage.

"I adore you."

"Quiero que para siempre."

"What does that mean?"

"It mean I want you forever."

Stuart brightened up and wriggled on him. "You got me!"

"You need to learn more Spanish? Yes?"

"Yes. Teach me. Teach me so we can whisper our words of love."

Miguel grinned broadly. "I am so lucky man."

"Grrr...me too, hot stuff. Me too." Stuart kissed him. "A whole day to play. It just doesn't get any better than this."

Rolling to his side so they were mirroring each other, Miguel asked, "I make us heuvos rancheros? A nice hearty breakfast to keep two men satisfied?"

"I love when you cook for me." Stuart felt as if he'd won the lottery. Miguel was the complete package. "Yes! Cook my favorite for me. I'll get the coffee going."

Before Stuart bounded out of the bed, Miguel held him back. "One more kiss."

Landing on top of him, Stuart sucked at Miguel's tongue and moaned. When they parted he grinned at Miguel in excitement.

"I never see you like this." Miguel laughed. "You look like little boy. You so like...a like jumping bean!"

Unable to express his passion and the thrill of taking his and Miguel's relationship to the ultimate level, Stuart spread out on top of him and pinned him underneath. "I have never wanted anything so much in my life as you and me together as a couple."

"No!"

"Yes. You complete me as a man, Miguel. You are everything to me."

After muttering in Spanish under his breath, Miguel replied, "Why we wait so long!" he whined loudly.

Cupping his face, planting a big kiss on his lips, Stuart answered, "Better now than never."

"Is true."

"Up. You made an offer I can't refuse." Stuart popped off the bed and hauled Miguel out of it. "A delicious breakfast." He swatted Miguel's bottom playfully as he tried to get clothing on.

"You loco!" Miguel cracked up. "You have no control. What I do to you? You used to be so calm. No more calm Stuart."

Stuart helped him draw the t-shirt over his head. "Nope.

No more calm Stuart. You've changed me into effervescent Stuart."

"I no know that word? Is good?"

Grabbing Miguel's coarse jaw, Stuart purred against his lips, "Is good." After kissing him, Stuart added, "Feed me, good looking."

"Si! Food for men, coming."

As Miguel raced to the kitchen, Stuart felt so much love for him, he tingled like bubbles all right. A fizzy swirl of contentment chased in his belly. Once he'd slipped on a pair of jeans, he bolted after his lover shouting, "I love windstorms!"

MALL MEN

Chris woke with a feeling of complete disorientation. Blinking his eyes, he noticed a small child staring at him. In surprise, Chris looked around and found Phil asleep on the mountain of pillows and sheets they had made to crash on.

"Phil." Chris shook him to wake him.

"Hm?"

"Wake up. It's morning and the store is open."

Phil bolted upright.

The little girl ran away.

"Shit!" Phil stood, tucking in his shirt and trying to smooth back his hair.

"Let's get the fuck out of here." Chris grabbed his elbow and escorted Phil to the escalators. He checked his watch and realized it was after nine.

In silence they descended to the ground floor and left via the entrance they had necked in front of the night before. The parking lot was sparsely occupied and a crew was righting a downed power pole.

"The world!" Chris shouted, "It survived!"

"Son of a bitch. It looks bad out here. Look at all the debris in the lot."

"Where's your car?" Chris asked, taking out his keys.

"There."

Out in the distance Chris noticed a gold Mazda RX8.

"You want to catch breakfast?"

"I want a shower."

"Your place or mine?" Chris purred.

Phil stopped and looped his arm around Chris tightly. "I

know you wanted to check on your place to see if it's okay."

"Perfect."

"But."

"I hate buts." Chris deflated.

"I don't know if I'm ready for a relationship, Chris."

"Okay." Chris couldn't believe how gorgeous Phil was in the light of day.

"I mean, I'm only twenty-five."

"And sex is so easy for a go-go boy."

"Well, yes." Phil chuckled.

"So? Was last night just a bout of hot sex with an Andreas Thorkildsen lookalike?"

"No. Don't be like that." Phil flicked back Chris's hair playfully. "I'm just not ready for anything exclusive. You know."

"You like your cock sucked by many men?"

"Yeah. I do. Many."

"You sure you want to come back to my place? It may cramp your style." Chris didn't feel badly. He wasn't in a position in his mind for a commitment either.

"I wouldn't mind a shower with you. And sex."

"Ahhh, penetration. We only exchanged blowjobs."

"Are you teasing me?"

"I am." Chris kissed Phil's chin.

"If you're not into me coming by, it's okay."

"Hm. I'm not sure. Are you a top or a bottom?" Chris teased.

"Either."

"Good. See that car?" Chris pointed to his Cadillac CTS.

"Yes."

"Sniff at its rear bumper."

"Can't wait." Phil hooked his arm around Chris's neck and embraced him, kissing him. "Shower, shave, and fuck."

"You ole' romantic you," Chris replied.

"You want romance? Go with a woman."

"No thank you."

"I didn't think so."

"I live only a few minutes from here."

"Good. See you there."

Chris nodded, taking his keys out of his pocket and as he walked to his car, a smile pasted itself on his lips. No, it wasn't true love, but he was too busy for a commitment and if he was honest with himself, he was relieved Phil was as well.

Checking his voicemail as Phil pulled up behind his car, Chris's only concern was his house, but they would soon see if it had survived.

Heading west to the coast, Chris kept eying the man in the car behind him, grinning contentedly.

When he arrived home he was relieved the place looked unscathed. Parking, getting out, Phil joined him in a cursory walk around the perimeter.

"Looks okay." Phil picked up a few pieces of driftwood that had washed up against the foundation and tossed them out onto the sand.

"Yes. It does. I'm very lucky."

"Nice place. I'd love to live on the beach."

Turning the key in the lock, Chris teased, "Play your cards right..."

"Funny man."

Chris instantly tried the light switch. The lamp lit up. "Yes! Power!"

"What a lucky guy."

"I'm about to get very lucky." Chris tossed his keys aside, taking off his shoes. "Strip for me, go-go boy."

Grinning in excitement, Phil slipped off his shoes and began pumping his hips as he undressed.

"Nice!" Chris crossed his arms, enjoying the show.

꙳

It was what he did best. Stripping for men. Phil hiked his shirt up, smoothing his hands over his rippled chest and tight abs. He licked his lips at Chris's enthralled expression, growing hard in his pants. I'm an exhibitionist, so what?

He was so relieved Chris was as handsome as he claimed, and in Phil's opinion, looked exactly like that gold medalist javelin thrower. He was thrilled to put on a show for him.

Pumping his hips, running his hand over the bulge in his jeans, Phil hammed it up. Music played in his head as he thrust his pelvis out and drew his shirt higher.

"Wow!"

Loving the look of lust in Chris's blue eyes, Phil removed his shirt and twirled it around his head before tossing it. With both hands he massaged next to his hard cock, growing harder by the minute at giving this hunk a private show.

Phil opened his zipper, drawing apart his jeans to titillate exposing his lower abdomen and some pubic hair. "Wanna fuck it?" he hissed, his hips humping the air.

Chris took off his own shirt, socks and slacks. Standing in his briefs he gawked at Phil as the performance continued.

Massaging his own nipple and stuffing his hand down his jeans, Phil touched himself and got off on Chris's excitement. There was nothing better than making men hot, especially ones as gorgeous as Chris.

"Jesus, Phil."

That made Phil smile. He lowered his pants down his thighs, showing off his huge erection under his briefs.

Chris made a move to come closer, stopping as if restraining himself from the urge, allowing Phil to continue.

"Am I making you want me?" Phil teased.

"Yes!" Chris rubbed his own cock excitedly.

Phil stepped out of his tight jeans and socks. Dipping his hand into his briefs, Phil played with himself while moving his hips to and fro sensually. "Want it?"

Hunger written all over him, Chris licked his lips, and Phil could see his Adam's apple move as he swallowed.

Slowly Phil began exposing his cock, nudging his briefs down his hip.

"Fuck this." Chris dove to his knees before Phil and opened his mouth for Phil's cock.

At the heat and wetness of Chris's mouth, Phil moaned and dug both hands into Chris's hair. "Suck it. Suck it." The dancing had gotten him as crazy as it had gotten Chris. He loved it.

Chris sucked him deep, moaning, digging his fingers behind Phil into his ass crack.

Shivering with the passion, Phil closed his eyes and pumped into Chris's mouth, fucking it. "Yes. Yes!"

Chris went wild, moaning and drawing hard on Phil's dick.

Gripped to Chris's head of hair as the orgasm rocked him, Phil opened his lips to gasp, pumping his seed into Chris's mouth. "Yes! Chris! Suck me!"

Tightening his hold on Phil's waist, Chris devoured him.

Phil's knees went weak as he shivered. "Baby...what a mouth! Holy shit!"

Chris hopped to his feet, dragging Phil with him.

Stumbling, his briefs around his ankles, Phil went flailing back onto Chris's bed. Still recovering from his climax, Phil panted, touching his own chest to feel his racing heart as Chris slid on a rubber.

When Chris was prepared, he nudged Phil to roll over. Trying to be accommodating after the fantastic blowjob, Phil knelt on the floor and rested his head on his arms on the bed.

Hot fingers penetrated his ass. "Oh, yes." Phil closed his eyes.

Soon a dick followed, very eager to be inside. Phil widened his position as Chris burrowed into him excitedly.

"Go-go boy," Chris hissed sensuously in Phil's ear.

Phil chuckled. He knew he was every gay man's fantasy.

"Let me fuck you, go-go boy."

"Fuck me." Phil relaxed, his cheek resting on his forearm and enjoying the internal massage.

When Chris amped up his thrusting, Phil sighed, delighted. In moments Chris was jerking his hips against him, grunting as he came. Phil grinned in pleasure. "Good one?"

"Ahhfuck...ahh..."

That means yes. Phil smiled in contentment.

Chris pulled out slowly. When he had, Phil tilted to look over his shoulder.

"Shower." Chris held out his hand.

Allowing Chris to help him stand, Phil kicked off his briefs that had hung on his ankle and followed Chris to the bathroom. As he watched Chris dispose of the condom and start the water in the shower, Phil whispered, "If I were to commit to a man, it would be someone like you."

Chris appeared amused.

"We can stay in touch." Phil wanted to see him again.

"Of course." Chris climbed into the crashing torrent gesturing for Phil to join him.

"I'm serious." Phil watched the water cascading over Chris's perfect physique. "I just wish I was older. You know, like thirty or something."

"I get it. You don't have to justify wanting to be single to me, Phil." Chris relinquished the showerhead to him.

As Phil wet down, he muttered, "I know. It's just that I didn't expect to meet such an amazing man."

"In the dark in the fitting room at Nordy's?" Chris laughed.

"Yes." Phil wasn't laughing.

"Me neither." Chris soaped up.

"Will you wait for me?"

"Wait for you?" Chris appeared puzzled.

Not wanting to tell Chris how crazy he was about him, Phil shook his head. "Never mind." He found the shampoo and washed his hair.

When Chris grabbed his jaw, Phil met his eyes instantly.

"I'm here anytime you want me."

Warmth spread across Phil's chest. "Thanks, Chris. I mean that."

"So do I, handsome. So do I."

FLAT OUT

Michael stretched and yawned tiredly. Opening his eyes, seeing light flooding into his bedroom through his slatted blinds, he suddenly remembered last night and the storm. Rolling over, Michael caught Greg staring at him contentedly.

"Hello." Michael chuckled. "Have you been up long?"

"No. Just a few minutes."

Michael looked back at his clock. It was flashing the incorrect time. "Power's on."

"Yes. I heard things starting up just a little while ago, you know, the fridge, your answering machine..."

Nodding, Michael crushed the pillow under his head and sighed deeply. "You have to rush off? Or can I make us breakfast and some coffee?"

"I have to be back at the mall later."

"I have an evening shift tonight as well." Michael ran his hand back though his hair, knowing he most likely had bed head. "Would you like to shower?"

"Yes. If you don't mind."

"Of course not. I can make the coffee while you do."

"That would be very nice of you."

His smile falling to a pout, Michael didn't know why, but he sensed something cold emanating from Greg. Remorse? Morning after regrets? "You all right?"

"I'm fine."

Michael didn't believe that for a minute. He climbed out of bed and slipped on his briefs. "Let me make sure you have enough towels."

"Thank you."

Refraining from grimacing at Greg in disappointment, Michael checked the bathroom and set out a few fresh linens. When he returned to the bedroom, Greg was sitting up, waiting.

"It's ready for you."

"Thank you, Michael."

"Don't mention it." Michael watched Greg make his way to the bathroom. Greg didn't making eye contact with him as he did. "Nice," Michael snarled to himself. Slipping on a shirt and his jeans, Michael headed to the kitchen to start the coffee dripping. He turned on the television to catch up on the news coverage of the night's storm. As he filled the carafe with water and the filter with coffee, he heard the shower start up. Trying not to grow upset with Greg's distant attitude, Michael watched video of the devastation the storm had left around the area and knew it would take ages to clean it up.

In a few minutes, while Michael sipped his cup of coffee and watched the broadcast, a very weary looking Greg appeared.

"Help yourself." Michael gestured to the empty mug and coffee pot.

"Thank you."

"My turn. Will you be here when I get out of the shower," Michael asked bitterly.

"Yes."

Without another word, Michael left the room. Taking off his clothing, he entered the bathroom and went through his routine of shaving, washing and getting ready for the day. All the while he was having doubts about Greg's interest in anything more than what they had. A one night fling. The lack of emotion in Greg was so palpable it was painful.

Once he had finished, Michael dressed in clean clothing and stood at the dresser mirror to tuck in his shirt and check his hair. I'm not bad looking, am I? What's with the attitude? You'd think any older guy would be hot for me?

When he returned to the kitchen, Greg had an empty mug in his hand and a vacant stare on his face. The news was still being spouted from the TV but it didn't appear Greg was listening.

Michael shut it off. "Would you like a piece of toast? I can make us something."

"Don't go to any trouble." Greg woke from his stupor and finally met Michael's eyes.

"What's wrong, Greg? Did I do something to upset you?" Michael knew he hadn't.

"No. Not in the least. Michael, I was very grateful for last night."

"Grateful?" Michael didn't know why, but that was an insulting comment.

Greg rose up to set his mug into the sink. "Yes. It was amazing and I really enjoyed it. I enjoyed you."

"And? But?" Michael waited for the punch line, the kiss off.

"And?" Greg just stared at him blankly.

"And you don't want to see me again?" Michael finished the sentence for him.

After a frown in response, Greg muttered, "My life is complicated right now."

"Uh uh." Asshole. Fuck off.

"I really did enjoy it. You're a lovely man, Michael."

"Look," Michael held up his hand to stop him. "I can't stand theatrics or games. Why don't you just go? I get the hint."

Greg moved quickly across the room to him, embracing him. "It's not what you think."

"It never is," Michael sneered. "I'm not in love, Greg. You won't break my heart, okay?"

An expression of pain flashed across Greg's face. "I could fall in love with a man like you."

Now Michael was growing angry. "I think it's time you left." Stop playing games with me!

"I want to see you again."

Nudging out of Greg's embrace, Michael crossed his arms over his chest defensively. "Sure, Greg. Call me when you 'uncomplicate' your life." Michael snorted at the joke.

"I will. I promise you I will."

Making his way to his front door, Michael opened it. "See ya."

"Michael," Greg sighed sadly.

"What?" Michael announced in aggravation. "I get it, okay? A one night thing. Go. I really don't want you here any longer."

"I'm sorry. I never meant to hurt you."

"Yeah, yeah, heard it all before." Michael looked away from him. A warm hand brought his attention back. He reluctantly met Greg's handsome gaze.

"I just need a little time."

"Whatever."

"I enjoyed last night. More than I can express."

Michael watched Greg's eyes fill with water and softened his anger at the sight. "Me too."

"Can I call you again?"

"Sure." *I'm such a fucking pushover.* Michael wrote his phone number down for him.

Greg pecked his lips. "Thank you."

Nodding, biting his lip, wanting more from Greg but obviously not going to get it, Michael watched him go. Greg looked back a few times before he drove off.

Slowly closing the door, Michael wished Greg was eager to begin a relationship. It seemed so right. But last night was obviously just a trick of the storm.

❧

Fighting back his emotions as he drove, Greg ground his jaw in anger. The passion from Michael last night consumed him. He hadn't felt that loved and wanted for a very long time, and he craved more. He craved Michael.

He's so beautiful, so giving. A charming, kind soul.

Greg wanted him so badly he ached.

Parked in his driveway, Greg inhaled and controlled his emotions before walking to his front door. The entire area was a mess with cleanup crews, men working on power lines, and emergency vehicles still racing around in the aftermath.

Before gathering his keys and raincoat, Greg slipped his ring back on his finger, then scuffed his way to his front door, turning the key in the lock.

"Where the hell have you been?"

The screech of her voice made him wince. "I was caught

at the mall. Some power pole came down and they kept everyone inside." He tossed his coat on the sofa, avoiding her eyes.

"You could have called."

"I tried. The lines were down." He reluctantly met her gaze. The hatred coming from a woman he had once loved made him sick to his stomach. She was a ragged hag, lost her looks, her confidence, her figure, and now she was just a bane of his existence.

"We're not legally divorced yet, Greg," she scolded. "You still have to answer to me."

"That's a laugh. Answer to you? You despise me." He glanced around. "Where are the girls?"

"At Janis's. Why do you give a shit?"

"Leave me alone. I have to go to work later this afternoon. Your constant hen-pecking drains the life from me."

"Good. I wish you were dead. Move out."

"I love you too, sweetheart," he snapped back sarcastically. "I am moving out. Believe me."

"Not soon enough. You make me sick."

"Then why the hell did you care where I was last night?" He paused before he entered his room to change his clothing. "You're a control freak, Donna. A fucking control freak. You hate my guts but you have to micromanage my every waking minute."

"Fuck you."

"Nice. I'm so pleased you're the mother of my daughters."

"Augh! Move out! I can't stand the sight of you."

"The feeling is very mutual." Greg closed himself into his room to change his suit for his later shift. As he did, he grew tired and sat down on the bed. Running his hand through his hair, he thought of Michael and felt his chest tighten up in agony. "You amazing man. Wait for me. Please, God, Michael, wait for me." Greg dabbed at his eye and continued to dress, hearing his soon to be ex-wife moving right outside his door. Peering down at the slip of paper Michael had given him with his phone number on it, Greg already had the urge to call him and make a date. But he knew in just a few weeks he'd be divorced, moved out, and ready for a new start. He just wished the timing was better. Pulling Michael along as he continued divorce proceedings seemed unfair. Michael should get a man who was free and clear, he at least deserved that.

"I'll be there for you, babe." Greg touched the corner of his eye. "Please, hang in there."

Movie House

Doug groaned and stretched his back. Blinking, he surveyed his bedroom and tried to kick-start his brain. Hearing breathing beside him, Doug peered over at the pillow next to him to see a handsome blue-eyed blond sleeping deeply.

A smile made its way to Doug's mouth. Hello, gorgeous! Doug rolled to his side, propping up his head in his hand so he could admire Carl.

"I figured you'd be taken." Doug tightened his frown wondering how hard it would be for Carl to extricate himself from his present relationship. He hated that. He didn't like interfering in anyone else's life, and...he wanted a man who was free and clear, not one that came with the baggage of a bad break up.

"Are you worth it?" Doug studied Carl's face intensely. "Gorgeous motherfucker. Loves to top. Gives great head. What's the catch?"

Doug brushed back a stray lock of golden hair from Carl's forehead. Slowly Carl's eyes opened at the touch. The crystal blue color of Carl's irises were mesmerizing. What a prize he was. The man who currently possessed this hunk will not be happy he strayed. Suddenly it occurred to Doug. "That's the catch."

A furrow appeared between Carl's eyebrows. "The catch?" His voice was gruff and sexy.

"I was admiring your good looks." Doug ran his hand down Carl's naked shoulder. "Ruminating over your attributes trying to decide what the catch was. You know, the one thing that's going to cause me grief."

"And?" Carl seemed to be more alert, shifting so he was facing Doug on the bed.

"Your boyfriend. Your present partner. He's the catch. I suppose that fact is too obvious to ignore."

Carl frowned. "He's no fucking catch, believe me."

"Really? Then how did he get you?" Doug felt a twinge of jealousy.

"He doesn't have me. Not anymore."

Carl paused to think about it. "That easy? All you have to do is decide it's over and it is? No consideration for your other half's feelings?"

"Stop." Carl dropped to his back on the bed.

"Uh huh. The catch." Doug smiled wryly. "I knew you were too pretty to be unattached. And my guess is your man will put up a fight to keep you."

"He has no choice. I want you."

"And what will that cost me?" Doug could only imagine. "Threats? Violence? Harassment?"

"I said stop. He won't do that."

"Is that a fact?" Doug found it grossly amusing. "So, this Mr. Whoever, will just say, 'Oh, sure, Carl, it was nice knowing you. Have fun with your next boyfriend'."

When Carl's expression darkened, Doug felt even worse. "He won't give you up without a fight, will he?"

His teeth bared, Carl snarled, "He has no choice! I'm not a fucking dog bone he can keep to himself. I have as much freedom as you do to choose a man. And I choose you."

Doug knew Carl was kidding himself. "You live with him?"

Carl's grimace hardened further.

"Is it your place or his?"

"His."

"Where will you move to?" Doug wondered if Carl was expecting an invitation. He would get one, as soon as Doug knew Carl was free and clear of this nastiness he was creating.

"I don't know."

Seeing Carl's pain, Doug cuddled with him to comfort him. Once he did, Carl let go of a deep stressful sigh.

"When you get your life sorted out, come here. But I don't

want to be involved in the mess. Okay?" Doug stroked Carl's blond locks at the back of his head affectionately.

"Yes. I do. It's my mess."

"It is." Doug kissed his forehead. "How long have you been with...whatever his name is?"

"Only nine months."

"Only?" Doug knew that was pretty substantial for a twenty-year-old gay male.

"He's very possessive. He drives me crazy."

"Uh huh." Talking about 'the other man' was certainly not turning Doug on.

"He's older than I am. He thinks he can run every aspect of my life. I'm sick of it."

"Where does he think you were last night?" Doug caressed Carl's rough cheek.

"Other than the movie house..." Carl shrugged.

"Ah. Missing person."

A second shrug preceded Carl's reply. "I don't give a shit. I was at the movie alone because we argued. He knows it's over."

"What were you waiting for? A man to fall back on?"

Carl flinched and made a move to climb out of the bed. Doug gripped his arm and dragged him back. "Not so fast."

"I don't need this shit from two men."

"You think I'm giving you shit?" Doug was very close to letting go, allowing Carl to leave. He didn't need 'this shit' either.

"No. I'm sorry." Carl embraced Doug and buried his face in Doug's neck, holding him tight. "I want you. You're perfect."

"I'm far from it. But I won't strangle you, Carl. I'm not like that."

"I know. I know you're wonderful."

Smiling, thinking Carl was slightly naïve in his trust of someone he knew less than twenty-four hours, Doug still tried to take it as a nice compliment, as it was intended.

While they lie pressed together, Doug felt Carl's cock moving against his hip. A smile made it to Doug's face. The attraction was winning out against the worry. After petting Carl's hair, Doug urged him to a kiss.

Carl went wild on him, pinning him down under him

on the bed and pressing his hard-on into Doug's crotch. "Let me fuck you."

The request sent the hairs standing on Doug's neck.

"I need to fuck you."

Doug shivered and closed his eyes.

Carl began gnawing at Doug's neck and jaw, leaning up over him to dry hump his body.

Chills rushed over Doug's length as their cocks slid past each other and bumped and ground together. Carl chewed on Doug's chin, his bottom lip, licking and kissing Doug's earlobe, sending shivers all over Doug's body. What was Doug supposed to say? No?

"Please?" Carl moaned in agony.

"Yes." Doug couldn't resist being yearned for, and begging? He loved that as well. Beg and you shall receive.

Anxiously Carl went for the nightstand. He tore off a condom and eagerly rolled it on. "Baby, baby!' Carl breathed in excitement. He urged Doug's legs backwards, opening his body up for the taking. A hiss of delight emerged from Carl's mouth. "You are perfect. Perfect!"

Doug had to smile at Carl's zeal. It was nice to be the object of desire. Very nice indeed.

As that slick hand coated his ass, Doug felt the first rush of pure pleasure tickle his skin. He wanted it. Make no mistake. Taking a man's cock up his butt was pure heaven to him.

"Ready?"

"Yes." Doug opened his eyes. The delightful preparation had lulled him off into a dreamland.

Carl pushed in, groaning in ecstasy. "Damn! Damn!"

Doug chuckled. He couldn't deny it. Being possessed by Carl felt incredible to him as well. Yes, having Carl in his bed would be pure pleasure.

"Jerk off. Jerk off." Carl began thrusting with determination.

Doug grasped his own cock and gave it what it and Carl were looking for. Tight friction. Keeping his gaze on Carl's pretty features, Doug watched Carl's stare move up and down, from his own eyes to his masturbating to their connection and back again.

"Yes. Jesus, Doug...I'm there. Ya there?"

Doug quickened his pace on his cock, his hand becoming a blur.

"Ah! I can't hold it. Look at you! Jesus!" Carl drove in deeply and grunted.

Doug could feel Carl's cock throbbing inside him. He gave up his own seed and sprayed his chest.

"Ahhfuck! Fuck!" Carl kept jamming his hips in deeply. Once he slowed down, he pulled out and dropped down, licking the cum off Doug's chest.

Doug's eyes sprang open. "Nice! You're a fucking keeper!"

Lapping contentedly, Carl seemed deep in a swoon. It made Doug smile. "Get free, Carl. Get free and come to me."

Panting, sticky cum on his face, Carl gasped, "Yes. Fuck. I have to be with you. Please. Let me just break up with him and I'll be yours."

Doug gently wiped at Carl's chin. "I'm here. I'm not going anywhere."

Carl crawled higher on Doug's body and cried, "I'll make it soon. Promise. Today. I'll do it today."

"Good." Doug petted his hair, smiling happily.

∽≈

Carl didn't want to leave. After a shower and breakfast, he knew he couldn't keep putting off the inevitable. Once he had helped Doug wash up the breakfast dishes, Carl reluctantly put his mobile phone to his ear to hear his messages.

"You son of a bitch. Where the fuck are you? You didn't go see a movie, you lying sack of shit!"

Carl flinched, deleting the message, unable to bear anymore.

"You okay?"

Meeting Doug's concerned eyes, Carl replied, "Jan's livid."

"I'd assume so." Doug leaned back against the sink counter. "Are you afraid of him?"

"A little." Carl felt his cheeks heat up in embarrassment. "He gets kind of crazy."

"Do you want me to come with you?"

"I thought you didn't want to be involved in my mess."

"I don't want you hurt. That's my priority. If you want, I'll hang out with you until you collect your things."

"To bring where? I have to get an apartment first."

Carl made a silly face at him. "Just move in here."

"I can't. We don't even know each other."

"I'll take my chances."

"Christ, Doug, I don't know your last name, what you do for a living...no, it's too much of a rush. I just need to find a place to stay for a little while."

"Can you stay with any family or friends temporarily?"

Carl wracked his brain for that answer. "Not really. I just need to rent a room somewhere until we can get to know one another better."

"Fuck that. Just move in."

"Doug!" Carl wanted to but he knew it was insane.

Doug sat with him on at the kitchen table. "My last name is Weinhart and I work in a music studio as a tech. Okay? Now you know me."

Carl laughed softly. "Brandt is my last name. I manage a commercial real estate office downtown."

"Good. Then it's settled. Come on. Let's get you packed and out." Doug stood and left the room.

Anxious about meeting Jan at their apartment while he was with Doug, Carl bit at his nail nervously.

They walked together back to Carl's car.

When they had the car in view Carl could see a maintenance worker repairing the line that had fallen onto his car overnight, his truck double-parked parallel to the curb. A fire truck blocked off the area with cones.

"Shit. Can I get out?" Carl kept moving closer.

"If not, we'll go back and get my car."

Approaching the fireman, Carl called, "Excuse me."

The firefighter spun around.

"This is my car. Any chance I can move it?"

"Sure. Hang on."

Doug leaned on Carl's back. "Cute!"

"All the firemen in LA are gorgeous. Are you just noticing that now?" Carl grinned back at Doug.

The diesel engine of the big red truck rumbled and hissed.

It moved up a few yards. A second fireman picked up the cones and shouted, "You're good to go!"

Carl waved, hurrying to get behind the wheel as Doug did the same next to him in the passenger's seat.

As they pulled out, Carl waved again in thanks.

Doug leaned down to get a good look at the young fireman. "Find 'em hot and leave 'em wet!"

Carl laughed. "I know!"

Feeling Doug's hand on his thigh for reassurance, Carl's mood darkened as he drew closer to Jan's and his home. "He may get physical."

"I presumed that. If that wasn't the problem, you wouldn't give a shit about coming here and clearing out."

Carl's stomach was in knots. He couldn't even imagine what Doug thought of him and his 'situation'. Trying to put himself in Doug's shoes, it wasn't a happy place to be for either of them.

Parking, shutting the engine off, Carl sighed. "It's what's kept me here. The intimidation. I know I shouldn't be afraid to move out. I should just fight the bastard. But he has belted me a few times already, and to be honest, I'm not as big or mean as he is and I always lose when we get physical. I hate to admit this but, I'm scared shitless of him."

Doug appeared very angry. "No. Please don't tell me you put up with abuse from the asshole."

"I won't tell you then." Carl shivered involuntarily in fear.

"Why didn't you call the cops?"

"He'd kill me. I can't. If the cops came, I'd be dead."

"Does he own a gun?"

"No."

"Can you tell if he's home right now?"

"Yes. He is. That's his pickup." Carl pointed to a battered Ford.

Doug cracked his knuckles. "Whenever you're ready. I'm primed to kick his ass."

Smiling at his confidence, Carl reached for Doug. "You don't have to do this. If you get hurt I'm never going to forgive myself."

"I won't get hurt. Are you kidding me?" Doug shook his

head at the absurdity. "You think I can't beat the shit out of this jerk?"

As if just getting his first look at Doug, Carl admired his large build and powerful frame. Maybe Doug could intimidate Jan. They would soon find out.

"Most of these dickheads are just overgrown bullies, Carl. One good ass kicking and they run away like beaten mongrels."

"I wish I had been the one to kick his ass though. I mean, why the hell should you be involved in this? Doug, I'm so angry with myself that you are." Carl exited his car and pocketed his key. "You sure you don't want to wait here?"

"No. Shut up and go inside." Doug nudged him.

Carl walked up the sloping cement steps and tried the knob. The door was unlocked. The minute he pushed it back, Carl heard Jan's voice.

"'Bout time, asshole."

Battle ready, Doug made sure he stood beside Carl. Carl waited for Jan to notice he was not alone.

"Who the fuck is that?" Jan rose up from the sofa he was slouched on, the television playing in the background.

"Get your shit." Doug nudged Carl.

Carl swallowed, trepidation adding to his worry. "I'm moving out, Jan."

"Moving out?" Jan puffed up. "I don't think so."

Doug stood between the two men looking very mean. "Get your shit, Carl!" Doug ordered, his eyes never leaving Jan's.

Carl felt his entire body tremble and hurried to the bedroom to pack. As he did he could hear their argument and cringed hoping nothing happened to Doug.

"What the fuck do you think you're doing with my boy-friend?" Jan shouted.

"He wants out. And you are going to let him get out."

"Out where? Where the hell's he going? Your place?"

"None of your fucking business."

"It is my business if you're stealing my piece of fucking ass!"

Carl slapped clothing into luggage as fast as he could. He knew the verbal argument was about to turn to into a brawl.

"Yours?" Doug's voice boomed in the small apartment.

"You don't own him. He's free to do as he pleases."

"Free? He's not free. He's mine. And no one is taking him anywhere!"

"Shit." Carl knew that was the invitation to punch something. He sat on his suitcase and struggled with the zipper. A crash was heard in the next room. "Oh God." He hefted his suitcase up, and raced to the living room.

Jan and Doug where locked up in fury, shoving each other over the furniture, clamped together with clawed fists and growling expressions of rage.

"Stop! Jan! Cut it out!" Carl raced over and began pushing Jan back. "You don't own me, you dickhead! Let him go! Jan! Grow the fuck up, you prick!"

Doug roared and broke free from Jan's grasp, his chest heaving. "Do you have everything?" he asked Carl appearing about to tear Jan's head off.

"I have my clothing packed, I just need my laptop and some toiletries." Carl glared at Jan. "Let me leave, Jan, enough! You know it's been coming. We do nothing but argue. Don't act like you never saw this coming."

"I blame you!" Jan pointed an accusing thing at Doug. "I'll kill you, you motherfucker."

Doug puffed up. "Come on! You think you're tough, ya dickwad? Come on!"

"No! Stop!" Carl roared. "Jan. I'm leaving. Okay? Deal with it like a human being and not an animal."

"Get your shit, and let's go," Doug screamed in rage.

Carl dashed out of the room for his computer, tossing his toiletries into a plastic bag, his heart pumping in his chest.

Jan yelled, "Carl! Don't go! You can't leave with him."

"Get used to it, asshole," Doug snarled. "He's done with you. And you leave him the fuck alone or I'll call the cops and get a restraining order put on you so you can't come near him. You got it?"

"Who the fuck do you think you are? His new boss?"

Carl grimaced, rushing around the bedroom wishing he could have leisurely packed and taken his time. This was madness.

He took what he felt were essentials, digging last minute

through drawers so he never had to come back. His camera, his checkbook, his photos. Christ, there was too much to take in one trip. He returned to the living room with his arms full. "I have to make a couple runs to the car."

"Go!" Doug waved, standing guard.

Carl sprinted out of the house, threw his stuff into the back seat and raced back. The minute he came through the door, Doug and Jan were back at it again. "No!" Carl grabbed Jan around his throat from behind and choked him enough to get him to release Doug. Doug let fly a right hook, knocking Jan to the floor.

"Get the rest of your shit!" Doug ordered, his chest heaving.

Carl felt sick to his stomach. This had to be his worst nightmare. Why couldn't Jan just let go? Carl had been trying to be nice about it, talking to him, making the slow moves, but nothing seemed to get through to Jan that it was over.

Carl grabbed another plastic bag and hunted for his belongings, tossing his CDs into it, his DVDs, small electronics. This wasn't how he wanted this to end. And certainly not how he wanted a new relationship to begin.

"You get up and I'll kick your fucking ass," Doug warned, pointing at Jan as he sat on the floor nursing a sore jaw.

Sweat pouring out of Carl's body, he took one last look around and gave up. With his suitcase in one arm, and a few plastic bags in the other, he stood at the door. "That's enough. I don't give a shit if I left some crap behind at this point."

Doug towered over Jan to give him one last warning. "He's through with you, got it? You look for him, you harass him? I'll kick your ass so hard you'll be shitting out of your mouth."

Carl touched Doug's arm. "Let's go."

"Cunt!" Jan spat out angrily.

"Let's go!" Carl jerked on Doug's sleeve.

As Carl jogged down the steep incline, Doug kept watching their back until they had loaded the car.

Carl took one last glance behind him and shook his head. "I didn't want it to end like this." He sat behind the wheel and sighed, rubbing his face in anguish.

"Just go before he decides to come out and start something." Doug fastened his seatbelt and slouched in the seat.

Carl drove them back to Doug's house feeling like shit. "You didn't need this. I can't believe I got you involved in this. I am so sorry, Doug."

"You're out. Hopefully he'll leave you alone."

Biting his lip, wanting Jan to be just a bad memory, Carl tried to focus on the driving.

"Why the hell did you get involved with that asshole in the first place?"

Carl knew the questions would come eventually. No one gets out of everything scot-free. "He was different in the beginning."

"He's not even nice looking. And he's in crappy shape. Was that different in the beginning as well?"

Carl hated having to justify his decisions to people. He chose from the heart, not from superficial looks or body shape. Just that this time he got it wrong. Jan was not kindhearted and giving as Carl thought he was when he met him. The man had turned into a monster.

"I'm sorry I got you involved. I wish you never met him. Doug, this is not a good way to begin a relationship."

Doug grew quiet.

Carl had a bad feeling Doug was reconsidering his offer after meeting Jan. Seeing the roadway clear after the fire truck and utility workers had finished, Carl parked but didn't shut off the car. "I'll go stay with my parents in San Diego."

"What?" Doug spun around in surprise. "Why?"

"I can't do this to you." Carl's emotions finally got the better of him.

"Baby."

At Doug's soft voice, Carl met his brown eyes.

"It's okay." Doug caressed Carl's cheek.

Unable to bite back his pain, Carl shook his head, but no words came out.

"Come here." Doug drew him into a hug and kissed Carl's neck. "It's okay. I want you with me."

"It's a really fucked up way to start, Doug."

Doug smiled adoringly at him, brushing back his hair. "I want you. I don't care about that beast."

"Are you sure?" Carl swiped at his eyes roughly.

"Yes. Positive. Unless you are having doubts about me."

"No. Are you kidding me? You helped me get away from that asshole."

"Then?" Doug opened his hands in a gesture of 'what now?'

"If you change your mind, and I get on your nerves, just tell me and I'll move out. Promise?"

"Promise." Doug smiled.

Carl wrapped his arms around Doug's neck and kissed him. When he parted from his mouth, he teased, "Bet you never expected all this from one night in the TomKat and a stormy blackout."

Laughing, Doug admitted, "No. You are right about that."

"So?" Carl tilted his head seductively. "Do I look as good to you now, in the light of day?"

"Purr, better." Doug cupped his face affectionately.

"Excellent. Douglas Weinhart, you amazing, amazing man."

Chuckling softly, Doug replied, "Stop, you'll swell my head."

"That's the idea." Carl gave Doug a wicked smirk.

"Come inside. Time to make more porno movies of our own."

Shutting the engine, Carl climbed out, carrying his belongings to his new home. With Doug behind him, helping him, Carl knew there was magic in that windstorm. Magic. And Doug was nothing short of a superhero in his eyes.

WHAT SHOULD NEVER BE

A Collection of Twelve Taboo Short Stories

DISCLAIMER

There are many of us who have fantasies that are too risqué to share. A few of us write those stories down for the amusement of others. Some, too nervous to expose their true sexual expressions repress their voices and live inside their minds. For those of you who know my work, and for those who don't, here lies a collection of sizzling erotic gay fantasies for your entertainment.

These shorts are based on the characters of my books. Every one of them tells a tale of the individual's darkest secret desire, all of which have never come to pass in the virtual realities of my novels. Yet each of the people in my universe does indeed have taboo thoughts and cravings they would love to fulfill if the world would only hide its eyes for just a moment.

But my pretend society is full of male heroes with conscience and loyalty. My stars are true-blue men who love with all their hearts and souls and who wouldn't harm their loved ones if their lives depended on it.

What if?

What if each character was entitled to one of his wickedest fantasies without fear of repercussion? What would they do?

In this series of short stories the men, and some women, who would never cheat, lie, or break their partner's hearts, gets to live out their wildest dreams. No consequences, no blame, no punishment. In this world the men and women are free to do as they choose, and some of their deepest carnal needs are truly too taboo for their 'real' worlds.

Come share the darkest sexual secrets of the men and women you have come to know and love in my universe.

Explore with them the forbidden fruit they have yearned for,
though would never dream of touching, sucking or fucking...
...in any other world than the realm of pure fantasy.

—GA Hauser

1

Ex-LAPD cop Steve Miller was home alone. His husband Mark Antonious Richfield was on a late photography shoot. Dangereux cologne had begun work on their spring ad campaign with their sexiest top model. That meant Steve had the night to himself.

Drinking a beer as he relaxed in front of the television in the den, Steve heard the front door open and close. A minute later, Mark's son, Alexander, poked his head into the room.

"Hey."

"Hey," Steve replied staring at the eighteen year old who was the spitting image of his stunning father.

"Where's Dad?"

"On a shoot. Where's Oliver?" Steve enquired of Alex's boyfriend.

"Obligated to spend some time with his grandparents. I declined." Alex stretched his back.

When he did, Steve gazed at the flat plane of Alex's stomach as it peeked between his shirt and jeans.

"I'm going to shower."

"Okay." Steve gazed back at the television, finishing his beer.

～

Hearing the noise of the water in the upstairs bath, Steve turned off the television set and placed the empty beer bottle on the side table. Rising to his feet, Steve climbed the stairs to the second floor intent on changing out of his jeans and into a pair of gym shorts to get more comfortable.

Pausing, seeing the door at the end of the hall was ajar, Steve felt his heart rate increase. Tiptoeing to the opening, he peered into the steamy heat seeing a flesh tone blur behind the glass shower doors.

Wet, Alex's long brown hair flowed to mid-back. His hips were narrow, his ass tight, his legs long. Gazing at Alex as he rinsed the soap off his face and hair, Steve licked his lips hungrily. Alexander Mark Lehman-Richfield was the spitting image of his thirty-eight year old dad, yet had the spirit and vitality of a very young man.

The water shut off. Alex stood dripping for a moment, wringing out his hair.

Steve's cock went wild under his jeans. The amount he wanted Alex was painful. But he was Mark's son, so that was taboo.

Alex pushed back the shower door, reaching for a towel. As he rubbed it over his head, Steve got a look at Alex's cock. Another attribute he had inherited from his gorgeous father, a big dick.

Even soft, it hung thick and long over his large testicles. Alex's chest was hairless but his treasure trail started below his navel and flared out at his pelvis to an almost jet black bush of pubic hair. Every muscle showed through Alex's bronze skin, a perfect six-pack abdomen, round pectorals with tiny dark erect nipples.

When Alex's head jerked up and he met Steve's eyes, Steve almost backed away and hid. Almost.

Now that Alex was aware he was being admired, Steve pushed the door wider. Son of a bitch. Look at you. Steve was in heat.

"Steve?" Alex asked innocently. "You need something?"

Do I need something? Steve laughed sadly. Before he entered the misty bathroom, Steve removed his t-shirt, tossing it on the carpet.

Alex appeared frozen as he stared at him.

Approaching Alex slowly, Steve wrapped his arms around those narrow hips and felt Alex's hot moist skin press against his chest. He picked Alex up, out of the bathtub and carried him into Alex's bedroom.

Throwing Alex onto the bed, Steve stared down at him as he unzipped his pants.

"We can't do this." Alex shook his head, his hair still wet and sticking to his cheeks and neck.

Steve stepped out of his jeans, briefs and socks, standing naked, ogling this amazing eighteen-year-old sex god.

"Steve?"

Crawling from the base of the bed, Steve began kissing Alex's shins, knees, thighs, making his way up his gorgeous body.

"Oh, God, we can't. Steve..." Alex moaned.

Already past the point of no return, Steve pried open Alex's thighs. As Steve panted to catch his breath, he found Alex's cock engorged and protruding from his pelvis like a mast. Dropping down on him, Steve rubbed his mouth over Alex's balls, inhaling him deeply, licking at the soft, warm dewy skin, all the while Steve whimpered in agony. When Steve caressed Alex's length, he found it as hard as steel. Eighteen-year-old cock. He remembered very well how that hard-on felt.

"Ah..." Alex shivered, elevating his hips off the bed at Steve's touch.

Leaning up over him, Steve sunk Alex's enormous cock into his mouth moaning in delirium. He'd waited forever for this moment. Spreading Alex's legs wider, Steve fondled those heavy balls excitedly.

Alex lit up, jerking his hips, instantly climaxing, pushing his cock further into Steve's mouth as he gasped. Tasting Alex's sweet cum, Steve sucked harder, drawing it as far into his throat as he could, finally savoring that delightful cream on his tongue.

"Ah! Steve! Ah!" Alex panted, his chest heaving.

Steve sat back to stare at him. Seeing rubbers and lubrication on Alex's nightstand, obviously left available for Alex and Oliver's coupling, Steve reached for one of the condoms, tearing it open with his teeth. After he was sheathed, he grabbed the gel. With Alex's large green eyes unblinking as they stared at him, Steve coated himself first before he dipped into that glory hole he had desired since Alex first showed up at their door months ago.

Instantly Alex reacted, his cock blushing reddish purple as it once again hardened to stone.

Eighteen-year-old dick! Steve loved it! He wasn't quite twice Alex's age. No. Not quite. But a thirty-three year old being able to taste this treat? Heaven.

Knowing very well Alex bottomed exclusively for Oliver, Steve didn't hesitate. Removing his fingers from Alex's ass, he pushed the head of his dick inside this sex nymph and burrowed up to his balls. Hearing Alex groan and feeling him quiver was worth everything he owned.

Raising one of Alex's legs at a time, Steve rested Alex's calves on his shoulders. Once he was deep inside Alex's ass, Steve gripped Alex's thighs and began screwing him the way he had dreamed of screwing him. Hard, deep, fast thrusts. "Jerk off!" Steve ordered.

Alex's hands instantly attached to his own cock.

This was fucking unbelievable. Steve knew it would be extraordinary. Look at this living young doll! That long hair drying and spread out all over the pillows, his emerald green eyes and long dark eyelashes. "Come! Alex, come!" Steve roared.

"Ah! Ah!"

Alex and his father sounded exactly the same during climax. It was uncanny.

"Give it to me!" Steve commanded.

"What?" Alex shook his head as he gasped for breath.

Frustrated Alex didn't get it, Steve released the grip of one hand and scooped up that sticky spatter, licking it off his fingers. "More!"

Finally understanding, Alex smeared his fingertips into his own cum and held his hand to Steve's mouth.

Sucking on Alex's fingers, tasting his cum, Steve hammered as hard as he could into that delicious body under him. When it hit, Steve nearly passed out from the intensity.

Opening his mouth, feeling Alex's hand slide down his jaw and throat, Steve unloaded the contents of his balls into Alex's ass. "Son of a bitch!" Steve screamed as the sensation washed up his spine and it felt as if his cock was exploding.

"Steve! Oh, God, Steve!"

Awash with aftershocks, Steve kept thrusting inside Alex. "Fuck! Fuck!" He couldn't stop. Didn't want to stop. He'd waited too long for this opportunity. Giving one last deep grinding plunge, Steve finally stilled his hips and hung his head.

"Steve!" Alex cried, "I love you! I love you so much!"

"Alex...holy fuck...Alex..." Steve moaned, staring down at the connection of their bodies. "That was the most amazing sex I have had in my life."

"Me too! Steve, my God!"

Pulling out, lowering Alex's legs to the bed, Steve licked the rest of the stickiness off Alex's smooth stomach, making his way to Alex's mouth with long wet laps of his tongue. When he reached Alex's lips, Steve wrapped his arms around him and devoured that fresh set of teenage lips and lost himself on that timid tongue.

≈≈

"Hey."

Steve blinked and looked up at the door to the den.

"I'm going to bed. I'm beat."

"Okay, Alex. Goodnight."

Alex pecked Steve's cheek. "What time is Dad supposed to be home?"

Steve checked his watch. "Any minute. You want me to send him in to say goodnight?"

"No. It's okay. See you in the morning."

"Goodnight, Alex." Steve waited for him to leave before resting his chin in his palm to continue to watch the evening news. He knew his fantasies would always be just that. Images in his head, nothing more.

2

Aura Stanton relaxed on her bed in her small but neat two-bedroom apartment in Cerritos, California. Slightly worn out from work, her belly full from a homemade dinner, Aura was in just her panties and her brother's worn-out, soft navy blue LAPD t-shirt. She was propped up on her pillows watching one of his gay romance DVDs.

At a sound at the front door, Aura lowered the volume to listen. Deep masculine voices reached her ears. She knew them well. Her brother Mickey, and his LAPD cop partner, Jeff Chandler.

The front door of the apartment banged shut making her jump. Trying to imagine what they were doing, Aura heard some angry conversation followed by the sound of someone getting slammed into a wall.

Knowing those two loved hot rough sex, Aura shut the DVD and got to her knees to try and hear them.

"Fuck you, Stanton!" Jeff snarled.

Another crashing sound followed. She imagined someone backed up against the wall again. Her skin broke out in chills and her crotch grew damp.

"Fucking asshole!"

Aura tried not to laugh at her brother's angry retort. Mickey was such a pussycat. Yeah, he was a trained marksman, but she knew the real man in that big brawny body was soft as putty. Especially in the arms of that hunk, Jeff Chandler.

"I think it's my turn to fuck you, Stanton!"

At Jeff's threat, Aura licked her lips and crept to the bedroom door, pressing her ear against it.

She could hear things in the living room overturning. Christ, those two are like wild animals!

Silence engulfed the apartment until she suddenly heard more slamming and crashing. Deep guttural moans echoed outside her room. "Zoiks!"

She peeked out. A light was on in Mickey's bedroom. Moving to the partially opened door she watched as Jeff tore off Mickey's clothing, practically shredding his gym shorts and t-shirt in his haste. When her brother ripped Jeff's shorts down his thighs revealing his naked ass, Aura gulped and felt her eyes dry out.

"Fuck you, pig!" Jeff shoved Mickey face down on the bed.

"You dirty cop! You fucking, dirty mother-fucking cop!" Mickey snarled.

As her eyes were glued to Jeff's naked back and ass, Aura felt her chest heave with her thrill. She watched Jeff reach for a rubber, kneeling up behind her brother who was face down on the mattress.

"Holy fuck!" She raced back to her room and tore through her closet. Stripping off her panties and her brother's t-shirt, Aura knew an opportunity like this was one in a million, and she wasn't about to pass it up.

In a box, unopened, an item purchased on impulse and wishful thinking, Aura demolished the plastic and cardboard to get at the product inside. A latex double dick attached to a black bikini. Shaking as she hopped into it, she slid one end of the dildo inside her, gasping at the penetration. Throwing the packaging up into the air recklessly to get at another smaller box, Aura trembled as she squirted a blob of lube onto her palm and rubbed it all over the protruding flesh-tone phallus.

Sprinting back to Mickey's bedroom, she found Jeff had Mickey's hips elevated off the bed and was giving her brother a good hard fucking. As they grunted like humping mongrels, Aura climbed onto the bed behind Jeff.

The minute Jeff felt her touch, he spun his head around in shock. "Aura!"

"Don't stop what you're doing, Jeff." She knelt behind him and pushed the tip of the dildo into Jeff's ass.

"Augh! Aura, what the fuck are you doing?" Jeff's body

went rigid.

"Aura?" Mickey asked in terror from under Jeff. "What the hell's going on?"

Aura pushed the strap-on as deep as she could inside Jeff, feeling the penetration increase in her as well. Wrapping her arm around Jeff's chest, Aura rested her cheek on his sweaty skin and began pumping into him.

"Ah! Holy Christ!" Jeff arched his back and thrust his hips into Mickey with more gusto.

"What?" Mickey shouted, "What the fuck is she doing?"

"Relax, Mouse," Aura purred. "Keep fucking him, Jeff."

Jeff's hips began moving in a rhythm which Aura matched. "Augh! Holy-fucking-Christ!" Jeff choked on his words and Aura felt his thighs go rock hard under hers. A delicious snarl came from Jeff as he went wild, jamming his hips into Mickey as Aura did the same to Jeff. The growling from Jeff's chest rumbled through Aura's, making her shiver in delight.

She inhaled deeply both their sweat and musky sex aroma and moaned in pleasure.

As Jeff began to climax, bucking into Mickey like he was riding a bronco, Jeff made the most exquisite masculine sounds. Aura's skin was covered with chills and her clit began to shiver with her own orgasm.

"Aaaahhhfuck! Mickey!" Jeff thrust hard into Mickey's ass under him.

Aura heard her brother's deep throaty grunts as he came. That's it, little brother, that's it. She felt the waves of her own climax spin over her body, rubbing hard against the double dildo so it ground into Jeff's ass at the same time.

With a deep groan, Jeff dropped heavily on top of Mickey, flattening him to the bed. Aura cuddled against Jeff's soaked back, smoothing her hands up and down the connection between Jeff and her brother, feeling the perspiration sealing them, making them one.

"Oh, God," Jeff moaned in disbelief.

"Good one, Officer Chandler?" Aura massaged his shoulders. Feeling her brother's body coated with sweat under Jeff's muscular physique, she caressed them both lovingly.

"Son of a bitch," Jeff whimpered.

"Jeff?" Mickey asked. "Did she fuck you?"

"Yes!" Jeff choked in awe.

"Aura?"

"I have a strap-on, Mickey. First time using it. My, oh my!" Aura gave Jeff's sweaty back a long wet lick before she climbed off. As she did, Jeff pulled out of Mickey, and they both rolled to their side to stare at her in awe.

She gazed at her brother, grinning wickedly.

"Jesus!" Mickey gaped at the size of the penis attached to Aura's body. He twisted to look at Jeff. "Are you all right?"

As Jeff tried to yank the rubber off his cock, still catching his breath, he laughed, "Am I all right? Did you just ask me that?"

"Never mind." Mickey shook his finger at his sister. "This is not going to be a regular occurrence, lady."

"No?" She grinned wickedly at a dazed LAPD cop. Jeff was lost on the little extra zing he'd experienced while giving her brother a damn good fucking.

"Son of a bitch," Jeff moaned, as if he couldn't believe what he had just done.

Aura climbed off the bed, strutting to the bathroom. "Time to wash up." She blew Jeff a kiss and left the room.

❧≈

Sighing sleepily, Aura picked up the cordless phone on her nightstand and dialed.

"Hello?"

"Hi, Mouse. Is it too late?"

"No, Jeff and I are still up, just watching TV."

"I miss you not living here anymore."

"Aw, poor thing. Why don't we all go out for dinner tomorrow night? It's our day off."

"Sounds great. You want me to come there?"

"No. We can pick you up. How about seven?"

"Perfect. Thanks, Mouse. I do get lonely without you." She lowered the volume on the DVD.

"You need a boyfriend, Aura."

"It's not as easy as it sounds, Mickey. I'm very particular."

"And you have a right to be."

"Okay. So, see you guys tomorrow."

"Okay, babe."

"Say hi to Jeff for me!" She heard her brother relaying it, next was Jeff shouting, "Hi, Aura!" Smiling warmly, she sighed, "Night, Mouse."

"Night, sis."

The line disconnected and she stared at the phone for a moment before setting it back on the nightstand. "Mickey, you are one lucky fucker." Raising the remote, Aura increased the volume of the movie she was watching and snuggled under the blankets, looking forward to dinner tomorrow with her two favorite men.

3

"This serial killer case is getting to me, John." FBI Agent Frank Skinner slid his semi-automatic handgun into his shoulder holster.

"Don't let it. We'll catch the fucker, Frank."

Frank put his suit jacket on over his shirt, covering the weapon. Checking his pocket for his hotel key, Frank sighed, "You ready to get cocky Agent Robbie Taylor?"

Agent John Green chuckled. "Fucking psychic. What will the bureau think of next? It's such a load of crap." After adjusting his holster, John nodded. "Yeah, let's get the long-haired hippy federal agent. He should be ready by now." John checked his watch.

Shutting off the lights as he left, Frank waited for his partner to lock their door before moving down the hall to the next room. As he rapped his knuckles on Robbie's door, Frank tried to imagine the sex Robbie was having with that handsome black Seattle cop, Dave Harris. Robbie didn't hide the fact that he was gay, yet he was very discreet when he had to be.

They waited a moment before Frank knocked again. Nothing happened.

"You think he went for coffee?" John asked.

"He's not supposed to go anywhere without informing us."

"Taylor?" John called through the door.

Frank met John's eyes. At the lack of an answer they exchanged concerned glances. John tried the doorknob. It wasn't locked so he pushed it back.

"Agent Taylor!" John shouted as he stepped inside the

hotel room.

"What the fuck?" Frank noticed the furniture was over-turned, paperwork was littered on the floor. Immediately Frank removed his gun from his holster. "Agent Taylor!" he yelled, clicking into FBI mode and checking the only other room, the bedroom. As Frank peered into the opening of the doorway, he found Agent Robbie Taylor gagged with his wrists tied to the bed, naked.

Hearing John announce after he checked the rest of the area, "No one else is here," Frank holstered his gun. "Well, well...Agent Taylor...finally get in over your head? Or you and Officer Harris have some playtime together and he got called away?"

John sat down beside Robbie, lowering the cloth gag.

"Very funny, Skinner." Robbie panted. "Why don't you fucking untie me?"

Admiring Robbie's taut muscular body and handsome good looks, Frank relaxed on the opposite side of Agent Green. "What's the rush?"

"Don't you even want to know what happened to me?" Robbie's blue eyes appeared to glow in the dim room.

"No. I don't give a crap." Frank ran his hand along Rob-bie's bare thigh. "What you get into on your own time ain't my business."

"What the hell are you doing?" Robbie gasped. "Agent Green! Get your fucking partner to untie me and stop grop-ing me!"

"Why?" John caressed Robbie's long brown hair.

"Why?" Robbie choked in surprise.

Licking his lips, Frank ran his palm over Robbie's soft cock.

"Hey!" Robbie tried to flinch away. "What the hell is wrong with you guys?"

Something caught Frank's eye. On the nightstand there were condoms and a tube of lubrication. Gazing at the tall, sexy FBI psychic again, Frank grew hard in his trousers. He bent over Robbie and sucked on his nipple.

"I don't believe this!" Robbie tried to squirm away. "Come on, guys, you can't be serious."

Frank exchanged wicked grins with John. "Are we serious, Agent Green?"

"Dead serious, Agent Skinner." John ran both his hand up Robbie's torso.

"Holy shit." Robbie shivered and closed his eyes.

That was all Frank needed to see before he responded. He stood, opened his zipper and reached for a condom.

"No. No way." Robbie shook his head.

Laughing as he rolled the condom on his cock, Frank replied, "No? I don't think you're in a position to say no, Taylor."

"I'll tell the director. You'll both be fired."

Frank and John laughed at Robbie. "Who will the director believe? The gay long-haired psychic? Or his two top special agents?" Frank crawled onto the bed between Robbie's knees.

"No! Frank, Jesus! I said no!"

As Robbie tugged at the bindings securing his wrists to the top of the bed, John helped Frank spread Robbie's thighs wider.

The minute Robbie's ass was exposed, Frank held Robbie around the waist and pushed the head of his cock into Robbie's butt. "Ahh, yes...son of a bitch that's as tight as pussy."

"You assholes!" Robbie tried to twist away.

"Who you calling an asshole?" John laughed as he pointed, "You're fucking hard, Taylor!"

"Is he?" Frank peered down at Robbie as he thrust in deep and fast. "Well, well. He likes it, John."

"I think he fucking loves it." John took his cock out of his pants and drew closer.

As Frank fucked this handsome FBI psychic, John knelt on the bed and poked his hard dick towards Robbie's lips.

A whimper of distress hissed out of Robbie's gorgeous mouth until it was filled with John's thick cock.

Watching John fuck Robbie orally, Frank went mad, driving as hard as he could into Robbie's hole. When John's body jerked in a spasm of pleasure and he gasped as he climaxed, Frank came, shivering down to his polished black shoes. Grinding as tightly to Robbie's body as he could, Frank opened his eyes, surprised to see Robbie's expression of ecstasy and feeling Robbie's cock shuddering under him.

Once John climbed off the bed and tucked his dick back into his trousers, Frank laughed, "Look, John. Our psychic came." Frank pulled out, tossing the spent condom on the floor and zipping his pants.

"Oh, God..." Robbie moaned, rocking his hips from side to side.

"Nice one." John admired Robbie as he recuperated. "Did I taste good, Taylor?"

"Unite me. Please." Robbie's chest rose and fell rapidly.

"Yeah. Maybe later." Frank straightened out his clothing and tilted his head for John to follow him to the door.

"Thanks, Taylor. We'll be back in a couple of hours. I'm sure you'll be hungry for more by lunch time." John laughed as he left the room.

Before he went, Frank paused to savor the act and the sight of Robbie bound and naked on the bed. "You have to admit, John. Taylor's one hot fucker."

"He's fucking gorgeous, but if you tell anyone I said that, I'll kill you."

Chuckling under his breath, Frank opened the door.

಄಄

Deep in thought as he checked he had his weapon and ID, Agent Frank Skinner peered behind him to see his partner, Agent John Green nodding he was ready. Opening their hotel door, Frank stepped out into the hall.

"Good morning, Agent Green. Agent Skinner." Robbie smiled as he approached them.

"You sound chipper," John sneered, walking passed Robbie down the hall to the elevator.

"What do I have to be moody about, John?" Robbie smiled.

As Frank walked behind Robbie, admiring his strut, Robbie spun around. Frank quickly met Robbie's eyes.

"You in a foul mood as well, Agent Skinner?" Robbie teased.

"We're in Seattle to catch a serial killer, Taylor, not play games," Frank grumbled as John pushed the elevator call button.

"And we will. I promise." Robbie brushed his long hair back from his face casually.

While they waited for the elevator, Frank tried not to be

obvious as he admired Robbie's good looks. Biting his cheek, Frank knew Officer Harris was one lucky SOB.

Once they were all inside the elevator, descending to the lobby, Robbie asked, "Starbucks anyone?"

"Yeah, yeah, whatever," John muttered.

"I love working with you two. You're so much fun." Robbie's eyes twinkled mischievously.

"Just shut up and go." Frank nudged Robbie when the doors opened.

"Oh! Stop manhandling me, Frank!" Robbie teased playfully.

A rush of humiliation flashed through Frank. Sure Robbie spied, his cheeks heat up and Frank turned aside.

"Did I flick a switch in you, Agent Skinner?" Robbie whispered as they walked to the parking garage.

"Just shut the fuck up. Isn't Officer Harris enough for you?"

"Mm. More than enough." Robbie winked.

As he followed Robbie into the parking area, Frank frowned deeply, knowing he better keep his fantasies to himself.

4

Sonja Knight chewed the back of her pen as she read over case law in the firm's library. Growing weary of the dry information, she set the pen down and rubbed her eyes gently. It was nearly five-thirty and she felt like calling it a night.

"Hey."

Raising her head to the doorway, Sonja found her law partner Jack Larsen standing there. "Hey." Sonja thought Jack was beautiful. His sandy blond hair and bright aqua blue eyes absolutely enthralled her.

"Any progress on finding relevant case law?" Jack moved closer, standing behind one of the chairs adjacent to where Sonja was seated.

"A little." Sonja gazed at Jack as he removed his suit jacket, draping it over the back of the chair. Instantly she could see how enormous Jack's body was under the fabric of his white dress shirt and maroon tie. Jack the gym junkie. It made her mouth water.

He pulled out the chair and relaxed his elbows on the table. "What have you got?"

Sonja slid a large tome over to him noticing Jack's substantial golden wedding band. Married. Jack had married Adam Lewis, the hotshot Hollywood agent, in a private ceremony at Mark Richfield's mother's estate in Paradise, California. Mark. The man who had married Sonja's ex-lover, LAPD cop, Steve Miller. It was a tangle. She tried not to think too much about Steve turning gay after they broke up. It had nothing to do with me! I ended it with him! What the hell did I have in common with a white LAPD cop and his racist moronic ex-police sergeant father?

"Yes. This will do nicely." Jack leaned over the text as he read.

Sonja loved the thick waves of Jack's fair hair, his darker brown eyebrows and sideburns. The man was perfect in her opinion. How Mark Richfield could resist him, pass him up when they actually lived together in the same house, was a mystery to her.

"Excellent work, Sonja. I can always count on you."

A whiff of Jack's cologne drifted past her. Sonja inhaled it deeply into her lungs. As she moved to get a look at the passage Jack was perusing, Sonja knocked her pen off the tabletop.

Reaching down for it, she caught sight of Jack's enormous quadriceps as he appeared like the Incredible Hulk, about to rip through the seams of his dress trousers. He was positioned in a comfortable straddle, the crotch of his pants showing off a large mound.

Son of a bitch!

Sonja inched off the chair, hopefully still appearing to Jack that she was searching for her pen. Nudging back the chair, she crawled in her stockings and mini skirt to that amazing sight.

Once she was crouching between Jack's legs, she touched both his kneecaps at once feeling him jump at the contact.

"Sonja?"

As he scooted out to get a look at her, she moved with him, smoothing her hands up those broad solid legs to cup his crotch.

"Uh...we can't do this, Sonja."

Can't we? She smiled as she opened his belt and top button of his trousers.

"Sonja. I'm gay. And married."

Think I care? She unzipped him finding him totally erect and blushing pink. Admiring her darker colored hands in contrast to his fair skin tone and blond pubic hair, she tilted Jack's cock towards her painted lips. Sonja moaned and licked the tip of his dick lightly. Hearing Jack whimper, his fingers digging into her shoulders, she felt her body surge with pleasure. Oh, yes, I knew you'd love it, Jack.

"Sonja..." he breathed.

Allowing the head of his cock to enter her mouth, Sonja felt Jack's length throb and tasted a drop of pre-cum on her tongue. Drawing him in deeper, brushing her lips against the fabric of his suit trousers, Sonja heard Jack's groan and her own body tingled.

Fuck this! She got out from under the table, yanked her thong and pantyhose down and sat on Jack's lap, forcing his length to push into her depth. Humping his cock while on his lap, Sonja buried her fingers into his thick blond waves and connected to his mouth. Loving the kiss, Jack's dominant masculine tongue action, Sonja felt her body rise to heaven.

As he broke the kiss to gasp, she stared at his expression of orgasmic bliss. Riding him hard, fast, and furious, Sonja witnessed Jack's climax and instantly felt her own spinning around her body.

"Ah! Sonja!"

"Jack! God, yes! Jack!" She held onto him as his cock throbbed deep inside her, feeling both their juices oozing between them. "Give me that mouth!" she ordered, grabbing his coarse jaw and sucking on his tongue and lips wildly.

He wrapped his arms around her and held onto her tightly. His cock pulsated gently as he lingered inside her.

"You're beautiful. Sonja, that was amazing."

"You know how long I've wanted to do that to you?" Sonja smiled.

"Better than Steve?"

"Hell yeah, better than Steve!" she retorted, laughing.

"Good."

❦

"Hey."

Sonja looked up from the dry reading to see Jack Larsen standing at the doorway.

"Go home. It's late."

Sonja checked her watch. "Christ, is it nearly six? I must be crazy still sitting here."

"You are. Go."

She pushed her chair out and stood, intending on leaving everything as it was for the morning.

"Goodnight, Sonja. See you tomorrow."

Before she was able to reply, Jack had vanished from the doorway. She moved quickly to look down the hall seeing his broad back before he turned a corner. "Goodnight, Jack. Say hello to Adam for me."

He waved but didn't turn around.

Sighing deeply, Sonja retrieved her purse and coat from her office. As she shut down her computer and the lights, she daydreamed about her life and the choices she had made.

By the time she stood in the parking garage, Jack's maroon Jaguar was already at the electronic gate, leaving.

A sweet smile on her lips, Sonja took out her mobile phone on her way to her own car. "Hello, Mama?"

"Hi, baby. How are you doing?"

"Good. You mind a little company for dinner?"

"Not at all."

"Great. I'm on my way." She hung up and dialed again. "Hello, Sonja."

"Hi, Chelsea. Look, I'm going to eat dinner at my folks' tonight. Is that okay?"

"Fine with me."

"Okay. See you later."

"Bye, Sonja. Say hi to them for me."

"I will." Sonja shut off her phone and sat behind the wheel of her car. Sighing softly, she whispered, "Adam Lewis, I hope you know how lucky you are."

5

Reaching across the wooden fence, mild-mannered accountant Owen Braydon stroked the long nose of a quarter-horse as it stood in the pasture. Taking a good look around, Owen admired his lover Taylor Madison's father's ranch in San Antonio. It was glorious with its rolling hills and grazing herds of horses and cattle. The large mansion attached to the nearly one thousand acre property was like a vision out of the old hit show Dallas.

They didn't come often to visit Taylor's family here in Texas, but when they did, it always felt like a vacation to Owen. Their home back in Denver was a shack compared to that seventeen bedroom monstrosity.

Waiting for Taylor to appear so they could take a leisurely ride into the open fields, Owen was surprised when Taylor's best friend Jude Rae Clark appeared beside him.

"What do you know!" Owen waited to see if Jude's law-graduate partner Logan Bleau would show up, but only the two Texans were headed his way.

Admiring their tight faded blue jeans, denim shirts, black cowboy boots and hats, Owen licked his lips and wiped the drool from his chin. The pair of them, Jesus. Owen always thought Jude and Taylor could pass for brothers. Matching six-foot-one-inch heights, thick wavy brown hair and brilliant blue eyes, they were hunks right off the pages of Playgirl magazine as far as Owen was concerned.

"Hey," Owen said as he approached the men, meeting them halfway. "I didn't know you were coming to Texas, Jude."

"It was a last minute thing," Jude replied in his deep

southern drawl.

"Where's Logan?"

"He had to stay in Denver. He's got a big case he's workin' on." Jude adjusted his black cowboy hat in the bright sun.

"We gonna chitchat or ride?" Taylor chided.

"Ride em', cowboys!" Owen followed Taylor and Jude to the stable, watching those matching struts as they moved side by side. Owen's dick was so hard he was about to combust.

In the dimly lit barn, Owen could smell the scent of fresh hay and horses as he surveyed the neat interior with its wall of western saddles and bridles.

"Go git one of the horses out of that stall, Owen." Taylor pointed to a door that was split in half separating top and bottom.

Nodding, Owen unbolted the lower half which was closed, and pulled it open. It was very dim inside the tiny stall. As he stepped in and looked around, he found it was empty. Spinning on his heels to say something about the missing horse, Owen blinked in surprise when Jude entered the confined space with him.

"Uh," Owen gestured, "There's no horse in here, Jude."

"I know." Jude grinned wickedly.

"You know?" Owen noticed the light go out in the main room of the stable. It made the stall he and Jude were in grow dark. A second later, Taylor appeared.

"Taylor?" Owen asked, just noticing him holding something. "What's going on? Aren't we going to ride?"

"Oh, we're goin' ta ride all right, Owen. You got that straight." Taylor began spinning a rope lasso gently.

"What are you going to do with that?" Owen asked nervously.

"I'm gonna do me some calf ropin'. Right, Jude?"

"Calf roping?" Owen tilted his head as Jude snickered devilishly.

"You ready for some good fun, Jude?" Taylor held up the rope.

"Let's go, partner." Jude made a move towards Owen.

As both men approached him aggressively, Owen backed up, smacking into the wall. The clean hay was soft under his leather soles.

While Jude unbuttoned and removed Owen's shirt, Taylor wrapped the rope around Owen's chest, coiling it around him to tie his arms to his torso.

"Holy shit." Owen began to pant in excitement.

His shirt was tossed aside. Jude got a grip on Owen once he was tied up, forcing him down to the hay covered floor.

Lying on his side, Owen watched helplessly as Jude removed his shoes and his lower half of clothing. When Owen was completely naked, both men paused to stare at him.

"Taylor?"

"Yeah, Jude?"

"I think I'm gonna enjoy this little adventure."

"I knew you would, good buddy."

"Uh," Owen gulped, "What adventure?"

"Now don't you worry yerself, sugar." Taylor unzipped his jeans.

Seeing Taylor's exposed cock poking out of his faded denim, that cowboy hat deepening the already dark shadow on his face and coarse jaw, Owen began to go mad for him. His cock grew hard and throbbed where Owen had trapped it between his own legs.

"Looks like he likes the idea, Taylor," Jude laughed, urging Owen to his knees.

Without the use of his bound hands, Owen's cheek pressed against the straw under him. It had a pleasant woody scent but was prickly against his skin.

As Taylor disappeared from Owen's sight, he could hear him and Jude laughing behind him. A leather bridle dropped down against his head. He jumped in surprise. Jude raised Owen's chin, tugging the leather straps down over Owen's face so the metal bit was under his jaw. "Holy Christ!" Owen gulped loudly.

"There. That's more like it," Taylor announced as he tugged on the reins, pulling Owen's head up.

As he waited, gasping for breath, Owen was so thrilled his eyes were wide in anticipation. Suddenly heat filled him from behind. He arched his back and cried out as a cock slipped deep inside his ass.

He had no idea who it was until the bridle was jerked back and his head with it. Jude was kneeling in front of him, his large engorged cock hanging out of his tight jeans.

"Now open up, like a good little cowpoke."

Owen parted his lips. Jude pressed his cock against his mouth.

As Taylor rode him like a broncobuster, Owen sucked Jude's cock deep and hard.

"That's it!" Taylor whooped, "What a good little filly you are, Owen Braydon. Yeeha!"

Owen closed his eyes as pleasure overwhelmed him. He sucked as hard as he could, straining to release his hands so he could stroke Jude's balls, but he couldn't. He was tied up and deliciously helpless to these two top men.

"Now don't you make me come, Owen," Jude chided. "I still want to do some bareback bronc riding myself."

When Jude slipped out of his mouth, Owen reached out his tongue, stretching after him, wanting more.

Taylor thrust in deep, as deep as he could, into Owen's ass. Owen heard Taylor's low throaty grunting and felt Taylor's dick pulsating inside him.

"What a pretty sight." Jude sighed, pulling on his own dick, rubbing the head of it on Owen's cheek and lips over the leather bridle straps.

"Jesus!" Taylor exclaimed as he pulled out. "That was mighty sweet."

"My turn."

Jude vanished from Owen's field of vision. A moment later, Taylor appeared, removing the spent condom from his still semi-erect cock.

"Look at that," Jude crooned, "This is the treat you get every night, Taylor? My, oh my!"

Owen shivered as Jude's thick cock pushed inside him. The sensation of pleasure was so intense, he almost fell onto his face on the hay. But Taylor was there to pull the leather reins up, making Owen hover over the ground. While Jude howled in delight behind him, Taylor rubbed the tip of his prick against his lips. "Give it a good lickin', will ya, Owen?"

His own dick thick and dripping from the craving, he

opened his mouth and tried to suck Taylor's cock. Tasting the flavor of the condom, Owen kept licking and swallowing his saliva until he couldn't taste anything but Taylor's skin and last drops of cum.

"Hold on to yer hats, fellers, cause I'm about to hit a hundred point ride!" Jude shouted, hammering into Owen so hard he was being knocked into Taylor's cockhead with his face repeatedly.

Owen felt like bursting from the scorching heat in his ass. Jude's cum felt as if it was filling every empty space in his body. The rapid throbbing of Jude's cock echoed in Owen's glory hole like a beating heart.

As Jude gasped, catching his breath, Taylor rubbed the sticky drop of his pre-cum over Owen's lips. "Ready fer round two, darlin'?"

"God yes..." Owen whimpered, his back tensing, his ass quivering.

Feeling Jude pull out, Owen sat on his heels to take a break and catch his breath. Sweat was dripping down from his forehead under the leather of the bridle.

"Move over, Jude Rae. It's time I had me a second go."

"He's all yours, Taylor. What a piece of fucking ass he is, buddy. I could fuck him all day."

"Good!" Taylor replied, "Cause we are!"

Owen moaned in ecstasy. "Fuck me, cowboys...fuck me."

❧❧

"Don't tell me yer watchin' that again?"

Owen spun around panicked to see Taylor standing at the doorway of their den in their home in Denver. Yanking his hand out of his pants, he blushed crimson and fumbled for the remote.

Taylor dropped down on the sofa next to him, cuddling him. "Brokeback Mountain? How many darn times have you watched that movie, Owen?"

Stammering in embarrassment, Owen muttered, "I forget."

"What is your fascination with cowboys?" Taylor wrapped his arm around Owen's shoulder tighter, kissing his cheek.

"I don't know." Owen shut off the video.

"Don't do that on my account. I'll go get dinner started." Taylor pecked Owen's face again and rose to his feet. "I should call Jude and Logan. See what their up to this weekend. Jude wanted to check with Logan before we made plans."

"Okay." Owen ran his hand through his hair, still mortified Taylor had caught him watching his favorite movie again. Taylor was supposed to be working late. After checking his watch, he realized it was 'late'.

"Right. You want a beer or anythin'?" Taylor asked as he left the room.

"No. I'm all right." Owen waited until he vanished. Once Taylor had, he reached inside his jeans and briefs to his cock, feeling the dampness from where he'd come from jacking off. He ejected the DVD, putting it away before slipping to the bedroom to change his clothing. About to step into fresh underwear, he looked up at the door as it opened. Seeing a wicked grin on Taylor's face, Owen paused in what he was doing.

"Get yerself over here, Owen."

Finishing tugging up his brief, Owen lowered his head and walked over to Taylor, feeling like a guilty little boy.

Taylor embraced Owen and kissed him. "I know you have a soft spot for cowpokes, Owen. No need to be ashamed. I think it's endearin'."

Owen didn't think if Taylor knew about his little fantasy life he would be so 'endeared'.

"Come on. Let me satisfy you again before dinner." Taylor coaxed him to the bed.

"I'd rather satisfy you."

"Whatever you want, darlin'."

Owen stripped quickly. "Take me from behind, Taylor."

"You got it, hot stuff."

As Owen waited on his hands and knees on the bed for Taylor to undress, he closed his eyes and drifted back to the ranch in San Antonio. "Oh yes...fuck me, cowboy."

6

"Alex? What are you doing here?" Jack Larsen stood up from behind his desk.

"I have to do a project for my humanity's class and I thought, what better person to ask about the meaning of our world than a lawyer."

The sight of Alex in his tight white t-shirt and threadbare blue jeans instantly had Jack in heat. Alex was the spitting image of his top model father, Mark Richfield. And Jack had loved Mark since college when both he and Mark were in their early twenties. Not much older than the lovely Alexander was at the moment.

Jack tried to loosen his shirt collar and tie as suddenly it felt as if there wasn't enough air to breathe in his office.

"So?" Alex sauntered closer, as sensual and feline as his stunning father. "Will you help me, Jackie-blue?"

Jackie-blue. Mark started calling him that after Mark moved out of their shared house and in with Steve Miller, the ex-LAPD cop. Where the hell Mark had come up with it, other than that old Seventies song by the Ozark Mountain Daredevils, Jack didn't know. Now Alex was calling him that as well? *Crap, he looks so fucking delicious I'm going to spurt.*

"Jackie?" Alex peered back at the open office door.

Seeing a wicked grin appear on Alex's pretty face, Jack began panting in agony when he closed and locked the door. "What are you doing, Alex?"

As he leaned back on the door, his hands behind his low back, Alex pushed his pelvis forward enticingly. "I'm here for some advice, He-man."

He-man. Another Mark-ism. Did Alex have to be Mark's carbon copy? The exact image of the young, long-haired seraph Jack had fallen for head over heels in college? Swallowing audibly, Jack watched as Alex licked his top lip with lewd intent. His vision drawn to Alex's movements, he watched as Alex ran his fingers down his zipper flap. Under that material was a substantial mound of flesh. Jack's own dick harden in his trousers.

"Look, Alex, I have work to do..." *I cannot stand this young man doing this to me. I'm losing it! It's bad enough Steve is going insane over him. I can't!* As Jack opened his mouth to say something, something like, "Please leave," Alex began tugging down his zipper with one smooth slide.

When the fabric parted over Alex's flat abdomen, Jack could see he'd gone commando, another trait he inherited from his sexpot dad. Rubbing his eyes and face in agony, Jack begged, "Alex, please go home." Hearing the rustle of fabric, Jack glanced up. Alex had removed his t-shirt and was smoothing his hand down his hairless torso.

Oh God! Jack ground his jaw as the yearning became unbearable. "Alexander! No!" *I'm married to Adam Lewis! And to your father, for that matter! I cannot touch you! It's bad enough you jacked off using my stunned limp hand at our beach house in Malibu. I cannot let this happen again. No!*

Alex closed the gap between them. Trying not to look, Jack couldn't help but peek through his fingers at this lithe twink. Alex had peeled his jeans down his hips, exposing his enormous erection. "You know you want it, Jackie."

Turning his back to Alex, Jack covered his face. "Why are you doing this to me?" he whined.

"Because I love older men, Jack. And I adore you. You're so fucking big I just want to squirm all over you."

At the first touch of Alex's hand on his shoulder, Jack flinched.

"Jackie..." Alex purred, trying to remove Jack's suit jacket from behind.

"No, Alex, please..." His reply was weak and lacked any force. Not only could Jack not resist, he allowed Alex to remove his suit jacket. Taking a deep breath, he looked over his shoulder. Alex was completely naked, his long brown hair flowed like silk down his shoulders to his chest. Following the line dissecting Alex's torso, Jack found both of Alex's hands stroking his cock and balls, holding up that package exactly the way his father does.

"Take it," Alex hissed, milking a drop of pre-cum out of his large mushroom-shaped cockhead.

Jack's skin covered in cool sweat and chills. He took one last look at the closed office door and reacted. Shoving everything off his desk, hearing pens, paper, and files scatter to the floor, he grabbed Alex around the waist and drew his naked body against him. Moaning as he dug his hand into Alex's incredible mane of hair, he kissed him, sucking on his tongue before fucking Alex's mouth roughly with his. Alex opened like a rose petal in his arms. It sent Jack into a tailspin.

Parting from Alex's mouth, Jack groaned so loudly it echoed off his office walls. He pushed Alex back on his desk and raised Alex's legs into the air. As Alex whimpered in longing, Jack dove between his thighs and sucked on that enormous dick. Christ, it had to be as big as Mark's. There was no way he was going to get the entire organ into his mouth, but it wasn't for lack of trying.

"Ah! Jackie!"

Jesus, even his moans sound like Mark!

Jack wrapped one hand around the base of Alex's thick cock, with the other he explored Alex's heavy soft balls and ass. The minute he pushed the tip of his finger into Alex's hole, Alex began bucking his hips, trying to penetrate deeper into Jack's mouth. Jack felt Alex's cock-head hit the back of his throat and tried to keep it there without gagging or pulling back.

Instantly with the deep-throating and hard-pulling sucking, Alex began to come. His big dick grew even thicker as it throbbed and spurted. It coated Jack's mouth and tongue with hot streams of spunk.

While Alex cried out in pleasure, Jack kept swallowing that eighteen-year-old sperm in bliss. As the last throes of orgasm engulfed Alex's entire body his cock had gone rigid and thickened even more, filling Jack's mouth, stretching his lips.

"Ohhh, Jackie, Jackie...this is why I love older men..."

Releasing Alex's cock with a wet pop, Jack panted as he stared down at him, wiping saliva off his chin where he had dribbled from sucking such a big prick. While Alex rocked his hips, closed his eyes and recovered, Jack opened his trousers and exposed his own length from his briefs. "You gorgeous fucker!" he gasped as he pushed the head of his cock between Alex's slick spit-covered crack. At the first thrust of Jack's hips, Alex inhaled sharply and arched his back in pain. But contrary to Alex's physical reaction, he shouted, "Yes!"

Staring at Alex's hairless chest, his thin furry treasure trail leading to a dense dark, almost black colored, mass of wiry pubic hair, Jack sank his cock deeper into this teen, balls deep. His eyes drinking in everything from Alex's expression of nirvana to his semi-erect cock, which had begun to twitch and respond to getting topped, Jack felt his loins explode with pleasure. "Son of a bitch!" He jammed his hips wildly, fucking this eighteen-year-old beauty with every ounce of muscle he possessed.

"Ah! Ah! Jack!" Alex grabbed his own cock and began fisting it like mad. "Fuck me! Fuck me!"

As orgasm washed up over him, Jack felt his entire body tense up and his sack go solid. Thrusting into Alex so hard he almost catapulted him off the desk, he held onto Alex's legs, keeping him in place. The cum rushing out of him and into Alex's hot hole, Jack ground his jaw and closed his eyes, overwhelmed with the strength of the climax. Under him Alex came again, crying out in ecstasy.

Gasping, unable to breathe, Jack stared down at the opalescent puddles on Alex's smooth chest and remembered wanting Mark when he looked like Alex, so badly he ached. His Mark Antonious. His glorious pretty boy with the long dark lashes and hair. "I love you, Alexander."

"I love you too, Jack. With all my heart."

⊱≋

"Jack?"

Blinking, surfacing from his daydream, Jack found Sonja rapping a knuckle at his partially opened office door.

"Yes?" Jack sat up in his chair.

"Court in fifteen minutes."

"Thanks." Jack nodded, straightening his desk absently until she vanished from his view. Pausing, Jack stared at a photo he had displayed on his desk. It was from the day of his wedding at Mark's mother's estate in Paradise, California. He and Adam, Mark and Steve, had wed that day, a polygamist arrangement that only the four of them, Alex and his boyfriend, Oliver Loveday, were aware of. In that photo, the four grooms were in black tuxedos. But there, standing in the middle of the quartet, in his dark suit, was Alexander Mark Lehman-Richfield looking like a living dream with his long flowing locks and emerald green eyes.

A smile formed on Jack's face. Yeah, so what? He and Steve fantasized about young Alexander. Was that a crime?

"Not according to the ex-LAPD cop or me," Jack chuckled softly.

"Jack?"

Hearing his law partners Jennifer and Sonja calling, Jack stood, buttoned his suit jacket and made his way to the hall, a contented grin planted on his lips.

7

Eli Walsh sipped his fifth gin and tonic. The club was packed tonight. More men filled the dance floor and lingered in the dark halls than usual. The music was so loud he couldn't hear himself think. The deep basso vibrated in his chest. As multi-colored lights spun around the writhing mass of male bodies, Eli focused on the go-go boys in cages that were dangling above the action, their slick, oily, hairless torsos wriggled to the beat. As he licked the alcohol off his lips, Eli imagined those nearly naked boys to be under twenty. He wasn't as attracted to the young ones as he was the slightly older men. Man. One man. Brock Hart.

Admit it. I'm crazy about him.

He and Brock were gym buddies, bar buddies, but Eli would have preferred it if he and Brock were fuck buddies.

"Ya can't always get what ya want," he sighed out loud, in no way being overheard in the din even by the drunken men standing right next to him.

But Brock Hart, the Wall Street stockbroker by day, was a predator at night. Brock ate men for fun. Or, Eli should say, men ate Brock.

When Brock actually tried to calculate how many blowjobs he'd received since he was nineteen, now that Brock and he were thirty, Eli fell off the chair. Over a thousand BJ's? Eli had yet to have his first.

He wasn't ugly. Well, maybe his light blond hair was thinning just a little at his forehead, but his body was a perfect ten. He was an athlete, a swimmer, played racquetball...no, he was still attractive. He was just picky. He didn't want a quick fuck or suck. I want a boyfriend not a one-nighter.

But Brock had pointed out to Eli how often they had attended that gay club. Twice a week for over a year. No boyfriend seemed to materialize from out of the mob. Why? Eli never could quite figure it out.

Finishing the drink, completely buzzed and thanking fuck it was Friday night and he had the weekend off from the banking world, Eli looked again for Brock.

The guy was so fucking gorgeous, within seconds of Brock lingering around with a drink to his lips or swaying on the dance floor, some young hunk offered to suck Brock's dick. Amazing.

Setting his glass on the bar behind him, Eli decided to take a walk around the packed room which stunk of exhaled booze and men's sweat and cologne, and search for the infamous man-eater, Mr. Hart.

Though he tried to utter, "Excuse me," as he made his way through the mob, after a while he gave up and simply held onto men's shoulders and guided them aside. He knew where he'd find Brock. It was a no-brainer.

Pushing back the door of the men's room, seeing several pairs of legs exposing from under the stall doors, some with trousers around their ankles, Eli scanned those feet for a familiar pair of Gucci shoes.

Last stall to check, Eli intended on taking a quick glance to see if it was Brock and then exit the men's room to get another peek at the dance floor where he obviously must have missed him.

As he crouched to have a look, he heard Brock's moan.

"Found ya." Eli smiled wickedly.

The stall wasn't closed all the way. As Eli investigated the position of the two pairs of feet under the metal door, he noticed Brock's facing outward and a pair of black leather boots covered over with black trouser legs, behind him, pointing the same way.

That confused Eli. Brock never took it up the ass. Never.

About to imagine he had the wrong stall, Eli heard the unmistakable sound of Brock's moaning sigh.

Pausing, making sure no one gave a crap what he was up

to, since several men were trying to get involved in three and four-ways of their own, Eli took a step closer to that stall and pulled the door open just enough to see in.

It was indeed Brock Hart. His slacks were down around his thighs, his belt hanging open, and one of the most amazing men Eli had ever seen in his life was fucking Brock anally. "Daniel," Eli mouthed without a sound.

Daniel's electric green eyes instantly opened and connected to Eli's. Eli felt a surge of power from them and his knees grew weak from just Daniel Wolf's kinetic gaze.

"Eli..." Brock moaned, appearing to be in a trance, making a slight attempt to reach out to him.

About to say something, but having no idea what, other than to apologize profusely for interrupting them, Eli's gaze swept downwards. Brock's cock was fully erect and dripping cum onto the floor in a thick, constant stream.

As Eli gasped in disbelief at the amount of spunk, Brock closed his eyes and groaned loudly as Daniel fucked him royally from behind.

Inhaling down a dry throat, Eli took one quick glance behind him before he crouched down at Brock's waist level. Right before he tasted his best friend's cum, Eli hesitated. He'd only sucked cock once before, in high school. He was dying for the opportunity to give Brock head. About to chicken out, thinking Brock would be furious with him to have broken the Brock Hart Rules of never having sex with a friend, Eli was stunned to feel Brock pushing his head towards that seeping slit. Yes!

Eli grabbed Brock's bare hips and opened his lips. The moment he allowed Brock's cockhead to penetrate his mouth, he was stunned at the amount of cum Brock was ejaculating. And judging from the puddle on the white tiles, Brock had been either dripping pre-cum or climaxing for some time. Impossible?

The taste of his best friend's love juice finally on this tongue, Eli began swallowing that treat. Brock roared another ecstatic cry of euphoria that echoed in the dim bathroom.

Closing his eyes and engulfing Brock's cock to the base, Eli ran his hands all over Brock's balls and thighs, swallowing again and again as his mouth filled.

At one point he peeked up to see if he could spy Brock's gorgeous expression of pleasure. Seeing Daniel had sunk his teeth into Brock's neck from behind, still fucking him hard, Eli gasped with his mouth full. Jesus! Daniel really was a vampire? Eli didn't believe Brock when he told him. He did now.

A crimson drop of blood ran down Brock's throat to his shirt collar.

It was Daniel's turn to moan.

In shock, Eli let Brock's cock slip out of his mouth, realizing he was still spurting out even more cum as Daniel drank his fill.

Staring in awe at the two men, locked together at the hips and neck, Eli held onto Brock's cock, pointing it downwards as it continued to pump out more spunk than was humanly possible.

"Ahhh! Daniel!!! Aaahhh!" Brock screamed as his cock pulsated in Eli's fist.

Sliding his palm over Brock's sticky thickness, Eli gazed up again at Daniel. Through Daniel's swoon, he opened his eyes.

Eli jumped out of his skin at the sight of those shocking green irises illuminated like the bulbs of Christmas lights on the snowy streets of Broadway and Fifth Avenue.

But Daniel wasn't looking at Eli any longer. He was looking through him. As bright red dripped down Brock's neck, staining his shirt collar, Daniel's lips were coated with it, like cherry lipstick.

"Ahhh! Daniel! No more...fuck!" Brock moaned in agony.

While Eli gaped in amazement, Daniel closed his eyes and drew back, licking Brock's blood off his mouth with a blood red tongue.

As Daniel disconnected his hips from Brock's ass, Eli felt Brock's cock go limp in his hand. Still fondling it gently, for he didn't think he'd ever get this opportunity again, Eli studied Brock closely as he recovered, gasping for air and reaching for the sides of the toilet stall to help him stay upright.

"Eli..." Daniel hissed wickedly.

It made the hair stand on Eli's neck. He avoided Daniel's hypnotic stare and gently tucked Brock's limp cock back into his briefs, helping him pull up his pants and fasten them.

"Thanks, Eli." Brock hung his head, his eyes closed.

"I'll be out at the bar." Eli stood tall and could see Daniel fastening his own slacks.

Before Eli left, he took one last look at the bloody trail that had oozed down Brock's skin, the long-haired fabulous demon behind him, and lastly, the unbelievable puddle of se-men on the floor near his feet. "You okay?"

"Yes." Brock nodded, not catching Eli's eye.

Stepping out of the stall, Eli washed his hands at the sink and noticed Brock's cum had dripped down his chin. Licking it off before he rinsed it, Eli shivered at the tangy taste and the chance to finally suck a cock he'd been yearning to suck for a very long time.

Once he'd splashed his face, Eli dried himself on paper towels and left the men's room.

"Gin and tonic, please." Eli bent over the bar to be heard.

꙰

Sipping his drink, Eli gazed at the go-go boys as they gyrated in their cages, yanking their tiny g-strings down their hips to expose the very base of their cock and balls. It was mesmerizing.

"Hey."

"Hey," Eli replied, having to shout in the noise, seeing Brock's flushed cheeks from his dancing.

"I'm heading out to my place with Daniel."

"Okay."

Leaning to Eli's ear, Brock asked, "Are you going to be okay, Eli?"

"Of course." Eli smiled.

"Get some action!" Brock implored, "Don't just prop up the bar every night."

Eli chuckled softly. "I'll try."

"See ya for racquetball tomorrow?"

"Yup." Eli just caught Daniel looming in the background. The sight sent a shiver over his skin.

As Brock waved at Eli and smiled, Eli sighed tiredly. One of these nights he'd have to do something other than live in his fantasy world. It wasn't working for him. He was feeling lonely and depressed.

An older man leaned on the bar next to him trying to flag down the bartender. Eli inspected his body when the opportunity presented itself. Shrugging indifferently, Eli shouted into the man's ear, "Can I buy you a drink?"

The man spun around to check Eli out. "Sure!"

Eli turned to face the bartender, leaning his shoulder against the man next to him, smiling at him. Maybe tonight I'll give casual sex a chance.

Nah... Eli laughed to himself. He wasn't Brock Hart and never would be.

8

Thankful for a day off from firefighting, Hunter Rasmussen shook out his towel and spread it on the warm sand. Removing his sunglasses as he pulled his t-shirt over his head, Hunter stuck them back on his nose and tossed the shirt on the towel. Next he slid his shorts down his legs and dropped them on top of his shirt. Surveying the sparse weekday crowd, Hunter was glad summer had reached an end and the school year had begun. The mobs abated substantially on the California waterfront, and he much preferred the calm serenity to the vacation madness.

Stretching out on the towel, Hunter scanned the few surfers and bathers in the water, enjoying the bright October sunshine without the scorching August heat.

A whistle blowing caught his attention. Sitting up, Hunter spotted a lifeguard in his red trunks and windbreaker standing at the rail of a nearby tower. "Is that Josh Elliot?" Hunter shielded his eyes in the glare. He and his lover Blake Hughes were good friends with Josh and his lifeguard partner, Tanner Cameron.

Getting to his feet to have a closer look, Hunter realized it was indeed, Josh. Heading over to say hello, Hunter checked his black Speedos discreetly knowing the minute he stood near the incredible lifeguard he'd get an erection. The guy was sex on a stick.

Seeing Josh still inspecting the water dutifully, Hunter admired Josh's prefect slender legs, thick shaggy brown hair, and chiseled features.

As Hunter drew near, Josh noticed him. Instantly a brilliant grin appeared on Josh's handsome face. "Hello, Hunter!"

"Hey, beautiful." Hunter stopped directly under where Josh was standing on the wooden platform. "Where's Tanner?"

"Off on his run down the beach. Are you here with Blake?"

"He's due later on. He had some errands to run."

"Oh? Blake left you on your own?" Josh's eyes swept over Hunter's body. "Naked?"

"Naked?" Hunter laughed uneasily. Josh certainly had a way of making him feel naked. Hunter cupped his hand over his hardening dick.

"Don't hide that on my account, hot stuff."

Shifting his feet in the sand, Hunter had an image flash of a get together he and Blake had with their two LAPD officer friends, Jeff Chandler and Mickey Stanton, as well as Tanner and Josh. While they all sipped beer and tequila on the patio, Josh sat on Tanner's lap and exposed his dick, giving the group a one-man show. It was an image Hunter would never forget.

Waking from his dream, Hunter came aware as Josh removed his windbreaker, staring at him as he did. Seeing Josh's well cut chest and abs, Hunter grew a full erection.

"Am I distracting the fireman?" Josh draped his jacket over the rail.

Taking a look around the sparsely populated beach, Hunter stared at Josh again. "Fuck yeah. You kidding me?"

"Come here."

"Huh?" Hunter felt his heart burst in his chest at the excitement. "Come where?" As he asked Josh that question, Josh pivoted on his heels and disappeared inside the lifeguard hut.

"Holy shit." Hunter bit his lip and looked around again. Before he reconsidered or thought about the betrayal to Blake and Tanner, Hunter raced up the ramp and into that dim shack. When he stepped through the door, Josh's large rigid cock was out of his red trunks and he was stroking it slowly.

"Jesus, Josh, don't do this to me."

"No one will know." Josh thrust his pelvis out enticingly.

Hunter felt his cock throb in his bathing suit as his erection had begun to creep upright and poke out of the top of the waistband.

"I love firemen." Josh licked his lips teasingly. "Find me hot, leave me wet...and satisfied."

"Oh God." Hunter glanced down at himself. His dick head was exposed completely from his tight black bathing suit.

Josh crossed the small space and stood in front of Hunter. He lowered Hunter's suit down under his balls, gripped both of their dicks together in his palms and began squeezing and pulling on them.

The shiver of pleasure nearly made Hunter topple over. Making sure he kept his gaze on Josh's amazing face, Hunter thought Josh was one of the prettiest men he had ever laid eyes on. Yes, Blake and Tanner were handsome, but Josh? As gorgeous as a woman with the body of a fit young man. Josh's green eyes appeared to glow as they were riveted to his own.

"You want to fuck me, Hunt?" Josh brushed his lips against Hunter's.

In response Hunter moaned in agony. This was so wrong.

"Or...suck it?" Josh used his dick to rub his pre-cum along Hunter's stiff length. "Or...I can suck you..." Josh dropped to his knees.

When Hunter felt Josh's full lips envelope his erection, his knees went weak. "Shit..." With both his hands he dug into that mop of thick brown hair and fucked Josh's mouth aggressively.

Before Hunter came, Josh pulled back with a breath. Hunter's cock bobbed in the air, slick with saliva.

"Fuck me, firefighter."

Still reeling from the blowjob, Hunter steadied himself on a wall as Josh dragged his red lifeguard trunks down and off his tanned legs. His snow white ass cheeks glowed in the dimness of the shack.

Josh spread his thighs wide and bent over a counter, offering his body.

"Holy shit. Holy shit." Hunter almost hyperventilated with the excitement.

"There's lube in my backpack."

Scrambling to get what they needed, Hunter tore open the pack and removed the tube. He slathered himself generously, rushing towards Josh before they were discovered. With two fingers Hunter entered Josh's back passage. Instantly Josh moaned and shivered, spreading his feet even wider. "I want your cock."

Gulping for air desperately because he was going crazy for this man, Hunter loosened that tight ring even further, pushing four fingers inside Josh passed the second knuckle. Josh's body tensed at first with a hiss of a sharp breath before Hunter felt that tight ring relax completely.

"Give me your cock, Hunter!"

Twisting his hand as he pushed in and out, working Josh's anus in ecstasy, Hunter could come just fist-fucking this beauty.

Once he was in past his third set of knuckles inside Josh's hot hole, Josh arched his back off the counter and yelled, "I'm gonna come! Hunter!"

Removing his hand, Hunter quickly jammed his dick into Josh's slick well-worked ass. From the prepping he had given Josh, Hunter slid in easily, right up to his balls.

"Harder!"

Wrapping his fingers around Josh's thick dick, Hunter began hammering ruthlessly into this treat. "Oh, yes...holy fuck..."

"Harder...deeper...fuck me, Hunt!"

Going into overdrive, Hunter slammed his hips against Josh's tight round globes making them shake, at the same time he jacked-off Josh's prick. Josh let loose a scream of pleasure as Hunter felt Josh's cock pulsating like mad in his fingers. The creamy spatter of Josh's cum dripped down the wall under the counter as ribbons of milky cream shot out of Josh's slit.

"Harder!" Josh gasped, choking with the effort.

Hunter drove in using all the power he had in his thighs and hips. He felt his balls go tight and the sensation of tingling began between his legs. It was so strong his knees gave out. As he shot his cum into Josh's worked hole, a huge load emerge from him, filling Josh to capacity and running back out down Josh's crack and thighs.

"Josh! Holy fuck!"

"Hunter...you are amazing...absolutely amazing."

"I love fucking you..." Hunter jammed his dick in a few last times forcing more of his own cum to ooze out of Josh's ass.

"Anytime, Hunter. Any fucking time."

❧❦

"You want me to spread sun block on your back for you, Hunt?"

Spinning around, Hunter found Blake sitting next to him on the towel, holding up a bottle of lotion. "Huh? Yeah. Okay." He cupped his hand over his crotch to hide his erection.

"Geez. You seem like you're a million miles away." Blake blobbed some cream in his palm and began massaging Hunter's shoulders.

"That feels nice." Hunter sighed, staring at the outline of his dick in his black bathing suit as his head drooped forward.

"Too bad Tanner and Josh aren't at their tower today, eh, Hunt? No Josh Elliot eye candy."

Hunter smiled. "No. No Josh eye candy today." He rubbed his finger down his length discreetly.

"We need to get together again soon. It seems there's always a big lapse between our visits."

"It's our schedules." Hunter moaned as Blake massaged his back with cream. "You'll put me to sleep."

Blake laughed. "Not until you do me."

"Deal." As Blake continued to rub lotion into his skin, Hunter peeked back at that tower. Some scrawny kid was manning it. Sighing heavily, Hunter closed his eyes and savored his lover's touch, keeping his fantasies to himself.

9

Sitting in his dark blue police uniform in the idling patrol car, LAPD Officer Jeff Chandler gazed out at nothing, bored with a slow day. Checking the dash for the time, seeing it was hours from the end of his twelve-hour shift, he rubbed his eyes and yawned.

The police radio crackled noisily, "Code-Twelve, audible residential alarm at the following location..."

Jeff tried to wake from his drowsy fog and pay attention.

"Resident on sight claiming false trip...need unit to verify."

Reaching for the mike on the dash, Jeff clicked the button to inform the dispatcher he would take the call. "Eight-Adam-One, roger, Code-one."

"Roger, Eight-Adam-One, Code-One," she acknowledged him.

Jeff hung up the mike and headed to the false alarm, reading the computer screen inside the car's compartment as the call appeared in print, checking the address. He registered it as vaguely familiar.

As he pulled in front of the large home in Bel Air, Jeff immediately recognized the house. It belonged to the Dangereux Cologne model, Mark Richfield and the ex-LAPD cop, Steve Miller. A smile formed on his lips. He loved those guys.

After letting the dispatcher know he arrived, he shut down the engine of the black and white patrol car. Jeff climbed out, switching on the portable radio in his belt with the microphone attached to his shoulder epilate.

When he turned his attention to the front door he found

the stunning androgynous Brit, standing waiting for him. The moment Mark recognized him, Mark grinned happily.

"You trip your damn alarm again, Richfield?" Jeff teased.

"I did. Come in, Officer Chandler."

Mark opened the door wider for him. Jeff entered the luxurious home and noticed Mark's eighteen-year-old son, Alex standing in the room. "Well! Hello!" Jeff greeted him excitedly. Alex was as gorgeous as his strikingly glamorous father. But added to that description was his youth and ridiculously long hair. In some ways, Alex had surpassed his father.

"Hey, copper." Alex, hands on hips, pushed his pelvis forward. It was no secret to Jeff and Mickey, Jeff's partner, that Alexander loved older men. And his dad? Mark made no secret about his desire for men in uniform.

"Well?" Jeff asked, already sporting a hard-on for this father and son combo, "Which one of you beauties set it off?"

"Me." Mark raised his hand. "I'm to blame. Arrest me, Officer." Mark held his hands out in front of him as if he wanted to be cuffed.

"Don't tempt me, gorgeous." Jeff's cock throbbed under his dark blue trousers. "Anyone else home?" He took a look around for Steve.

"Nope, just us." Alex sauntered closer. "Christ, you're so fucking good looking in that uniform, Officer Chandler. Wanna pat me down?"

"Alex," Mark chided softly. "Don't torment the poor man on duty."

Jeff keyed his microphone and informed the dispatcher it was indeed a false alarm, immediately asking for a break after. She granted him one. "Off duty now." Jeff grinned wickedly.

"Oh?" Mark stepped closer. "And? Off duty and can play?"

"Yes!" Alex pumped his fist.

"Ya got me for fifteen minutes. Do your worst." Jeff held out his arms to his sides in invitation.

"No time to waste!" Mark grabbed Jeff's hand and raced up the stairs to his bedroom, Alex in hot pursuit.

The minute Jeff entered the master suite, Mark began unfastening his heavy gun belt. Helping Mark drop the weighty gear to the floor and lower his uniform trousers, Jeff instantly began stripping Mark of his clothing as well.

When a tongue lapped at his ass, Jeff jolted and tuned to look over his shoulder. Alex was naked on his knees behind him, spreading his cheeks and licking at his rim. "Holy Christ!"

"You like it, copper?" Alex asked wickedly.

While his son was busy molesting his rear, Mark unzipped Jeff's uniform shirt, revealing his Kevlar vest and white t-shirt.

"I like!" Jeff's cock stood at attention as that eighteen year old devoured his butt like a pro.

Once the three of them were naked, Mark led Jeff to his large king-sized bed.

"The two of you?" Jeff gasped. "Jesus! It doesn't get any better than that!"

Both Mark and Alex lay back on the bed side by side. "Come and get it." Mark craned his finger.

Jeff dove between them, pulling them both closer, under him. Feeling Alex and Mark licking at his face and ears, perfectly matched bookends, their hands on his back and ass, Jeff groaned in agony. "Shoot me. I've died and gone to heaven."

Alex giggled. "Yes, shoot me. Shoot your spunk into me."

"Fuck! I don't know which one of you I want to fuck first!" Jeff squirmed on them in bliss. Finding each of their cocks hard and ready, he stroked those amazing lengths simultaneously. Through the grapevine he'd heard rumors they were ten inches and shivered in disbelief. "Jesus, guys!"

"Fuck me first," Alex whimpered, thrusting his enormous shaft through Jeff's hand.

Scooting lower on the bed, Jeff sucked on Alex's long thick dick while he fisted Mark's. Hearing both their groans was pure gold. The minute he tasted Alex's pre-cum he swapped over sucking Mark. Mark's cock was just as delicious as his son's.

After he'd devoured each for a few moments, he leaned up on his elbows, resting on their thighs. "Kiss."

"Sorry?" Mark tilted his head, his shoulder-length hair sticking to his sweaty face and neck as he panted for breath.

"Kiss!" Jeff urged.

Alex and Mark exchanged looks.

Jeff's body went into overdrive as the thought of that

gorgeous father and son duo swapping spit pushed him over the edge.

Gently, Mark reached behind Alex's head and urged him close. When their lips touched, Jeff growled like a wild animal and knelt up on the bed, jacking off as he stared in absolute astonishment that they did it. "Fuck!"

As their kissing intensified, and Alex reached down for his father's huge cock, Jeff shouted, "Yes! Oh, God! Jack each other off! Please!"

While they were lip locked, Mark reached downwards. Jeff led Mark's hand to Alex's stiff dick. Jeff was gasping so hard he couldn't catch his breath. "Come! Come! Oh, my fucking God, I'm so hard I'm going to explode."

Mark fisted Alex faster, as Alex did the same to him, both groaning in pleasure as they kissed more passionately.

"Aahhhfuck!" Jeff came, his stream arcing like a fountain across the two naked men under him as long strings of cream coated their tanned flesh.

"Ah! Ah!"

Jeff's eyes sprang open to see which Richfield climaxed first. As his jaw hung in shock, both of those gorgeous men came together, spraying Jeff's abdomen and pubic hair with their spunk. "Yes! Holy mother-fucking-god!"

"Ah...Dad...holy shit..." Alex moaned.

"Alex, you're delicious," Mark purred.

Blinking his eyes in disbelief that the two of them had done his bidding, Jeff jolted in excitement as Alex and Mark sat up to lick their cum off his skin. "I swear this is the best fucking break I've ever had in my life."

The men chuckled softly, their hot tongues cleaning up the mess they made.

"Ahhh, God...I'm in heaven!"

≈≈

"Jeff?"

"Huh?" Jeff turned in the car seat to Mickey.

"Are you falling asleep?"

"No." Jeff rubbed his face tiredly.

"It's dead." Mickey tried to stretch in the tight space.

"Maybe we should look around for a traffic stop or something to kill the time."

Jeff stared at Mickey as he sat relaxed in the passenger's seat of their patrol car. After giving the parking lot they were in a good look around, Jeff dove onto Mickey's lap, opening his gun belt and trousers.

"Ah! Chandler! Now?"

"Now, Stanton!" Jeff dug Mickey's soft cock out of his briefs and sucked it.

"Fuck, I love working with you." Mickey spread his legs wider.

That flaccid dick hardened up in his mouth. Yeah he had some pretty strange fantasies. So? No one had to know but him.

"I love you, Jeff," Mickey crooned, digging his hands through Jeff's hair.

"Mm!" Jeff replied in agreement, sucking harder.

10

Bryan Buck sat across the kitchen table from his older brother Jordon. Not only was Bryan envious of his Wall Street stockbroker brother's brains, he was jealous of his culinary skills as well.

"Are you going to be involved in another play once Hair is done its run on Broadway?" Jordon asked, sipping the crisp white Riesling from a stemmed glass.

"I'm hoping so. I've already had two auditions and a call back for the next one."

"What's this play about?" Jordon placed the glass down carefully on the table and continued to eat the seafood paella he had prepared.

"It's from a new playwright. I've never heard of him or the play." Bryan studied his brother's handsome features in admiration. All right, admit it. Jordon is nicer looking, smarter, bigger, and everything else better than I am. Christ, who has time to work out in the gym every day?

"What's the name of it?"

"Joe Orton Slept Here."

Jordon laughed. "Uh huh."

"Yeah, well." Bryan blushed as he replied, "It's for the lead so I'm not complaining."

"I assume it's a gay play then. You know. Orton inspired?" Jordon rested his fork on the empty plate, relaxing, raising his glass again.

"Yes. Gay actors, gay play," Bryan said. "And speaking of gay..." He narrowed his eyes at his brother. "How's life fucking the ex-teen-porn star, Tyler Holliday?"

Jordon's calm demeanor changed to rage. Bryan knew how protective Jordon was over his lover's reputation, but he just couldn't help but push his brother's buttons.

"Don't talk about him like that." Jordon stood abruptly and began clearing the empty plates off the table.

Crossing his legs as he watched Jordon, Bryan sipped his wine smugly. "Oh? Still a wee bit sensitive about your lover's first life?"

"I said shut up." Jordon began loading the dishwasher.

Once he'd finished his wine, Bryan brought the glass and his plate to the sink where Jordon was standing. "Ex-porn star, ex-wedding planner, and now top model with Spencer and Epstein's agency. My how he has grown."

Twisting the sink tap closed, Jordon glared at Bryan. "Are you trying to get me angry? What's the deal? Because it's working."

Bryan handed his brother a towel for his wet hands. "I love bringing out the fire in you, Jordon. It's more than that lame blonde bimbo flight attendant you were engaged to ever could."

"Now you're bringing up Fawn?" Jordon groaned in exasperation. "Maybe it's time you went home, Bry."

Staring at Jordon's deep brown eyes, his chiseled jaw, his strapping six foot one inch height, all solid muscle, Bryan felt his body react against his will. "I don't want to go home."

"Then stop pissing me off." Jordon closed the door of the dishwasher. "You want dessert?"

"Yes..." Bryan hissed seductively.

"Fine." Jordon inched passed him and opened the refrigerator.

While Jordon's back was turned, Bryan admired his tight ass in his clinging black trousers.

"What are you in the mood for? I have some Dean and Deluca cheesecake."

On the premise of peering into the fridge, Bryan leaned over Jordon's body, pushing his semi-hard cock into his brother's butt. "Anything." Bryan closed his eyes, inhaling Jordon's masculine cologne.

"Well, decide. I'm not having anything so tell me what

you want."

Running his fingers lightly down Jordon's sides to his hips, Bryan held tight and pushed his pelvis into his brother's bottom.

Jordon turned to look over his shoulder. "What the hell are you doing?"

"What I want isn't in the refrigerator, Jordon." Bryan ground his stiff cock into Jordon's ass crack.

Jordon bolted upright and closed the refrigerator door, frozen where he stood.

Moaning softly, Bryan smoothed his hands around the front of Jordon's slacks caressing his large soft package.

"Oh God, no way, Bryan."

As Bryan kneaded the soft fleshy mound under his brother's slacks, he noticed Jordon did not pull away. Closing his eyes, Bryan rested his cheek on Jordon's broad back and swayed in a gentle dance as he massaged between his brother's legs.

Feeling Jordon's chest expand as his respirations quickened, Bryan opened the buckle of Jordon's belt, his button, and his zipper. Pausing, Bryan waited for Jordon to stop him.

Assuming he gave Jordon enough time to end this incestuous act, Bryan dragged Jordon's pants down his hips. He felt Jordon stiffen, but again, he did not stop him.

Lowering both Jordon's briefs and trousers to the floor, Bryan knelt behind him and admired what he knew would be a perfect set of buns. "Son of a bitch."

Jordon's torso expanded with a deep inhale followed by a long slow exhale.

Bryan parted his brother's ass cheeks and lapped at his rim.

An agonizing groan came from Jordon in response.

Ever since they were teens, Bryan thought his brother was gorgeous. Perfect build, prefect hair and teeth, Hollywood movie star features, captain of the football team, prom king, Jordon should be the actor, not him. Bryan knew he wasn't ugly, far from it. But nothing, in his opinion, compared to his brother, Jordon Buck. And only a man as gorgeous as Jordon could have netted that living gay fantasy, Tyler Holliday. Bryan couldn't, but it wasn't for lack of trying.

His saliva was running down Jordon's inner thigh. Stiffening up his tongue, Bryan penetrated Jordon's ass ring.

"Ah!" Jordon jumped in shock. "What are you doing to me, Bryan? Are you insane?"

"Doesn't Tyler do this?" Bryan wiped at his chin and continued to lick at that puckered rim.

"Tyler is my lover! You're my fucking brother!"

"Incest is best." Bryan ran kisses all over Jordon's tight ass globes.

"You're insane," Jordon mumbled, rubbing his eyes.

Holding Jordon's waist, Bryan forced him to turn around. Seeing Jordon's cock protruding like a stiff rod from his slacks, Bryan smiled. "Uh huh...not turned on? I beg to differ."

"Go away. Do you have any idea what Mom would do if she knew about this?"

"Mom?" Bryan choked in disbelief. "Who gives a shit about Mom? I want to know what my brother's spunk tastes like."

"You're sick!" Jordon tried to slink back but he was trapped by the kitchen counter.

"Am I?" Bryan aimed Jordon's cock towards his mouth and enveloped the head of his dick, swallowing it inch by inch.

Jordon's entire body tensed and he ended up on his toes, gripping the counter with white knuckles.

"Mm!" Bryan drew him in so his nose was being tickled by Jordon's dark bush. I knew you'd taste fucking fantastic!

"No...oh, come on, Bry, no..." Jordon whined.

Bryan waited for him to push him back, make a move to end the perversion. Jordon didn't. As a matter of fact, Jordon was pumping his hips in a nice rhythm into his mouth. Bryan dug between Jordon's legs for his balls. While he manipulated the large soft sacks in his fingers, he increased his suction and speed. A blast of pre-cum melted on his tongue. Bryan moaned in pleasure.

"No! No!" Jordon pleaded as his groin geared up for a climax.

Waiting eagerly for his brother's spunk to shoot out, Bryan pushed his index finger up Jordon's slick saliva-coated ass and massaged his prostate.

"Augh! God help me!" Jordon's knees gave out and he fell back against the kitchen counter.

The pulsating of Jordon's cock commenced with a jutting blast of thick tangy cum. Bryan crooned in delirium as mouthful after mouthful of spunk entered him. Shivering at his brother's orgasmic moans and jerking muscles, Bryan continued to milk him gently, getting every drop. When Jordon's cock began to soften, Bryan pulled back, releasing it with a wet pop, allowing his dick to settle against those long dangling balls. He gazed up at Jordon's expression as he recuperated.

"Well?" Bryan asked wickedly.

"We'll burn in hell." Jordon panted.

"I'd rather laugh with the sinners than cry with the saints."

"Fine, Billy Joel, but I'll never get over the shock or the deed." Jordon bent down to pull up his clothing.

Grinning contentedly as Jordon stuffed his spent cock back into his briefs, Bryan sighed deeply.

⋙⋘

"Bry? Oh, Bryan to earth?"

Blinking, Bryan looked across the kitchen table at his brother.

"You want seconds?" Jordon pointed to his nearly empty plate.

"No. I'm good." Bryan sat up, his face suddenly feeling flushed as he hoped to hell his brother wasn't clairvoyant and could read his thoughts.

Jordon stood, setting his plate in the sink. A sound of the door to the penthouse opening reached Bryan's ears.

As he waited, the glorious ex-teen porn star turned top model, Tyler Holliday entered the room.

"Hello, Bryan."

"Tyler." Bryan tried to smile politely at him.

"Hey, babe." Tyler swung Jordon into a hug with one arm around Jordon's waist.

As they kissed, Bryan felt a pang of jealousy.

"How was work?" Jordon asked, preparing a dish of food for Tyler. "If I'd have known you would be home so soon, I would have waited."

"No. I had no idea when the shoot would finish. It's fine." Tyler sat in the seat Jordon had been in, across from Bryan. "Was it good?"

"It's always good if Jordon cooked it." Bryan watched as his brother set a full plate in front of his lover and poured wine for Tyler before joining them at the table.

"So?" Tyler asked once he'd eaten a couple of bites, "How's your love life, Bryan? Still enjoying Adrian Tripp?"

Yeah, but he's not either of you. "Yes. We still see each other on occasion."

"More wine, Bry?" Jordon held up the bottle.

"No, Jordon. I should go." Bryan didn't think he could watch his brother lavish affection on another man.

"Already?" Jordon appeared hurt. "I thought you'd hang around for dessert. I bought cheesecake from Dean and De-luca."

Bryan paused to stare at Jordon at the comment. "What I want you don't have in your fridge."

"Huh?" Jordon tilted his head in confusion.

"Nothing." Bryan found Tyler giving him an odd look as well. "I'll see you guys."

"Let me walk you to the door." Jordon hurried behind Bryan.

"Bye, Tyler."

"See ya, Bryan."

As they approached the front door, Jordon whispered, "Are you okay?"

Stopping, turning around, Bryan cupped his brother's face in one hand.

Jordon jolted but waited before pulling back.

"Have a nice night, Jordy."

"Jesus, Bry. Don't kiss me."

An empty sensation filled Bryan. "I wouldn't dream of it."

"Good." Jordon backed away from him to open the door. "Call me."

"I will." Giving Jordon a soft smile, Bryan waved as he stood at the elevator while Jordon waved back before closing his door. Once he was alone in the hall, Bryan's smile faded to an ache. "Man, am I fucked up or what?" He took his phone out of his pocket and dialed. "Hey, Adrian. Wanna fuck? ...Good. I'll be at your place in fifteen minutes. Bye." He hung up, took another look at his brother's door before he entered the elevator.

11

Alexander Mark Lehman-Richfield stood in front of the bathroom sink after blow-drying and brushed his long hair as he stared at himself in the mirror.

Ever since he'd discovered Mark Richfield was his real dad, Alex's life had gone from miserable to fantastic. Leaving behind an abusive step-father, sharing a bedroom with a set of ten year old twin brothers who tormented him constantly, and the near poverty of living hand to mouth with a school teacher mother and auto mechanic father all suddenly had changed. Now Alex drove a brand new cherry red Mustang, had a gold watch on his wrist, could be out and gay without abuse from his family, and, not to mention, was surrounded by stunning older gay men.

Yes, Oliver, Angel Loveday's son was his 'boyfriend' and he loved Oliver dearly, but...he had cravings and a sex drive to challenge even the most restrained eighteen year old.

Brushing his long locks until they shined like silk, Alex whispered to his reflection, "So many men, so little time."

He knew they all wanted him. Well, almost all. Adam Lewis never made overt sexual advances or gave him the lascivious looks that Jack Larsen and Steve Miller had. But Alex knew his dad would go ballistic if he flirted with those guys again. He just wished there was some way to get his cake and eat it. Eat it all.

He wanted a chance to have a onetime sex orgy with those men, and not hurt Oliver or his dad.

"But there isn't." Alex set the brush down on the sink counter and shook back his hair. The feather-cut bangs on his forehead hung to his eyelashes in front and the tips of his long tresses came down to his nipples. It was a woman's look. Alex knew he grew it long to look slightly feminine. His body was slim and feline, his eyelashes were dark and framed his green eyes like they were painted with liner.

He pushed his pelvis out seductively at his reflection. "Want some?" he purred.

At a noise on the first floor, Alex perked up. He opened the bathroom door and listened. Men's voices, laughter, made its way to his ears.

He glanced down at his nakedness, knowing he should slip on a pair of jeans to see what was going on downstairs. Before he left the bathroom he found Steve, Jack, and Adam joking around and roughhousing with each other on their way to the master bedroom suite.

Holding his breath until they noticed him standing there, Alex paused.

Steve was the first to spot him. He came to such an abrupt halt, Jack and Adam body-slammed him from behind.

"What?" Adam asked in confusion.

When Alex met Adam's brown eyes, Adam sighed, "Oh."

"What are you doing, Alex?" Steve demanded in a deep voice.

"I was just finishing up from a shower." Alex pointed behind him to the bathroom. "Where's Dad?"

"On a late modeling shoot."

Alex leaned over to have a look behind Steve. Jack was desperately trying not to stare at him. "Hi, Jackie."

"Go get some clothing on, Alexander," Jack chided.

"Do I have to?" Alex sauntered closer.

"Oh my!" Adam laughed nervously as he gave Alex's body a good inspection.

"Alex," Steve moaned, rubbing his face tiredly. "Get some jeans on, will ya?"

Drawing closer, Alex asked innocently, tilting his head to the side like a little girl, "Whatcha guys going to do? Have sex together?"

Jack groaned in agony. "Is anyone else dying here?"

Steve continued down the hall towards Alex, with the

two men in tow. Once Steve was standing in front of Alex, he reached out to the very tip of Alex's long hair and fingered the ends.

Alex again strained to get a look at Jack and Adam over Steve's broad shoulder. They were both ogling his nude body. "Mm..." Alex ran his hand over his hairless chest to his flat washboard abs. "Want some?"

"Yes," Adam replied smugly. When the other two glanced at him, Adam defended, "Am I the only honest one of the three of us?"

Alex chuckled. "I think so, Adam. Wanna be the first to fuck me?"

"Yes!" Adam began removing his shirt.

"No." Steve spun around to stop Adam. "We can't."

"We can." Alex slithered between their bodies, rubbing against the men as he entered Steve and Mark's bedroom. Leaping on the bed with a bounce, Alex lay on his back, his hands behind his head and smiled brightly.

The three thirty-something men slowly entered the room, standing at the foot of the bed to stare down at Alex hungrily. In response, Alex slowly spread his legs and bent his knees, exposing his ass. "Any takers?"

"Fuck!" Jack dug his hand through his blond hair. "Steve! Do something!"

"I know what I'm doing." Adam stripped his clothing off.

"Ahh, I love a man who can make a decision. Got lube?" Alex teased.

Opening the nightstand, Adam found what he needed and knelt between Alex's thighs on the bed.

Alex glanced at Jack and Steve who were watching, spellbound. "You guys know you want in. Who's got dibs next?"

Instantly Jack began yanking off his shirt.

"I don't believe this," Steve sighed, closing and locking the bedroom door. "If Mark finds out he'll go insane."

"He won't find out." Adam pushed Alex's legs back so Alex's knees were against Alex's chest.

"That's it, Adam. Fuck me good." Alex reached out to comb his fingers through Adam's long brown hair. It was nearly the length of his dad's, down to his shoulders, and Alex knew it was because Jack wanted it long so Adam resembled his father.

Once he had made his cock slick with lube, Adam moved two fingers inside Alex's tight rim to loosen it. "Relax, my pretty boy."

"Mmm..." Alex closed his eyes and forced his body to let go. In moments Adam had his tight ring softened and responding to his massage. "I want your dick, Lewis."

"You're going to get it." Adam removed his fingers and pushed his cockhead inside Alex's hole. "Alexander, you are a prince."

"More like a queen." Alex laughed as he hissed out a breath of air, commanding his body to let go of its tight hold on Adam's dick. When Alex felt his ass muscles release, Adam pushed in deeper. They worked it slowly until Adam was buried up to his balls.

Allowing his passage to get used to the size of Adam's cock, Alex finally opened his eyes to see both Steve and Jack naked, looming in the background, playing with each other.

"How's it feel, pretty boy?" Adam's cock pulsated in his tight hole.

"Good. Fuck me." Alex pushed his hips higher, forcing Adam deeper.

Bracing himself on his hands, Adam pulled out to the head of his cock and thrust in quickly.

Alex gasped and his back raised off the bed at the mixture of pleasure and pain. "More!"

Adam grunted deeply, tightening his hold on Alex's legs and increasing the speed and power of his pelvic thrusts.

"Ah! Ah!" Sizzling heat scorched Alex from the inside out as his cock began spurting cum onto his chest and under his jaw.

"Oh, yes!" Adam shouted in excitement when he witnessed it.

Instantly Alex felt Adam's body unload its juicy contents into his ass. With his eyes clamped shut, Alex used his other senses to savor Adam's climax. That hot pulsating in his asshole, the scent of his and Adam's sweat, Adam's gasping breaths.

As slowly as he went in, Adam backed out. Once he had detached himself from Alex, he groaned and pushed his dark hair away from his dripping face and forehead.

Gazing at Jack's expression of pure lust, Alex crooned, "Come to me, Jackie-blue. Fuck your boy toy."

Steve released his hold on Jack's cock and nudged him to the bed.

Feeling the mattress shift as Jack's enormous muscular body drew near, Alex's heart rate rose once more. "All lubed and ready for you, He-man."

"Are you sure?"

"Am I sure?" Alex laughed at the absurdity.

After Jack glanced over his shoulder to Steve, and Adam, who had recuperated and was now an observer, Jack inched closer.

Seeing Jack's cock swollen, blushing red with thick veins running along the shaft, Alex quivered in anticipation. "Take it, Jackie. You couldn't have Dad at eighteen, but you can have me."

Jack closed his eyes and his jaw tightened. Alex watched those enormous muscles in his cheeks twitch.

"You big, brawny god, fuck me, Larsen." Alex raised his hips.

With an animalistic growl, Jack grabbed Alex's waist and drew him onto his lap. Alex gasped as Jack's thick cock began to burrow inside his worked hole. Holding Jack's enormous deltoids as he settled down on that long dick, Alex slowly let gravity draw him down to a seated position on Jack's massive quadriceps. Once they were tightly sealed together, Jack snarled, "Fuck me, Alex."

A shiver raced over Alex's sweaty skin. He tightened his fingers around Jack's girth and began to raise and lower on that stiff pole between his legs. As he concentrated on increasing the speed and depth, Jack began licking the sweat and spent cum off Alex's jaw and neck, chewing Alex's skin.

"Ahhh," Alex closed his eyes as his head fell back.

Obviously not moving quickly enough for him, Alex felt Jack encircle his hips and begin lifting him up and down on his thighs.

The penetration increased at once, and Alex's dick was back upright. "Yes! Jackie!"

Another rumbling snarl came from Jack's broad chest. He threw Alex backward, still deep inside him, and began fucking him with his body in a straight, stiff line between Alex's spread knees. The rhythm became intense and Alex's cock sprang to life, bobbing and seeping pre-cum.

Staring up at Jack, looking at the underside of Jack's jaw, his conservatively cropped thick head of blond hair and clean shaven chin, Alex shivered in delight.

"Fuck me, Jackie! Harder!"

Jack's teeth showed beneath his top lip as he rammed into Alex's ass, until his face contorted with ecstasy and his body jerked in what felt like a convulsion. Once again heat filled Alex's hole, overflowing from what Adam had left behind. Feeling it ooze down his crack, Alex moaned happily and smoothed his fingers up Jack's solid forearms. "Good one, Jackie?"

"Oh my fucking God..." Jack hung his head, drops of sweat rolled off his nose to Alex's dewy skin.

Waiting as Jack slowly withdrew and climbed off the bed, Alex gave Steve a big smile. "Last but most certainly not least."

Without the slightest hesitation or preparation, Steve leapt onto the bed, pinned Alex's hands over his head and jammed his dick into that well lubed hole.

Alex inhaled in surprise and felt his dick spurt pre-cum.

Steve grabbed a handful of Alex's hair and forced Alex's lips to his own. When they kissed, Steve piston-fucked Alex like a madman. Alex needed to scream the climax was so intense, but his tongue was being sucked hard into Steve's mouth.

For a second time he shot out his cum in thick pelting wads onto both their chests. As Alex hit the heavens with an orgasm that rocked him to the core, Steve finally joined him, jerking back from their kiss and hammering into Alex as he howled in pleasure.

"Augh! Augh!" Alex tried to catch his breath as his entire body erupted in chills. Watching this macho ex-cop shiver from his climax, Alex couldn't be any more in love.

Steve choked for air as he tried to recover. The moment he could function, Steve dropped down on Alex's body and began licking all the cum off his chest.

"I love you! Love you!" Alex cried, wrapping his legs and

arms around Steve, locking them together.

≈≈

"Alex?" was called through the bathroom door.

Blinking in surprise, Alex grabbed a towel and wrapped it around his hips, running water in the sink to rinse the sperm down the drain. "What do you want, Dad?"

"We're going out for dinner. How long do you need to get dressed?"

"Five minutes."

"What have you been doing in there? It's been ages. Stop preening."

Alex opened the door to glare at him. "I'm not preening."

"You'll get conceited," Mark warned, wagging his index finger at him. "Don't idolize your reflection."

"I wasn't doing that."

"Go. Is Oliver joining us?" Mark nudged Alex into his room.

"Yes. He should be here soon." Alex checked the time, tossing his towel down on the bed and finding a pair of briefs.

Hearing Steve's voice, Alex froze and looked at the open door and his waiting father.

"When are we going?" Steve peeked into the room, saw Alex getting dressed and backed up quickly.

"As soon as Oliver gets here and Alexander stops wasting time!" Mark scolded.

Continuing putting on clothing, Alex argued, "I'm not wasting time!" He tugged a pair of dress slacks on. "Steve, you can come in. I'm decent."

"I'll wait downstairs." He heard Steve say and then footfalls on the steps.

Alex sighed in defeat.

"What is it?" Mark entered the room.

"Nothing. Can you find me a shirt to go with these?" Alex gestured to his slacks.

Mark hunted in his closet. When he came out with a selection he handed it to Alex. "Are you all right?"

"Yes. Fine." Alex buttoned the top and tucked it in.

Mark cupped his face and forced him to meet his eyes.

Alex felt the steely glare of his dad's emerald green gaze. "You have Oliver."

"I know, Dad."

"Be content with him."

"I am. I love him."

"Good." Mark kissed Alex's cheek and left the room.

As he sat to put his socks on, Alex pushed his long hair aside from his face. "Can't stop me from fantasizing though, can ya, Dad?"

Once he was trotting down the stairs he found Steve opening the front door to Oliver. Smiling excitedly at his lover, Alex rushed to him and embraced him. "Hello, my love!" Alex kissed him hotly.

"Wow!" Oliver beamed at him.

"All right, boys. Sex later. Dinner now. We're meeting Adam and Jackie. Get moving or we'll be late." Mark ushered them to the attached garage. Alex slipped his shoes on quickly.

As they followed Steve out of the kitchen door to his Mercedes, Alex grabbed Oliver's hand, giving him a wicked smile. Oliver returned it.

The moment they were in the back seat together, Alex pounced, pushing Oliver onto the seat and smothering him with kisses.

"Boys!" Mark admonished.

"Tough! Live with it." Alex continued to kiss Oliver.

"Leave them alone, Mark," Steve whispered. "There's nothing wrong with Alex being with Oliver."

Yeah, Dad. If you stop me from making love to Oliver, I may look for it elsewhere, beware!

"Wow. You're hornier than normal. What's got you all hyped up?" Oliver pushed Alex's hair back from his face.

"You. You, Loveday, you." Alex smiled down at him.

"Good." Oliver drew him close for more kisses.

Alex sighed happily. Yeah, he had his fantasies, but in reality, all he wanted was Oliver Loveday.

12

Dylan Conway felt sweat roll off his skin as he left the playing field. His cleats clattered in the noisy corridor along with an entire pro-football team's heavy trod, shouting, cheering, high-fiving, over a well-earned victory.

His helmet in his hand dangling at his side, Dylan felt several teammates still jumping against him, and slapping his back and butt enthusiastically.

"You're amazing!"

"What a pass into the end zone! Man, you're the best fucking thing that's happened to this lousy team in ten years!"

"Son of a bitch, Conway! You were on fire out there!"

Dylan grinned at their adoring comments. "Thanks, guys. But it was a team effort. I couldn't do it without you." Dylan shoved one of the large offensive linemen. "And particularly you! Christ, Warren, you never let their defense get near me. Thanks, man!"

"Gave you time, bro! It was what you needed to pass."

"Jesus. Best fucking offensive line in the league. That's what I have around my ass." Dylan shook his head, setting his helmet above his locker on a shelf.

"And what an ass it is."

Dylan gave another teammate an affectionate smile. "Growl!"

A big dark-skinned sweaty defensive tackle purred, "Get in the shower, QB, and let us show you our gratitude."

Inhaling the enormous man's sweat, Dylan pulled his jersey over his head. "Can't wait, sweetie."

Someone from behind helped him take off his shoulder

pads. When he turned around he found another enticing grin. "I love it when we win." Dylan's dick became rock hard.

"We'll be waiting," was whispered as his ass was stroked.

A surge of pleasure cascaded over Dylan's body. Kicking off his cleats, he dragged his tight uniform pants down his thighs along with his jock strap and cup. Tugging off his socks, standing naked, Dylan looked around. A dozen men were in various stages of undress, all glancing at him hungrily.

Yes, his cock was sticking out like a flag from his body, so what? These guys knew how hot they made him.

Strutting down the middle of the line of big muscular men, Dylan gave each one a wicked grin as he passed. A flurry of activity followed as the men hurried to disrobe.

In a long tiled hall with showerheads poking out of either side, Dylan turned on the water, waiting until it billowed with steam. Male laughter and deep voices echoed off the white ceramic. Soaking under the soothing spray as it pelted his dirty, aching muscles, Dylan closed his eyes and relaxed.

When a dozen of the fifty members of his team began to surround him, Dylan felt goose bumps rise on his arms.

Large strong hands began to rub soap on his back and ass. Suddenly he was in the middle of a whirlwind of men every color of the rainbow, all dripping with male testosterone. Walls of ripped muscles and tattoo covered flesh fought to be near him, seeking a taste or touch.

He dropped his head back and groaned in pleasure, the noise echoed off the surroundings which mixed with the sound of panting breaths and raspy moans.

The first cock, slick with soap, made its way towards his ass.

"Yes, give it to me." Dylan quivered in excitement. As soothing hands and fingers ran all over his wet soapy skin, the man behind him pushed his cockhead passed Dylan's tight rim.

Dylan gasped and forced himself to relax as the large prick inched its way inside him.

"That's it, QB...you just let your teammates take good care of you."

Dylan hissed out a breath, letting his tight muscles release with it. That dick moved in to the hilt. He felt his own dick get harder as he braced his hands on the dripping white tile.

Being fucked by a massive defensive lineman, Dylan took the entire weight of the man on his back and lavished in his thrusting hips. Dylan cried out in bliss, "Yes! Fuck me!"

A guttural growl preceded the rapid pulsating of the big man's cock. Dylan felt it fill his ass with burning heat. The minute he pulled out, another soon replaced it.

Fingers pinched his nipples raw, manipulated his balls like play toys, dug into his saturated hair, caressed his back and neck, yet avoided touching his aching cock and making him come.

Another big defensive lineman had his way with him. Then the cornerback, next the linebackers, nose tackles, safety...

Only to be followed by his delicious offensive line; his receivers, halfbacks, fullbacks, not to mention the tightest of tight ends.

He knew he'd be sore. He didn't care. God, how he loved his men! "Take me! Fuck me to heaven...oh, Jesus, keep fucking me!"

After an hour of having nearly half the pro team's dicks up his ass, Dylan felt arms surround him and a breath in his ear hiss, "Best for last?"

An intense shiver washed over Dylan's length. "My love, my baby...make me come!"

"You got it, lover."

Finally two hands gripped his swollen prick to give it relief. And the last and best dick of the night was burrowed balls deep inside him.

"Anything for our winning quarterback."

"Sean...oh God, Sean!" Dylan rocked into Sean's slick palms, still bracing himself on the wet tiled wall. He knew there were dozens of men present, lingering, watching.

"How's that, my love?" Sean crooned in his ear.

"Ah! Ah! Ahhffuck!" Dylan shot out ribbons of cum, which coated the wet wall and oozed down it.

As Sean's pelvis slapped his ass with loud wet cracks, Dylan felt his lover's body go rigid and pulsate in his well-worked hole.

Hearing Sean's throaty grunts was reward enough for Dylan.

As Sean recuperated, resting his head on Dylan's back, the men each kissed Dylan's cheek whispering, "'Til the next win, QB," as they left the showers.

"I love my job," Dylan whimpered, rocking his forehead against his forearm as he pressed on the wall.

"And I love you." Sean pulled out gently, still hugging Dylan tight.

≈≈

"You awake?"

"Huh?" Dylan had been leaning on the arm of the sofa with his chin cradled in his palm. Blinking wearily, he gazed at Sean as he sat next to him. "Yeah, just beat."

"Want to stop watching this?" Sean pointed the remote control at the television set.

"No. I want to see the rest of it." Dylan repositioned himself to cuddle Sean.

"Nice wood." Sean gazed at Dylan's crotch.

"I always get wood when I watch this video."

"I know. The ex-porn star turned pro football player watching a porn film about a football star. Christ, the irony."

"Shut up and let me watch it." Dylan stuffed his hand between Sean's thighs.

Sean kissed Dylan's ear and whispered, "You'd want to get gang fucked by the team, wouldn't you?"

"No. Come on." Dylan laughed uneasily.

"Liar."

Dylan met Sean's eyes. "All right. I may fantasize getting it like that, but in reality I just want you."

"Yeah?"

"Yeah!" Dylan wrestled Sean down onto the couch under him.

After they kissed, Sean asked, "You really have fantasies about being screwed by the rest of the team?"

Seeing Sean's look of disbelief, Dylan replied, "Nah. I was just kidding."

"Damn!" Sean laughed.

"Shut up and kiss me."

"You'll miss the rest of the video."

Dylan took the remote control and stopped the DVD. "There. Where were we?" Dylan drew Sean's mouth to his.

Yes, fantasies were fun. But that was all they were. Fantasies.

The End

ABOUT THE AUTHOR

G.A. Hauser was born in the shadow of the Manhattan skyline in the suburbs of New Jersey in the sleepy town of Fair Lawn. After graduating with a degree in Fine Arts from a university in New York, she gave up the idea of being a starving artist and headed for Seattle. For over a decade she lived in Rain City, and the last eight of those years she wore a blue police uniform working for the Seattle Police Department as a patrol officer. She's been writing since 1990 but it wasn't until she reached the wet British Isles that she published her first book, *In The Shadow of Alexander*. She lived in Hertfordshire, England for six years and from there she was able to travel and see the wonders of the world. She's back in the good ol' USA once again and is convinced *there's no place like home*.

Breinigsville, PA USA
15 March 2011
257725BV00001B/20/P